PRAISE FOR *I LOVE DICK*

"I know there was a time before I read Chris Kraus's *I Love Dick* (in fact, that time was only five years ago), but it's hard to imagine; some works of art do this to you. They tear down so many assumptions about what the form can handle (in this case, what the form of the novel can handle) that there is no way to re-create your mind before your encounter with them"

—Sheila Heti, *The Believer*

"For years before I read it, I kept hearing about Chris Kraus's *I Love Dick*. I mainly heard about it from smart women who liked to talk about their feelings...Then I read it. I was nearly two decades late to the party—*I Love Dick* came out in 1997—but I loved the party anyway. I was finally *part* of it, and it made me feel even more part of it—part of *something* —to have men making asinine comments on the 4 train, pointing at the cover: *Good to know what you like!* I knew I was holding white-hot text in my hands, written by a woman who had theorized what these guys were doing—with me, with their dick jokes—even before they'd done it. *I Love Dick* is a 'novel' about a woman named Chris Kraus and her unrequited, increasingly obsessive love for a cultural critic named Dick. (What I could have told those men on the subway: *See? Dick is actually a cultural critic!*) Kraus keeps writing to Dick, keeps calling Dick, even makes her husband a collaborator in her pursuit of Dick, and all the while keeps getting rebuffed by him. She brings us deep into the folds of her relentless pursuit—'marching boldly into self-abasement,' in the words of her friend, the poet Eileen Myles. She gives us female desire without shame or passivity, and follows abjection 'into something bright and exalted, like presence'"

—Leslie Jamison, *The New Yorker*

"Kraus's *I Love Dick* is a written in a clear prose capable of theoretical clarity, descriptive delicacy, articulate rage and melancholic longing"
—*The White Review*

"[*I Love Dick*] changed my life… It explained the problem of heterosexuality to me in terms that I had never thought about before. I had been attracted to books by and about gay people or at least people with fluid sexuality for a long time, and had not spent much time thinking about why that was. Worlds without straight men appealed to me; I liked the idea that there could be narratives that didn't operate on the presumption of women's dependence on men for love, money, and support. *I Love Dick* was the first work of fiction I'd ever read that acknowledged that women who were attracted to men and wanted to have relationships with them were not going to somehow create relationships that existed outside of all existing economic and social structures; that women who love men are going to have to come to terms with their complicity in their own repression and subjugation, and find ways to address it. This is not all the book's about, of course, but that was my first and most lasting takeaway"
—Emily Gould, *n+1*

"*I Love Dick* detonated something in me, but it's been a slow demolition. With each quiet, contained blast I grow more sure that by recognizing our own billboards of desire and failure, and perhaps even finding some dignity there, we are also moving the culture towards the 'subversive utopia' that so many women, artists or not, hoped and hope for"
—Stephanie Wong, *The Rumpus*

"An exploration of desire as something other than passivity or inadequacy and relentless romantic pursuit not as self-degradation but a kind of generative, creative act. Kraus is interested in the dynamics of exposure itself: why we judge acts of self-exposure as self-absorbed or needy, especially if they come from a woman; how any trace of the self can become a kind of shameful stink, the whiff of some failure of imagination or, worse yet, self-pity or self-aggrandizement"
—*New York Times*

"Chris Kraus' first novel, *I Love Dick*, reads like *Madame Bovary* as if Emma had written it. Kraus spins out the Emma-syndrome of dissatisfied feminine boredom through a chronicle of the '80s art world. Her book is a damningly intelligent form of 'confessional' literature, part love letter and part public document"
—*Artnet*

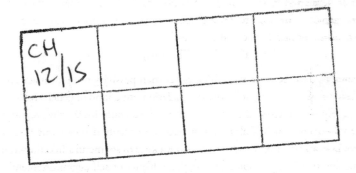

CH
12/15

ALSO BY CHRIS KRAUS

Aliens & Anorexia
Torpor
Summer of Hate
Video Green: Los Angeles Art and the Triumph of Nothingness
Where Art Belongs

I

LOVE

DICK

CHRIS KRAUS

TUSKAR ROCK PRESS

First published in Great Britain in 2015 by Tuskar Rock Press,
an imprint of Profile Books Ltd
3 Holford Yard
Bevin Way
London
WC1X 9HD

First published in 1997 by Semiotext(e), Los Angeles, CA

1 3 5 7 9 10 6 4 2

Designed by Hedi El Kholti

Printed and bound in Great Britain by Clays, St Ives plc

A CIP record for this book can
be obtained from the British Library

ISBN 978 1 78125 647 3
eISBN 978 1 78283 254 6

FSC
www.fsc.org
MIX
Paper from
responsible sources
FSC® C018072

ACKNOWLEDGMENTS

I want to thank the following people who helped with their encouragement and conversation: Romy Ashby, Jim Fletcher, Carol Irving, John Kelsey, Ann Rower and Yvonne Shafir.

Thanks also to Eryk Kvam for legal counsel, Catherine Brennan, Justin Cavin and Andrew Berardini for proofreading and fact-checking, editors Ken Jordan and Jim Fletcher, Marsie Scharlatt for insights and information on the misdiagnosis of schizophrenia; and Sylvère Lotringer as always for everything.

CONTENTS

PART I: SCENES FROM A MARRIAGE

SCENES FROM A MARRIAGE

December 3, 1994

Chris Kraus, a 39-year-old experimental filmmaker and Sylvère Lotringer, a 56-year-old college professor from New York, have dinner with Dick _____, a friendly acquaintance of Sylvère's, at a sushi bar in Pasadena. Dick is an English cultural critic who's recently relocated from Melbourne to Los Angeles. Chris and Sylvère have spent Sylvère's sabbatical at a cabin in Crestline, a small town in the San Bernardino Mountains some 90 minutes from Los Angeles. Since Sylvère begins teaching again in January, they will soon be returning to New York. Over dinner the two men discuss recent trends in postmodern critical theory and Chris, who is no intellectual, notices Dick making continual eye contact with her. Dick's attention makes her feel powerful, and when the check comes she takes out her Diners Club card. "Please," she says. "Let me pay." The radio predicts snow on the San Bernardino highway. Dick generously invites them both to spend the night at his home in the Antelope Valley desert, some 30 miles away.

Chris wants to separate herself from her coupleness, so she sells Sylvère on the thrill of riding in Dick's magnificent vintage Thunderbird convertible. Sylvère, who doesn't know a T-bird from a hummingbird and doesn't care, agrees, bemused. Done. Dick gives her copious, concerned directions. "Don't worry," she interrupts, flashing hair and smiles, "I'll tail you." And she does. Slightly buzzed and keeping the accelerator of her pickup truck steady, she's reminded of a performance she did called *Car Chase* at the St. Mark's Poetry Project in New York when she was 23. She and her friend Liza Martin had tailed the steelily good-looking driver of a Porsche all the way through Connecticut on Highway 95. Finally he'd pulled over to a rest stop, but when Liza and Chris got out he drove off. The performance ended with Liza accidentally-but-really stabbing Chris' hand onstage with a kitchen knife. Blood flowed, and everyone found Liza dazzlingly sexy and dangerous and beautiful. Liza, belly popping out of a fuzzy midriff top, fishnet legs tearing up against her green vinyl miniskirt as she rocked back to show her crotch, looked like the cheapest kind of whore. A star is born. No one at the show that night had found Chris' pale anemic looks and piercing gaze remotely endearing. Could anyone? It was a question that'd temporarily been shelved. But now it was a whole new world. The request line on 92.3 The Beat was thumping, Post-Riot Los Angeles, a city strung on fiber optic nerves. Dick's Thunderbird was always somewhere in her line of sight, the two vehicles strung invisibly together across the concrete riverbed of highway, like John Donne's eyeballs. And this time Chris was alone.

Back at Dick's, the night unfolds like the boozy Christmas Eve in Eric Rohmer's film *My Night At Maud's*. Chris notices that Dick is flirting with her, his vast intelligence straining beyond the po-mo rhetoric and words to evince some essential loneliness that only she and he can share. Chris giddily responds. At 2 a.m., Dick plays them a video of himself dressed as Johnny Cash commissioned by English public television. He's talking about earthquakes and upheaval and his restless longing for a place called home. Chris' response to Dick's video, though she does not articulate it at the time, is complex. As an artist she finds Dick's work hopelessly naive, yet she is a lover of certain kinds of bad art, art which offers a transparency into the hopes and desires of the person who made it. Bad art makes the viewer much more active. (Years later Chris would realize that her fondness for bad art is exactly like Jane Eyre's attraction to Rochester, a mean horse-faced junky: bad characters invite invention.) But Chris keeps these thoughts to herself. Because she does not express herself in theoretical language, no one expects too much from her and she is used to tripping out on layers of complexity in total silence. Chris' unarticulated double-flip on Dick's video draws her even closer to him. She dreams about him all night long. But when Chris and Sylvère wake up on the sofabed the next morning, Dick is gone.

December 4, 1994: 10 a.m.

Sylvère and Chris leave Dick's house, reluctantly, alone that morning. Chris rises to the challenge of extemporizing the Thank You Note, which must be left behind. She and Sylvère have breakfast at the Antelope IHOP. Because they are no longer having sex, the two maintain their intimacy via deconstruction: i.e., they tell each other everything. Chris tells Sylvère how she believes that she and Dick have just experienced a Conceptual Fuck. His disappearance in the morning clinches it, and invests it with a subcultural subtext she and Dick both share: she's reminded of all the fuzzy one-time fucks she's had with men who're out the door before her eyes are open. She recites a poem by Barbara Barg on this subject to Sylvère:

> *What do you do with a Kerouac*
> *But go back and back to the sack*
>   *with Jack*
> *How do you know when Jack*
>   *has come?*
> *You look on your pillow and*
>   *Jack is gone...*

And then there was the message on Dick's answerphone. When they came into the house, Dick took his coat off, poured them drinks and hit the Play button. The voice of a very young, very Californian woman came on:

> Hi Dick, this's Kyla. Dick, I—I'm sorry to keep calling you at home, and now I've got your answering machine and, and I just wanted to say I'm sorry how things didn't work out the other night, and—I know it's not your fault, but I guess all I really wanted was just to thank you for being such a nice person...

"Now I'm totally embarrassed," Dick mumbled charmingly, opening the vodka. Dick is 46 years old. Does this message mean he's lost? And, if Dick *is* lost, could he be saved by entering a conceptual romance with Chris? Was the conceptual fuck merely the first step? For the next few hours, Sylvère and Chris discuss this.

December 4, 1994: 8 p.m.

Back in Crestline, Chris can't stop thinking about last night with Dick. So she starts to write a story about it, called *Abstract Romanticism*. It's the first story she's written in five years.

"It started in the restaurant," she begins. "It was the beginning of the evening and we were all laughing a bit too much."

She addresses this story, intermittently, to David Rattray because she's convinced that David's ghost had been with her last night for the car ride, pushing her pickup truck further all the way up Highway 5. Chris, David's ghost and the truck had merged into a single unit moving forward.

"Last night I felt," she wrote to David's ghost, "like I do at times when things seem to open onto new vistas of excitement—that you were here: floating dense beside me, set someplace between my left ear and my shoulder, compressed like thought."

She thought about David all the time. It was uncanny how Dick had said somewhere in last night's boozy conversation, as if he'd read her mind, how much he admired David's book. David Rattray had been a reckless adventurer and a genius and a moralist, indulging in the most improbable infatuations nearly until the moment of his death at age 57. And now Chris felt David's ghost pushing her to understand infatuation, how the loved person can become a holding pattern for all the tattered ends of memory, experience and thought you've ever had. So she started to describe Dick's face, "pale and mobile, good bones, reddish hair and deepset eyes." Writing, Chris held his face in her mind, and then the telephone rang and it was Dick.

Chris was so embarrassed. She wondered if the call was really for Sylvère, but Dick didn't ask for him, so she stayed on the scratchy line. Dick was phoning to explain his disappearance the night before. He'd gotten up early and drove out to Pear Blossom to pick up some eggs and bacon. "I'm a bit of an insomniac, you know." When he'd gotten home to Antelope Valley he was genuinely surprised to find them gone.

At this moment, Chris could've told Dick her own far-fetched interpretation: had she, this story would've taken another turn. But there was so much static on the line, and already she was afraid of him. She feverishly considered proposing another meeting, but she didn't, and then Dick got off the phone. Chris stood in her makeshift office, sweating. Then she ran upstairs to find Sylvère.

December 5, 1994

Alone in Crestline, Sylvère and Chris spent most of last night (Sunday) and this morning (Monday) talking about Dick's 3 minute call. Why does Sylvère entertain this? It could be that for the first time since last summer, Chris seems animated and alive, and since he loves her, Sylvère can't bear to see her sad. It could be he's reached an impasse with the book he's writing on modernism and the holocaust, and dreads returning next month to his teaching job. It could be that he's perverse.

December 6–8, 1994

Tuesday, Wednesday, Thursday of this week pass unrecorded, blurred. If memory serves, Tuesday that term was the day that Chris Kraus and Sylvère Lotringer spent in Pasadena, teaching at Art Center College of Design. Shall we attempt a reconstruction? They get up at 8, drive down the hill from Crestline, grab coffee in San Bernardino, hop on the 215 to the 10 and drive for 90 minutes, hitting LA just after traffic. It's likely they talked about Dick for most of the ride. However, since they planned to move out of Crestline in just 10 days, on December 14 (Sylvère to Paris for the holidays, Chris to New York), they must've also briefly talked logistics. A Restless Longing…driving through Fontana and Pomona, through a landscape that meant nothing, with an inconclusive future looming. While Sylvère lectured on poststructuralism, Chris drove out to Hollywood to pick up some publicity photos for her film and shopped for cheese at Trader Joe's. Then they drove back out to Crestline, winding up the mountain through darkness and thick fog.

Wednesday and Thursday disappear. It's obvious that Chris' new film isn't going to go very far. What will she do next? Her first experience in art had been as a participant in some druggy psychodramas of the '70s. The idea that Dick may've proposed a kind of game between them is incredibly exciting. She explains it over and over to Sylvère. She begs Sylvère to phone him, fish around for some sign that Dick's aware of her. And if there is, she'll call.

Friday, December 9, 1994

Sylvère, a European intellectual who teaches Proust, is skilled in the analysis of love's minutiae. But how long can anyone continue analyzing a single evening and a 3-minute call? Already, Sylvère's left two unanswered messages on Dick's answerphone. And Chris has turned into a jumpy bundle of emotions, sexually aroused for the first time in seven years. So on Friday morning, Sylvère finally suggests that Chris write Dick a letter. Since she's embarrassed she asks him if he wants to write one too. Sylvère agrees.

Do married couples usually collaborate on *billets doux*? If Sylvère and Chris were not so militantly opposed to psychoanalysis, they might've seen this as a turning point.

Crestline, California
December 9, 1994

Dear Dick,

It must be the desert wind that went to our heads that night or maybe the desire to fictionalize life a little bit. I don't know. We've met a few times and I've felt a lot of sympathy towards you and a desire to be closer. Though we come from different places, we've both tried breaking up with our pasts. You're a cowboy; for ten years, I was a nomad in New York.

So let's go back to the evening at your house: the glorious ride in your Thunderbird from Pasadena to the End of the World, I mean the Antelope Valley. It's a meeting we postponed almost a year. And truer than I imagined. But how did I get into that?

I want to talk about that evening at your house. I had a feeling that somehow I knew you and we could just be what we are together. But now I'm sounding like the bimbo whose voice we heard, unwittingly, that night on your answerphone…

Sylvère

Crestline, California
December 9, 1994

Dear Dick,

Since Sylvère wrote the first letter, I'm thrown into this weird position. Reactive—like Charlotte Stant to Sylvère's Maggie Verver, if we were living in the Henry James novel *The Golden Bowl*—the Dumb Cunt, a factory of emotions evoked by all the men. So the only thing that I can do is tell The Dumb Cunt's Tale. But how?

Sylvère thinks it's nothing more than a perverse longing for rejection, the love I feel for you. But I disagree, at bottom I'm a very romantic girl. What touched me were all the windows of vulnerability in your house...so Spartan and self-conscious. The propped up *Some Girls* album cover, the dusky walls—how out of date and déclassé. But I'm a sucker for despair, for faltering—that moment when the act breaks down, ambition fails. I love it and feel guilty for perceiving it and then the warmest indescribable affection floods in to drown the guilt. For years I adored Shake Murphy in New Zealand for these reasons, a hopeless case. But you're not exactly hopeless: you have a reputation, self-awareness and a job, and so it occurred to me that there might be something to be learned by both of us from playing out this romance in a mutually self-conscious way. Abstract romanticism?

It's weird, I never really wondered whether I'm 'your type.' ('Cause in the past, Empirical Romance, since I'm not pretty or maternal, I never *am* the type for Cowboy Guys.) But maybe action's all that really matters now. What people do together over-shadows Who They Are. If I can't make you fall in love with me for who I am, maybe I can interest you with what I understand. So instead of wondering 'Would he like me?', I wonder 'Is he game?'

When you called on Sunday night, I was writing a description of your face. I couldn't talk, and hung up on the bottom end of the romantic equation with beating heart and sweaty palms. It's incredible to feel this way. For 10 years my life's been organized around avoiding this painful elemental state. I wish that I could dabble like you do around romantic myths. But I can't, because I

always lose and already in the course of this three-day totally fictitious romance, I've started getting sick. And I wonder if there'll ever
be a possibility of reconciling youth and age, or the anorexic open
wound I used to be with the money-hustling hag that I've become.
We suicide ourselves for our own survival. Is there any hope of dip-
ping back into the past and circling round it like you can in art?

Sylvère, who's typing this, says this letter lacks a point. What
reaction am I looking for? He thinks this letter is too literary, too
Baudrillardian. He says I'm squashing out all the trembly little
things he found so touching. It's not the Dumb Cunt Exegesis he
expected. But Dick, I know that as you read this, you'll know these
things are true. You understand the game is *real*, or even better than,
reality, and better than is what it's all about. What sex is better than
drugs, what art is better than sex? *Better than* means stepping out
into complete intensity. Being in love with you, being ready to take
this ride, made me feel 16, hunched up in a leather jacket in a corner with my friends. A timeless fucking image. It's about not giving
a fuck, or seeing all the consequences looming and doing something
anyway. And I think you—I—keep looking for that and it's thrilling
when you find it in other people.

Sylvère thinks he's that kind of anarchist. But he's not. I love
you Dick.

Chris

But after finishing these, Chris and Sylvère both felt they could do
better. That there were things still left to say. So they began a second
round, spending most of Friday sitting on their living room floor in
Crestline passing the laptop back and forth. And they each wrote a
second letter, Sylvère about jealousy, Chris about the Ramones and

the Kierkegaardian third remove. "Maybe I'd like to be like you," Sylvère wrote, "living all alone in a house surrounded by a cemetery. I mean, why not take the shortcut? So I got really involved in the fantasy, erotically too, because desire radiates, even if it is not directed towards you, and it has an energy and beauty, and I think I was turned on to Chris being turned on to you. After awhile it became difficult to remember that nothing really happened. I guess in some dark corner of my mind I realized if I wasn't going to be jealous, my only choice was to enter this fictional liaison in a sort of perverse fashion. How else could I take my wife having a crush on you? The thoughts that come to mind are pretty distasteful: *ménage à trois*, the willing husband … all three of us are too sophisticated to deal in such dreary archetypes. Were we trying to open up new ground? Your cowboy persona meshed so well with the dreams Chris has of the torn and silent desperate men she's been rejected by. The fact that you don't return messages turns your answerphone into a blank screen onto which we can project our fantasies. So in a sense I did encourage Chris, because thanks to you, she's been reminded of a bigger picture, the way she was last month after visiting Guatemala, and we're all potentially bigger people than we are. There's so much we haven't talked about. But maybe that's just the way to become closer friends. To share thoughts that may not be shared…"

Chris' second letter was less noble. She started off by rhapsodizing once again about Dick's face: "I started looking at your face that night in the restaurant—oh wow, isn't that like the first line in the Ramones song, *Needles & Pins*? 'I saw your face/It was the face I loved/And I knew'—and I got the same feeling from it that I get everytime I hear that song, and when you called my heart was pounding and then I thought that maybe we could do something together, something that is to adolescent romance what the Ramone's cover of the song is to the original. The Ramones give *Needles & Pins* the possibility of irony, but the irony doesn't undercut the song's emotion, it makes it stronger and more true. Søren Kierkegaard called this "the Third Remove." In his book *The Crisis In The Life Of An Actress*, he claims no actress can play 14-year-old Juliette until she's at least 32. Because acting's art, and art involves reaching through some distance. Playing the vibrations between here and there and then and now. And don't you think reality is best attained through dialectics? PS, Your face is mobile, craggy, beautiful…"

By the time Sylvère and Chris finish their second letters, it's the end of the afternoon. Lake Gregory shimmers in the distance, ringed by snowy mountains. The landscape's fiery and distant. For now both of them are satisfied. Memories of domesticity when Chris was young, 20 years before: a China eggcup and a teacup, painted people circling around it, blue and white. A bluebird at the bottom of the cup, seen through amber tea. All the prettiness in the world contained in these two objects. When Chris and Sylvère put away the Toshiba laptop it's already dark. She fixes dinner. He returns to working on his book.

EXHIBIT B: HYSTERIA
                    PART I. SYLVÈRE FLIPS OUT

Crestline, California
December 10, 1994

Dear Dick,

This morning I woke up with an idea. Chris should send you a short note breaking out of this stuffy, referential delirium. Here's how it should read:

"Dear Dick, l am taking Sylvère to the airport Wednesday morning. I need to talk to you. Can we meet at your place?"

Love,
Chris

I thought it was a brilliant coup: a piece of reality shattering this twisted hotbed of emotions. Because after all, our letters were so self directed, *marriage a deux*. Actually that's the title I thought of for this piece before I went to sleep and I wanted to communicate it to Chris as soon as she woke up. But it had the opposite effect. After last night's brainstorming, she'd somehow put aside her infatuation with you. She was back on the safe side—marriage, art, the family—but my concern reignited her obsession and suddenly we were thrown back into the reality of unreality, the challenge at the bottom of it all. Outwardly it has to do with Chris' apprehension about turning 40, or so she says. I'm afraid my letters have been too high-minded and patronizing. Anyway, let me try again—

Sylvère

California scrubjays screeched outside the master bedroom. Sylvère sat propped against two pillows, typing, looking out through the glass doors across the deck. No matter how many times they tried to change it, so long as he and Chris slept together their days rarely started before noon. While Chris still dozed, Sylvère would make the first coffee of the day and carry it back to the bedroom. Then Chris would tell Sylvère her dreams, and after that her feelings, and Sylvère would be the best, most subtle and associative listener she'd ever find. Then Sylvère would go to make the toast and second coffees. As the caffeine hit, the conversation shifted, became more general, ranging over everything and everyone they knew. They dug each other's references and felt smarter in each other's presence. Sylvère and Chris were among the five most well-read people they each knew, and this a constant miracle, since neither of them had been to good schools. She felt so peaceful with him. Sylvère, Sylvalium, accepted her so totally and she took little sips of coffee to clear her head of morning dreams.

Sylvère never dreamed and rarely knew what he was feeling. So they played a game sometimes that they'd devised to tease his feelings out: Objective Correlative. Who was Sylvère's metonymic mirror? A student at the art school? Their dog? The Dart Canyon Storage man?

Fully awake around 11, the conversation usually peaked with a passionate discussion of checks and bills. So long as Chris continued making independent films they'd always be juggling money, thousands here and thousands there. Chris spent time buying or acquiring long-term leases to three apartments and two houses which they kept rented at a profit while holing up in rural slums. She kept Sylvère apprised of the status of their mortgages, taxes, rental income and repair bills. And luckily, beyond this primitive foray into acquisition, with Chris' help Sylvère's career was becoming lucrative enough to offset the losses incurred by hers. Chris, a diehard feminist who often saw herself as spinning on a great Elizabethan Wheel of Fortune, smiled to think that in order to continue making work she would have to be supported by her husband. "Who's independent?" Isabelle Huppert's pimp demanded, spanking her in the backseat of a car in *Sauve Qui Peut.* "The maid? The bureaucrat? The banker? No!" Yeah. In late capitalism, was anyone truly free? Sylvère's fans were mostly young white men drawn to the more "transgressive" elements of modernism, heroic sciences of human sacrifice and torture as legitimized by Georges Bataille. They scotch-taped xeroxes of the famous "Torture of a Hundred Pieces" photo from Bataille's *Tears of Eros* to their notebooks—a regicide captured on gelatin-plate film by French anthropologists in China in 1902. The Bataille Boys saw beatitude in the victim's agonized expression as the executioner sawed off his last remaining limb. But even more inexcusably, they were often rude to Chris. Going out to Exchange Ideas with Sylvère Lotringer in bars after his lectures in Paris, Berlin and Montreal, the Boys resented any barrier (especially a wife, and an unseductive one at that) between themselves and the great man. Chris responded by milking money from Sylvère's growing reputation, setting ever-higher fees. Would the German money and the $2,000 from Vienna be enough to pay her lab bill in Toronto? No. They'd better hit up Dieter for per diem. Et cetera. Around noon, after Coffee Number 3, too buzzed to think about anything but money, they hit the phone.

Dick's presence in their lives was a vacation from this kind of scheming. It was a foray into scheming of another kind. That Saturday when they drank their morning coffee they were already planning a second round of letters, juggling Sylvère's laptop between toast and coffee mugs. Sylvère, a great reviser, didn't like the sound of his first letter. And so he wrote:

Crestline, California
December 10, 1994

Dear Dick,

Last night I fell asleep thinking of a great title for our piece: *Ménage à Deux.* But when I woke up it seemed too conclusive and too lame. Have Chris and I spent this past week in turmoil just to turn our lives into a text? While making coffee I came up with the perfect solution, a way of instantly reshuffling the cards. Because Dick, Chris and I have been debating whether we should send the letters that we wrote to you last night. It's a crazy distillation of our mental state and you, poor Dick, do not deserve to be exposed to such a masturbatory passion. I imagine our 14 pages emerging line by line from your deserted fax. To even consider sending them was crazy. These letters weren't meant for you; they were a dialectical resolution of a crisis that never was. So that's why I thought of sending you this terse injunction:

> *Dear Dick, I'm taking Sylvère to the airport Wednesday morning. I need to talk to you.*
>
> Love,
> Chris

What are you going to do with that? Probably not answer!

Sylvère

⚜

All his life since age 19, Sylvère Lotringer had wanted to be a writer. Carrying a huge tape recorder on the back of his Vespa motorscooter around the British Isles, he'd made interviews in faulty English with all the literary greats—T.S. Eliot, Vita Sackville-West and Brendan Behan—for a French communist literary magazine. He was away from his Holocaust survivor family on the scabby rue des Poissonières for the first time and this was freedom. Two years later, studying at the Sorbonne with Roland Barthes, he wrote an essay on *The Function of Narrative Throughout History*. This was published in a prestigious literary magazine called *Critique*. The rest was history. His. He became a specialist of narrative, not a creator of it. Because the French draft for the Algerian war was on, he started trundling between teaching jobs in Turkey and Australia and finally America. Now 40 years later he was writing about Antonin Artaud, trying to find some link between Artaud's madness and the madness of World War 2. In all these years Sylvère'd never written, really, anything he loved or anything about the War (same thing). And he remembered how David Rattray'd said once about Antonin Artaud: "It's like the rediscovery of the truths of Gnosticism, the notion that this universe is crazy…" Well Artaud was plenty crazy and so was David. And maybe now instead of just being unhappy Sylvère could be crazy too? So he continued:

"That night with you, we caught the Western bug. Your bug. I mean, Chris and I are sensible people. We don't do anything without *a reason*. So you must be responsible. I have the feeling you've been watching all these days with a John Wayne grin, manipulating us from a distance. I really resent that part of you, Dick. Intruding on our lives. I mean before that night Chris and I had a good thing going. Perhaps not passionate but comfortable. We could have gone on like that forever and then you came, the rambling man, with all these expatriate philosophies that we've outgrown ourselves over the past 20 years. This is really not our problem, Dick. You're leading a ghost town life, infecting everyone who comes near you with a ghost disease. Take it back, Dick. We don't need it. Here's another fax I thought of:

Dear Dick, Why did you do this to us?
Can't you leave us alone?
You're invading our lives—why?
I demand an explanation.

> Love,
> Sylvère

✧ ✦ ✧ ✦

Were these letters sendable? Chris said yes, Sylvère said no. If not, why write them? Sylvère suggested writing until Dick returned their calls. Okay, she thought, believing in telepathy. But Sylvère, not in love but enjoying the collaboration, understood they might be writing him forever.

Crestline, California
December 10, 1994

Dear Dick,

Come to think of it, why'd you even call us Sunday night? The night after our 'date' with you in Antelope Valley. You were supposed to be this cool guy smoking a cigarette behind his bedroom door on Sunday morning, just waiting for us to clear out. It would've been totally in character not to call. So why did you call? Because you really wanted it to continue, right? You came up with this lame excuse about going to get breakfast—at 7:30 in the morning in this tiny town where the grocery store is 3 minutes away? It took you three hours, Dick, to get that fucking breakfast. So where'd you go? Did you sneak out to meet the bimbo girl who left her abject message on your answering machine? Can't you spend a single night alone? Or were you already fighting the invasion of your mental universe by this couple of cynical rapacious libertines? Were you trying to defend yourself; or was it a trap you set, tightening it the following night with your apparently innocent call? Actually, that night I picked up the receiver for a moment and heard your voice. Such a small voice, too, for such enormous stakes. You've been holding our destiny in your hands for the last few days. No wonder Chris didn't know what to say. So what's your game, Dick? You've gone too far into it to keep hiding in the distance, biting your nails and listening to *Some Girls* or some *other* girls. You have to deal with what you've created. Dick, you have to respond to the following fax:

> *Dear Dick I think you won. I'm totally obsessed with you. Chris will be driving across America. We have to talk this over—*

> Sylvère

What do you think of that, Dick? I promise not to do you any harm. I mean, I'm on my way to France to see my family, they have security at the airport, I can't afford to be caught carrying a gun. But it's time to put an end to this craziness. You can't go on messing people's lives up like this.

> *Love,*
> *Sylvère*

Chris and Sylvère laugh hysterically, sitting on the floor. Because Chris is a 90 wpm typist she and Sylvère maintain eye contact while he talks. Sylvère's never been so prolific. After plodding along at a rate of about 5 pages a week on *Modernism & The Holocaust* he's exhilarated by how fast the words accrue. They take turns giving DICK-tation. Everything is hilarious, power radiates from their mouths and fingertips and the world stands still.

Crestline, California
December 10, 1994

Dear Dick,

Two days ago Sylvère and I were discussing methods of disposing of dead bodies. I thought the best place might be in a rural storage facility. We visited one this week in Crestline and it occurred to me that a body could be left for quite some time so long as the rent was paid. Sylvère, however, objected that the corpse would rot and smell. We discussed refrigeration, but as far as I recall the bins have no electric outlets.

Highway medians are a notorious place for corpse disposal, and a real commentary on the public architecture of the '80s, wouldn't you say? Like Self Serve Filling Stations (and doesn't that description say it all?) they're a densely yet anonymously travelled public space where no one seems to be in charge. You don't see people picnicking around the highway, do you? It's not a place where children play. Medians are seen only from fast moving vehicles: a perfect condition for disposing of remains.

For a long time now I've been interested in dismemberment. Did you ever read about the Monika Beerle murder in the East

Village, circa 1989? The case was apocryphal of conditions in New York at that time. Monika'd come from Switzerland to study Martha Graham dance. She made money part-time topless dancing at Billy's Lounge. She met a guy named Daniel Rakowitz hanging around the outside of her building and she liked him. One thing led to another and she invited Daniel to move in. Maybe with someone sharing rent she could cut down on dancing? But putting up with Daniel Rakowitz was worse than Billy's Lounge. He disappeared for days, then brought groups of crazy people from the Park back home. She said he'd have to leave. But Daniel wanted Monika's rent-stabilized apartment lease. And maybe he set out to kill her, 'cause the New York City Council, in the wake of AIDS, had passed a bill entitling non-related roomates to inherit leases of the deceased. Or maybe he just hit her in the throat with the broom handle accidentally too hard. But Daniel Rakowitz found himself alone on 10th Street with her corpse.

Getting rid of bodies in Manhattan must be very hard. It's bad enough trying to get out to the Hamptons without a car or credit card. A carpenter friend loaned him a chainsaw. Parting out the arms-legs-head. He jammed the different body parts in garbage bags and hit the street like Santa Claus. A leg turned up at Port Authority Bus Terminal in the trash. Monika's thumb came floating to the surface of some Welfare Soup in Tompkins Square Park.

And then there was the airline pilot in Connecticut who killed his wife, strapped a rented woodchipper onto the bed of his pickup truck and drove around the streets of Groton in a snowstorm, chipper whirling skin and bones. Sylvère says this story reminds him of the *Romance of Perceval*. The blood must've been a sight.

Speaking of Sylvère, he now thinks the best way of disposing of a body would be to cement a basketball hoop above it. This presumes a suburban setting (perhaps like yours). The land I own is in the Town of Thurman, upstate New York, 3000 miles away—although I will be driving there next week.

Dick, did you realize you have the same name as the murdered Dickie in Patricia Highsmith's Ripley books? A name connoting innocence and amorality, and I think Dick's friend and killer confronted problems much like these.

Love,
Chris

Crestline, California
December 10, 1994

Dear Dick,

On December 15 I'll be leaving Crestline to drive our pickup truck and personal belongings and our miniature wire-haired dachshund Mimi back to New York. Six or seven days, three thousand miles. I will drive across America thinking of you. The Idaho Potato Museum, every landmark that I pass, will draw me closer to the next and they'll all be meaningful and alive 'cause they'll trigger different thoughts of you. We will do this trip together. I will never be alone.

Love,
Chris

Dear Dick,

I bet if you could've done this with Jane you never would've broken up with her, right? Do you envy our perversity? You're so priggish and judgmental but deep down I bet you'd like to *be like us*. Don't you wish you had someone else to *do it* with?

> *Your friend,*
> *Sylvère*

Crestline, California

December 10, 1994

Dear Dick,

Sylvère and I have just decided to drive out to Antelope Valley and post these letters all around your house and on the cactuses. I'm not sure yet whether we'll hang around next door with a video camera (machete) to document your arrival, but we'll let you know what we decide.

> *Love,*
> *Chris*

Crestline, California

December 10, 1994

Dear Dick,

We've decided to publish this correspondence and were wondering if you'd like to write an introduction? It could read something like this:

"I found this manuscript in the drawer of an old kitchen cabinet that I picked up at the Antelope Valley Swapmeet. It makes strange reading. Obviously, these people are very sick. I don't think there's much film potential in it because none of the characters are likeable.

"Still, I believe these letters will interest the reader as a cultural document. Obviously they manifest the alienation of the post-modern intellectual in its most diseased form. I really feel sorry for such parasitic growth, that feeds upon itself..."

What do you think?

Love,
Sylvère

PS: Could you Express Mail us a copy of your latest book, *The Ministry of Fear*? We feel that if we're going to write for you we should get more familiar with your style.

Love,
Chris

Crestline, California
December 10, 1994

Dear Dick,

Chris and I have spent the whole morning lying around with our computer thinking about you. Do you think this whole affair was just a means for Chris and me to finally have sex? We tried this morning but I think we've gone too far into our morbid imaginations. Chris continues to take you seriously. She thinks I'm sick, now she'll never touch me again. I don't know what to do. Please help—

Love,
Sylvère

PS: Thinking about it further, these letters seem to open up a new genre, something in between cultural criticism and fiction. You told us how you hope to revamp the writing program at your institution along these lines. Would you like me to read from it in my Critical Studies Seminar when I visit next March? It seems to be a step towards the kind of confrontational performing art that you're encouraging.

Regards,
Sylvère

By now it was 2 o'clock in the afternoon. Sylvère was triumphant, Chris was desperate. All she'd really wanted, for the past seven days was a chance to kiss and fuck Dick ____, and now all hope was receding, their meeting grew more distant every day, leaving ever-fewer pretexts for her to call. Clearly the letters were unsendable. And Sylvère was so excited by their writing, and aroused by it, and he knew that if there wasn't another event soon, another point of contact to fuel Chris' expectations, all this would end. For all these reasons, the pair decided they would write a fax.

FAX TO: DICK ____
FROM: CHRIS KRAUS & SYLVÈRE LOTRINGER
DATE: DECEMBER 10, 1994

Dear Dick,

It's a pity that we missed each other Sunday morning. It's funny, both of us thought a lot about your video—so much that we've had an idea for a collaborative piece, inspired by and hopefully involving you. It's kind of like, Calle Art. We've written about 50 pages over the last few days and were hoping we could shoot something with you out in Antelope Valley soon before we leave (Dec. 14).

Basically our idea was to paste the text we've written all over your car, house and cactus garden. We (i.e., Sylvère) would videotape me (i.e., Chris) doing this—probably a wideshot of all the papers flapping in the breeze. Then, if you like, you could enter and discover it.

I guess the piece is all about obsession, although we wouldn't think of using images that belong to you without your agreeing to it. What do you think? Are you game?

Best regards,
Chris & Sylvère

But of course the fax was never sent. Instead, Sylvère left one more message on Dick's answering machine:

"Hi Dick, it's Sylvère. I'd like to talk to you about an idea I had, a collaborative piece we could do before I leave on Wednesday. I hope you won't find it too crazy. Call me back."

Expecting no more response from Dick than they'd had all week, Chris left to do some errands in San Bernardino. But at 6:45 p.m. that Saturday, December 10, around the time that she was driving up the mountain, he called.

Upper Crestline seemed so dismal that night. A liquor store, a pizza parlor. A single row of woodframe facaded storefronts from the '50s, Depression-era recollections of the West, half boarded up. Wendy and Michael Tolkin had visited last month with their two daughters. Michael's film *The New Age* had just come out, following his other great films, *The Rapture* and *The Player*. He was a Hollywood intellectual and Wendy was the wittiest and nicest psychotherapist Sylvère and Chris had ever met. After expressing their delight in Crestline's quaint-ness, Wendy remarked: It must be very lonely living in a place you don't belong. Chris and Sylvère had no children, three abortions, and they'd been shuttling between low-rent rural slums on both coasts for the past two years in order to put money into Chris' film. And of course Michael, who was Sylvère's friend, really, because Sylvère was someone in LA who knew more than he about French theory, couldn't, wouldn't, do anything to help her with the film.

When Chris got home and Sylvère told her he'd talked to Dick, she nearly swooned. "I don't want to know!" she cried. And then she wanted to know everything. "I have a little present, a surprise," he said, showing her the audiotape. Chris looked at Sylvère as if seeing him for the first time. Taping their phone call was such a violation. It gave her a kind of creepy feeling, like the time the writer Walter Abish'd discovered the tape recorder Sylvère had hidden underneath the table when they were having drinks. Sylvère laughed it off, calling himself a Foreign Agent. But to be a spy is being no one. Still, Chris had to hear it now.

EXHIBIT C: TRANSCRIPT OF A PHONE CONVERSATION
             BETWEEN DICK _____ AND SYLVÈRE LOTRINGER

December 10, 1994: 6:45 p.m.

D: So, could we talk about the possibility of your coming out in the next semester—

S: Yeah. I guess the easiest for me would be between March 10 and 20. Do you want me to do something about cultural anthropology? Is that what you're doing now?

D: If it's not something you're interested in, we can maybe, uh, forget about it but—(inaudible).

S: Yeah?

D: (inaudible)—I don't know if you'd be enthusiastic about you know summarizing James Clifford and other discourses around anthropology, but if you want to do something more original, more, uh, primary, it's up to you.

S: Okay. And the fee would be 2500 dollars for two lectures and one seminar?

D: Two lectures and a seminar and maybe some studio visits.

S: Oh. Marvin said the crits paid extra…500 dollars more?

D: Uh, look, I'll see what I can do. I hope coming here is worth your while.

S: (inaudible) Well, I want it to be worth your while too.

D: We'll get a clearer picture of what's coming up in the semester in the next couple of weeks, and well, I can phone you in New York. (Inaudible)

S: Well, that's what I wanted to talk to you about. We—I want to sound you about a project that's a little weird, but I know you don't mind things that are weird—(laughs)—(silence) Right?

D: I don't think so, it depends. There's weird and weird. There's weird, and there's impossible weird. Impossible weird is more interesting.

S: Well okay, I might have something you're looking for then. (Laughs) Well, let me—it's a, uh, it's a collaborative project we were thinking of possibly doing before we leave on Wednesday, otherwise we'd have to postpone it to the end of January. And, uh, it started really with our visit to your place. And how we didn't reconnect in the morning—

D: (Inaudible)

S: Yeah, it was very odd. And then you—

D: I got back about 10:30 and you'd gone.

S: Uh huh, uh huh.

D: I'd crept out the back. I didn't expect you to know that I'd done that, but I thought I'd find you here so that was very weird.

S: Uh huh. Chris thought that somehow you were in your bed and you were just waiting for us to leave because you were in a different mood.

D: (Inaudible)

S: Yeah?

D: I'd just gone out and done a few errands and—I'm a bit of an insomniac so I'd driven around to Pear Blossom and Palmdale and I picked up some eggs and bacon. That was what I'd been doing.

S: Uh huh. So. What happened was, we had a very strange thing, I don't know how I can summarize it but basically, Chris felt very attracted to you.

D: (Snickers, exhales)

S: And uh, then we started talking about it, and writing you letters?

D: (Laughs, exhales)

S: (Laughs) and uh, these letters included you, both as yourself and as some sort of object of, you know, seduction or desire or fascination or something, and then—Well, I wrote a letter and she wrote a letter and we planned to send them to you and get you involved in a kind of fax correspondence. But somehow it got a little out of hand and we started riffing around it and getting paranoid and writing all these letters.

D: (Laughs, exhales)

S: And it kind of grew...into a, um, 20, 30, 40 pages and then it became impossible to send you that or sound you about it or involve you (laughs)—So we thought maybe we should do something a little bit more drastic to involve you in some way, and that's what I wanted to sound you about. We, uh, we got the idea that maybe we should just go back to your place before we leave on Monday or Tuesday with a video camera. Is that something you would like? I mean, I didn't want you to feel invaded in your territory and all that, but basically it would turn into some kind of an art piece with a text that could be, maybe, hanged on the cactuses and your car and something like that? And you'd come upon it and you know, we'd basically improvise from there.

D: (Inaudible)

S: *The Invasion of the Heart Snatchers.* Uh, it's a Calle Art piece. You know, like Sophie Calle? (Laughs) And it involves—I mean we've been caught up in a strange storm for several days, it just got a little out of hand—in our emotions and there's all these ups and downs where we connect and disconnect and somehow it seems so strange that you may not be connected to it at all, because we were totally convinced that you were a part of it—(Laughs)—But then we couldn't get hold of you, and, well, I don't know if you had a sense of it but we had such storm in a teapot here. (Laughs)

D: You mean a—tempest?

S: (Laughs) Yeah. Anyway what do you think about it?

D: Well I, I, uh, I need a little bit of breathing space to work out the—, wade through what you've told me—(Laughs) But uh, I mean it's—if we can just ah… Let me think about it yet.

S: Of course.

D: And I'll phone you back tomorrow and say what my dreams are and—kind of—creating a disposition in relation to this project.

S: Okay that's perfectly legitimate. In any case we liked your piece a lot, the video, seeing you rambling got us rambling too. After all, Chris is a filmmaker and she's working in video too.

D: Maybe the timing isn't great but the timing never is, I suppose. Let's think about it and I'll give you a call tomorrow.

S: Okay we'll be here all day.

D: Thank you for letting me in on the secret. I will think about it. Bye bye.

S: Okay you too. Yes don't tell anyone. Take care. Bye bye.

And then Chris went alone into her room and wrote a letter, thinking she would send it, about sex and love. She was all confused about wanting to have sex, sensing that at this point if she slept with

Dick the whole thing would be over. THE—UNEXAMINED—LIFE—IS NOT—WORTH—LIVING flashed the titles of a Ken Kobland film against the backbeat of a carfuck 1950s song. "As soon as sex takes place, we fall," she wrote, thinking, knowing from experience, that sex short circuits all imaginative exchange. The two together get too scary. So she wrote some more about Henry James. Although she really wanted both. "Is there a way," she wrote in closing, "to dignify sex, make it as complicated as we are, to make it not grotesque?"

Sylvère must've known that she was writing and at the same moment, in his room, he wrote:

"Dear Dick, it's funny how things have a way of turning around. Just when I thought I was taking some initiative I find myself in the position of the Dumb Dick, pushed around by other people's drives. Actually what hurt me most was how confused and disoriented Chris was, reverting to her reaction to younger crushes that I wasn't around to witness the first time. And then the difference between our ages widened to the half century. And I felt old and sad. And yet we're sharing something."

And yet being together as a couple was all either of them could imagine. Did they read their "private" letters to each other out loud? Probably. And then they made love, thinking about what? The absent Dick? At any rate they were on the bus again, committed to the game. Lying in bed beside Sylvère, Chris wrote this post-coital letter:

Crestline, California
December 10, 1994

Dear Dick,

It's several hours later and we've just had sex and before that spent the last two hours talking about you. Since you've come

into our lives our house has turned into a brothel. We smoke cigarettes, knock ashtrays over without picking them up, lay around
for hours. We've only worked halfheartedly and for a few hours at
a time. We've lost all interest in packing for the move, or trips
ahead, the future, consolidating our possessions or moving forward with our work and our careers. It isn't fair that you're so
unaffected. Are you spending Saturday night thinking about
Sylvère's phone call? I doubt it. Sylvère says you're right to tune it
out, because this correspondence has nothing to do with you. He
says it's just about us as a couple, but that's not true.

When I was 23 my best friend Liza Martin and I invited a
famous rock star known for his forays into the bizarre to fuck us
as if we were one person. Under the guidance of two artists we
revered, Richard Schechner and Louise Bourgeois, we'd been
developing a schizophrenic twin act in the backrooms of several
topless bars (Oops the phone is ringing. Is it you? No, it's just
another fax about the fucked up EDL of my movie from the negative cutter in New Zealand, which I've become so indifferent to.)
Anyway we told him Liza'd do the physical part of sex, I'd do the
verbal. Together we incarnated the cyborgian split projected on
all females by this culture. We even offered _____ his choice of
venue: the Gramercy Park Hotel or the Chelsea. But _____ never
answered. Easier I guess to fuck a bimbo than get involved with
such weird girls.

And now Sylvère and I are the weird girls. I never dreamed I'd
do anything like this again, especially never with Sylvère. But
frankly I feel like I've come to the end of something with the
movie. I don't know what will happen next and maybe you've fallen
into the vacuum. Don't you think the only way of truly understanding things is through Case Studies? I read a book last month

about the Guatemalan Coca Cola strike by Henry Frundt: a total reconstruction of events through documents and transcripts. By understanding one simple thing—a strike—it's possible to understand everything about corporate capitalism in third world countries. Anyway I think a case study is what we've started to create with you.

I feel like I'm awaiting an execution. Probably all this will come screeching to a halt tomorrow morning when you call. There're just a few hours left for the whole story (what story?) to unfold.

Love,
Chris

Crestline, California
December 10, 1994

Dear Dick,
I wonder what I'd do if I were you.

Love,
Sylvère

PS: We decided we will leave you alone for the rest of the night.

They were delirious, ecstatic. Chris had wished so many times that she could reach inside Sylvère's head or heart and exorcize his unhappiness. On Saturday, December 10, they rested, blissful and exhausted, finally inhabiting the same space at the same time.

Crestline, California
December 11, 1994: Sunday morning

Dear Dick,

I guess it's been a case of *infatuation*. Funny I haven't thought to use that word before.

You are the fourth and a half person (Shake, the Good Yvonne, the Bad Yvonne and David B., the Jesuit) I've been infatuated with since living with Sylvère. Mostly this infatuation-energy is about wanting to know someone.

It's funny, with the two Yvonnes, the sex-infatuation part came after already knowing them quite well, adoring them and wanting to be with them in other ways. Whereas the sex-infatuations that're male (you, Shake, the priest) leap out of nowhere, based on not knowing them at all. As if sex could provide the missing clues. Can it? In the cases of the males it's like I felt some kind of hint of who that person was floating underneath the surface. Wanting sex to realize things I knew.

Before I got together with Sylvère I'd usually get dumped by guys as soon as they found someone else more feminine or bovine. "She's not like you," they'd say. "She is a truly nice girl." And it hurt 'cause what turned me on in sex was believing that they knew me, that I'd found somebody to understand. But now that I've become a hag, i.e., accepted all the contradictions of my life, there's nothing left to know. The only thing that moves me now is moving, finding out about another person (you).

I know how lame these letters are. Still, I wanted to use the last few hours before your call to tell you how I feel,

Love,
Chris

Dear Dick,

We're under the gun now. In a few hours you might blow our whole story into shreds and reveal it for what it is: a strange perverse machine to get to know you, Dick. Oh Dick, what am I doing here? How did I ever get into this strange, embarrassing situation, telling you on the phone about my wife's infatuation with you? (I'm calling her my "wife," a word I never use, to emphasize the depth of our depravity...)

Would Chris have fallen in love with you if I hadn't been there to make it so embarrassing? Is knowledge a desperate form of acceptance? Or does acceptance transcend itself in knowledge to reach more interesting ground? "Knowledge" is supposed to be my concern...

So I was thinking about you, longing for a crisis, a bright future to keep death away. Do we have any right to push our fantasies on you? Is there any way they can connect that would be beneficial to us all? I understand what we have to gain from it. But what would I do if I were you, Dick? If you'd wanted the complexity of human relationships you wouldn't have moved alone out to the Antelope Valley. It reminds me of something Chris said the other day: the best place to hide a corpse is under everybody's eyes. And you're so close to everything but so difficult to grasp.

So why would you want to blow your cover, such a fragile eggshell, to enter a game you've refused to play anymore? The thing that's most embarrassing isn't telling you my wife's in love with you—that's just transgressive, and so ultimately acceptable. What's more embarrassing is to strip the whole intrigue bare, to bring it down to raw desire, like the "..."s in Chris' story when she imagines making love to you. Does knowledge stand for "..."? Does it need to be eroticized to find its point? And why should any point be finer than the raw "..."s of our desires? We know what the "..."s stand for. And what does your name stand for, Dick?

> *Here is mine,*
> *Sylvère*

Crestline, California
December 11, 1994

Dear Dick,

I disagree with Sylvère about your living situation. He thinks that it's escapist, as if living alone is an evasion of the inevitable coupledom, rejecting life. It's what parents say about the childless. But I think your life choices are totally valid, Dick.

> *Love,*
> *Chris*

Crestline, California
December 11, 1994

Dear Dick,

Noon. (Already). We're still waiting for your call. We think we'll switch now to the conversational mode since all our time between these letters has been spent talking about you anyhow.

> *Love,*
> *Chris & Sylvère*

Sunday, December 11, 1994: 12:05 p.m.

C: Sylvère what're we gonna do if he doesn't call? Are we gonna call him?

S: No, we can continue this without him anyway.

C: But you're forgetting that I really *want* for him to call. I'm tingling all over waiting for the phone to ring. I'll be really disappointed if he doesn't call.

S: Well this time you should talk to him. Why let us two white guys decide the course? I got him in. It's your turn now.

C: But I'm afraid he's not gonna call at all. What then? Do I call him? It's already feeling like the Frank Zappa song *You Didn't Try And Call Me*.

S: He'll call, but not today. He'll call when it's too late.

C: Oh Sylvère, I hate that.

S: But Chris, that's why he'll do it that way.

C: If he doesn't call today I think I'll have to disengage. Because, you know, I'll lose respect. We've done *so much*. All he has to do is call.

S: But maybe he'll realize we've already done everything in his place. Why disturb it?

C: I disagree. He should be curious. If some one called me and said they'd written 50, 60, 70 pages about me overnight I'd definitely be curious. You know, Sylvère, I think if this whole Dick thing falls through I'll go to Guatemala City. I have to do something with my life.

S: But Chris. The Antelope Valley *is* Guatemala.

C: I'll just be so disappointed if he doesn't call. How can you continue loving someone who doesn't pass this first and really basic test?

S: What test? The adultery test?

C: Nooo. The first test is to call.

Since their telephone has call-waiting, Chris phones her unshockable friend Ann Rower in New York.

TEN MINUTES LATER—

S: What did Ann think?

C: Ann thought it was a great project, more perverse than just having an affair. She thinks it'd make a good book! When Dick calls shall we tell him we're considering publication?

S: No. The murder hasn't happened yet. Desire's still uncon-summated. Let the media wait.

C: (whining) Whyyyyyyy??

SEVEN HOURS LATER—

C: Look Sylvère, this's hopeless. We're leaving in two days and I can't think past this phone call. I got a fax this after-noon from a producer who wants to see my film. I didn't even read it. Maybe it's already thrown away.

(Pause)

It's an impossible situation! I don't even know what I want from Dick anymore. Nothing good can come of this. The only thing I'm thankful for is that it's not the '70s and I didn't already fuck him. You know that anguish? Waiting by the phone until the burn and torment finally goes away? Our only hope is for some resumption of our normal lives. What seemed so daring just looks juvenile and pathetic.

S: Chris, I already told you he wouldn't call. He has a ten-dency to pull away. We've taken the decision for him. Deciding on his thoughts. Remember the introduction that we wrote for him? In a sense Dick isn't necessary. He has more to say by not saying anything and maybe he's aware of it. We've been treating Dick like a dumb cunt. Why should he like it? By not calling he's playing right into his role.

C: You're wrong. Dick's response has nothing to do with character. It's the situation. This reminds me of something that happened when I was 11 years old. There was this man at the local radio station who'd been very nice to me. He let me talk over the air. Then one day a cloud came over me, I started throwing rocks into the windshield of his car. It made sense while I was doing it but later I felt crazy and ashamed.

S: Do you want to throw a rock through Dick's Thunderbird?

C: I already have. Though mostly I've debased myself.

S: No.

C: Of course. I've projected a total fantasy onto an unsuspecting person and then actually asked him to respond!

S: But Chris, I think his embarrassment isn't in relation to you or me but to himself. What can he do?

C: I hate being thrown into such a physical state. When the phone rang during dinner my face flushed, my heart was pounding. Laura and Elizabeth drove all this way to visit us and I like them but I couldn't wait for them to leave.

S: Isn't that experiencing life to the hilt?

C: No, it's just a dumb infatuation. I'm so ashamed.

S: But even if his silence hurts you, isn't that what attracted you to him? The fact that he was inaccessible. So, I think there is a contradiction there, at least nothing to feel ashamed of—

C: I took terrible liberties with another person. He has every right to laugh at me.

S: I doubt he's laughing. Perhaps biting his fingers.

C: I feel so teenage. When you're living so intensely in your head you actually believe when something happens you've imagined, that you caused it. When Leonora OD'd on bad acid from my boyfriend Donald, he and Paul and I sat up all night in the park and made a pact that if Leonora wasn't out of Ward 16 tomorrow we'd kill ourselves. When you're living so intensely in your head there isn't any difference between what you imagine and what actually takes place. Therefore, you're both omnipotent and powerless.

S: You're saying teenagers aren't in their heads?

C: No, they're so far in that there's no difference between the inside of their heads and the world.

S: So what's happening in Dick's head now?

C: Oh Sylvère, he's not a teenager. He's not experiencing any feeling of infatuation for me. He's in a normal state, well, whatever's normal for him, wondering how to deal with this horrible mawkish situation.

S: If he's thinking about it, he'll call tonight. If not, he'll call on Tuesday morning. But he will definitely call.

C: Sylvère, this is like the Institute of Emotional Research.

S: It's funny how what we're after is so fleeting and so easily lost. The only way we can recapture any feeling is by evoking Dick.

C: He's our Imaginary Friend.

S: Do we need that? It's so mixed up. At times we reach these peaks of real possession at his expense, but through it we're able to see him more clearly than he ever would himself.

C: Don't be so presumptuous! You keep talking about Dick as if he was your little brother. You think you have his number—

S: Well, I don't have the same take on him as you do.

C: I don't *have* a *take*. I'm in love with him.

S: It's so unfair. What has he done to deserve this?

C: Do you think we're doing this because we're anxious and confused about leaving California?

S: No, leaving's our routine. But what would've happened if he'd been involved and willing?

C: I would've fucked him once and then he'd never call.

S: But what makes all this legitimate is that you didn't. What thinking about it's brought up is the essential thing. You know, I was picturing Dick before as a wicked, manipulative creature. But perhaps he's keeping silent just to give us time…

C: To get over him. He wants us to get over him.

S: Chris, what sort of strange zone are we entering? To write to him is one thing but now we're writing to each other. Has Dick been a means of getting us to talk, not to each other but to someTHING?

C: You mean that Dick is God.

S: No, maybe Dick never existed.

C: Sylvère, I think we're entering the post-mortem elegiac form right now.

S: No. We're just waiting for his call.

8:45 p.m.

S: It's so unfair. I guess these silent types make you work twice as hard and then you can't escape because you yourself create the cage. Maybe that's why you feel so bad. It's like he's watching, watching you do this to yourself.

C: Misery and self-loathing is the essence of rock & roll. When stuff like this happens you just want to turn the music up really loud.

TWO HOURS LATER—

(Dick hasn't called. Chris writes another letter and proudly reads it to Sylvère.)

C: Crestline, California
                                                 December 11, 1994

Hey Dick—

It's Sunday night, we've been through hell and not quite back, but now that you've been semi-informed about "the project" I guess it's only fair to bring you up to date: we're ready to call it off. We've travelled galaxies since Sylvère talked to you last night about shooting video at your place... Well, the video was not the point, we just wanted to find a mechanism for involving you in the process. Since then I've embraced/discarded several other art ideas but all we really have're these letters. Sylvère and I are wondering if we should submit them to Amy and Ira at High Risk or publish them ourselves in Semiotext(e)? In three days, we've written 80 pages. But I'm miserable and confused and judging by your silence you're not into any of this at all. Let's let it rest.

Bonne nuit,
Chris

S: Chris you can't send that. It makes no sense at all. You're supposed to be intelligent.

C: Okay, I'll try again.

EXHIBIT E: THE INTELLIGENT FAX

(printed on Gravity & Grace letterhead)

Sunday night

Dear Dick,

Well the "tempest in a teapot" seems to've passed without your entering it, which's fine with me. What is it we've been doing here over the last few days? I've been in limbo since disengaging emotionally from the movie and when this THING—the "crush"—came up, it seemed interesting to try and deal with dumb infatuation in a self-reflexive way. The result: 80 pages of unreadable correspondence in about 2 days.

It was interesting, though, to plummet back into the psychosis of adolescence. Living so intensely in your head that boundaries disappear. It's a warped omnipotence, a negative psychic power, as if what happens in your head really drives the world outside. Kind of a useful place to move around in, though maybe not so interesting to you.

In the future I'd like not to have to leave a room if you happen to be in it, so it seemed best not to leave things hanging.

Do let me know if you'd like to read (perhaps selections from) the letters. Through all the haze, at least some of them relate to you.

All best,
Chris

At midnight they transmit the fax. They go to bed but Chris can't sleep, feeling like she's compromised herself. Around 2 she slips into her office and scrawls the Secret Fax.

EXHIBIT F: THE SECRET FAX

> *Dear Dick, The idée fixe behind the tempest was that I'd like to see you Wednesday night after Sylvère leaves for Paris. I'd still like to do this. If you fax me yes or no after 7a.m. Wednesday I'll get your message privately.*
>
> > Chris

She punches in Dick's fax number, index finger hovering over *SEND*. But something stops her and she goes back to bed.

⋘⋆⋙

December 12, 1994

This morning as they lie in bed drinking coffee Chris says nothing to Sylvère about the Secret Fax. Instead she wonders about the difference in the prefix numbers in Dick's fax and phone lines. Tiny wisps of doubt gather into a thunderhead. When she checks the numbers in Sylvère's notebook she shouts: "Oh my God! We sent the fax to Dick at school!" (Curiously, Dick's school has only one fax machine. It's in the President's office. The President was a nice man, a Jewish liberal scholar married to a friendly acquaintance of Chris' from New York. Just two weeks ago, the four had spent a warm and animated evening at the President's home...)

The situation is now so globally embarrassing there's no choice but to phone Dick and alert him to the arrival of the fax. Miraculously,

Sylvère reaches Dick on the first call. This time he doesn't tape the conversation. Chris hides her head underneath the pillows. Sylvère returns, triumphant. Dick was gruff, annoyed, Sylvère reports, but at least we've headed off disaster. Chris sees him as a hero. She's so in awe of Sylvère's bravery she spontaneously confesses all about the Secret Fax.

And now Sylvère can't avoid the reality of this anymore. This is not another coffee-game they've invented. HIS WIFE LOVES ANOTHER MAN. Upset, betrayed, he writes a story.

EXHIBIT G: SYLVÈRE'S STORY
             INFIDELITY

Chris thought a lot about deceiving her husband. She'd never understood the comedies of Marivaux, all that sneaking around behind closed doors, but now the logic of deception dawned. She'd just had sex with Sylvère (who thanked Dick afterwards) and Sylvère expressed his deep undying love for her. Wasn't time ripe for betrayal?

Because in a sense, the story had to end this way. Isn't it what Sylvère intended, really, when he practically forced Chris to write "The Intelligent Fax"?

Sylvère and Chris had been together for ten years, and she fantasized confessing her adulterous virginity to Dick—"You're the first." Now the only way to get what she wanted (age 40 looming fast) without hurting Sylvère's feelings was to sneak. Sylvère also longed for an elegant conclusion to this adventure; didn't the form dictate that Chris end up in Dick's arms? And it would end there. Dick and Chris wouldn't need to ever do this again; Sylvère would never have to know.

But Sylvère couldn't help thinking Chris had betrayed the form they'd both invented by excluding him.

[And here Chris picks up the story, hoping to make Sylvère understand—]

Chris thought she was acting valiantly on her and Sylvère's behalf. Didn't someone have to bring the story to a close? Driving up North Road this afternoon, Chris felt she understood Emma Bovary's situation very well. The lonely move from Crestline looming; the drive across America. Three starved coyotes stood along the road. Chris thought about Emma's sensitive Italian Greyhound running farther from the coach towards certain doom. All is lost.

[Together, they continue—]

Ever since Sylvère's brave phone call that morning to a justifiably annoyed Dick, they realized they'd be hanging together now. Dick would never answer. The form would never be fulfilled. Sylvère would never be offered a job at Dick's school.

Sylvère pretended not to mind. Hadn't he and Chris behaved like true patricians, i.e., reckless lunatics? Would anyone else have dared to put someone in Dick's position through such a trip? We're artists, Sylvère said. So we're allowed.

But Chris was not so sure.

Eventually they would subtitle this *Does the Epistolary Genre Mark the Advent of the Bourgeois Novel*? But that was later, after another dinner with some noted academic friends at Dick's.

Crestline, California
Monday, December 12, 1994

Dear Dick,

I, we're, writing you this letter that we will never send. Finally we've figured out what the problem is: you think we're dilettantes. Why didn't we realize it before? I mean, Dick, you're a simple guy. You don't have time for the likes of us. You're like all the other boyfriends, guys, who'd confess proudly after shagging me regularly for six months, a year: "I've met someone. I really like her. Karen-Sharon-Heather-Barbara's not like you. She is a truly nice person." Well. Are we not Nice People in your eyes?

Is it a class thing? Even though we share your background, you think we're decadent sophisticates. That we are somehow…insincere.

What now? Were we wrong in trying to be close to you? Here are some events from the background of our lives:

We're leaving California, moving house for about the hundredth time in the last two years. Anxiety's become routine.

Chris got a letter today from Berlin: her film will *not* be in the Festival.

Chris received several faxes full of bad news, hidden costs, delays, from the post-production coordinator in New Zealand.

These events took us off the Dick Track for a while and we were so relieved to get back on it in a house already packed away.

Then Sylvère got a call from Margit Rowell, Drawing Curator at the MOMA. Would he like to edit a catalogue on Antonin Artaud? It's an important exhibition. The gap between us widens. Then the cleaning women showed up followed by the Carpet Shampoo man. Chris paced between everyone, frantic about your reaction to her fax.

Dick, why are we so bored with our lives? Yesterday we decided not to take this house again next summer. Perhaps we'll rent one on the other edge of your town?

Do you attract this kind of energy? Are we like the famous burglar who enters people's homes to steal small talismans—a pack of condoms, a cheese knife?

We can't bring ourselves to finish this letter.

Signed,
Chris & Sylvère

10:55 p.m.

We're thinking about calling Dick again to tell him that the video was a half-baked idea. This is how delirium works: we're laughing and excited and at this moment it makes perfect sense for us to call. After all, Dick's been "with" us for the past two hours. We're forgetting Dick never wants to hear from us again. Calling now would be the final straw.

Writing this has been like moving through a kaleidoscope of all our favorite books in history: *Swann's Way* and Willam Congreve, Henry James, Gustave Flaubert. Does analogy make emotion less sincere?

Time heals all wounds.

Dick, you're so intelligent but we live in different cultures. Sylvère and I are like the Ladies of the Heian Court in 5th century Japan. Love challenges us to express ourselves elegantly and ambiguously. But meanwhile you were Back at the Ranch.

Billets Doux; Billets Dick: A Cultural Study.

We put you to the test; we failed.

December 13, 1994

Tuesday dawns in disappointment. Sylvère and Chris spend the day moving things into Locker #26 at the Dart Canyon Storage Bins. For $25 a month they can postpone discarding their broken wicker chair, sagging double beds and thrift store couch forever. Chris hauls the furniture from the truck upstairs to Level 2 alone while Sylvère barks instructions. Because he has a plastic hip he can't lift anything heavier than a *Petit Larousse*, but he does consider himself an expert packer/mover. By the third trip it's completely clear that their stuff won't fit into Locker #26, a 4x8 enclosure. For 15 dollars more they could've had Bin #14, an ample 10x12, but Sylvère won't hear of it, these unnecessary expenses. *I'm very organized!* he cries (just as concentration camp survivors boasted about their ability to "organize" a smuggled egg or contraband potato). He keeps re-visioning how to stack the floor lamps, mattresses, 300 pounds of books and Chris is screaming at him, sagging under the weight of all this shit, (*You Cheap Jew!*) as she drags junk out of Bin #26 to the hall and back again. This makes him even more determined. But finally it all fits when they agree to throw away the gilded cage they'd bought in Colton at the Pets'R'Us liquidation sale for 30 bucks, a bargain. The bird had long since flown away. Driving back through Ensenada at the end of their cheap and dusty impromptu vacation in Baja last September, they'd bought a small green conure parrot on the roadside, hiding it under the carseat when they drove across the border. Loulou—they'd named it for Félicité's pet in Flaubert's *A Simple Heart*—had been Sylvère's Bird Correlative. He fed it lettuce leaves and seeds, confided to it, tried to teach it words. But one sunny autumn day he left the cage door open on the deck so Loulou could get a better view of the freshly snow-capped peaks above Lake Gregory. As he watched, astonished and then quickly broken-hearted, Loulou flew from the birdcage to the railing to the giant pine and finally out of view. They'd bought every bird accessory but the wing-clip. "He chose freedom," Sylvère repeated sadly.

Because most "serious" fiction, still, involves the fullest possible expression of a single person's subjectivity, it's considered crass and amateurish not to "fictionalize" the supporting cast of characters, changing names and insignificant features of their identities.

The "serious" contemporary hetero-male novel is a thinly veiled Story of Me, as voraciously consumptive as all of patriarchy. While the hero/anti-hero explicitly *is* the author, everybody else is reduced to "characters." Example: the artist Sophie Calle appears in Paul Auster's book *Leviathan* in the role of writer's girlfriend. "Maria was far from beautiful but there was an intensity in her gray eyes that attracted me." Maria's work is identical to Calle's most famous pieces—the address book, hotel photos, etc.—but in *Leviathan* she's a waif-like creature relieved of complications like ambition or career.

When women try to pierce this false conceit by naming names because our "I's" are changing as we meet other "I's," we're called bitches, libellers, pornographers and amateurs. "Why are you so angry?" he said to me.

There are no messages from Dick that evening on the answering machine. The house is empty, clean. After dinner Sylvère and Chris sit together on the floor and turn the laptop on.

EXHIBIT H: SYLVÈRE AND CHRIS' LAST CRESTLINE LETTERS

Tuesday, December 13, 1994
Crestline, California

Dear Dick,

I'm leaving for France in less than 24 hours. The clock is ticking though you seem unaware of it. This is a perfect tragic space.

It's such a bitch. This morning I felt some remorse, some empathy with you. It's been such a persecution game. But then again when you think of all the dozens of pages written, millions of words that've crossed our minds about you and all we ever did was phone you twice and send one miserable fax? I mean the discrepancy is mind-blowing.

Last night we thought we had it nailed, and in a sense we do. There's no way of communicating with you in writing because texts, as we all know, feed upon themselves, become a game. The only way left is face to face. When Chris woke up this morning I made my decision. She should go back to Antelope Valley alone and meet you, Dick.

But by the end of the afternoon I started having doubts. This morning I left a message with the President of your school thanking him for a pleasant evening. Imagine the scene: the President mentioning to you that I might join the faculty next year, Chris arriving on your doorstep just when you thought the devilish couple had flown away. What would you do? Say "Hi" or reach for your airgun? Maybe it's not such a good idea. Let's try another:

Chris arrives in Antelope Valley around sundown and settles in your favorite bar. She leans against the door sipping a long-necked beer and waiting for your car to drive by. Should she call your house? But she knows you're screening calls.

Here's another: you drive past the bar and notice that her truck is parked outside. You pull up by the bar, take your hat off and go inside. She looks up modestly across the long empty table of this cantina and sees your frame hovering in the door. The rest is history.

Scene Number Three: Chris books a room at a motel in a nearby town. She considers phoning you, decides against it, then on impulse drives to Antelope Valley and installs herself at your favorite bar. After a while she strikes up a conversation with the barman. Does he happen to know anything about this gringo living by himself on the edge of town? A nice guy, but somewhat strange? Chris fires questions at the soft Chicano cowboys who make a living keeping the undocumented Guatemalan orange pickers in line. Do they know your girlfriend? Do you have a girlfriend? Do you come here often? Do you go home alone? Do you talk? What do you say? "Whatsamatter?" the leathery-white American barkeep asks. "Are you a cop? Has he done something wrong?" "Yes," Chris says. "He won't return my calls."

You see? It's no use hiding.

So long for now,
Chris & Sylvère

Tuesday, December 13, 1994
Crestline, California

Dear Dick,

None of these ideas are right. The closest I can come to touching you (and I still want to) is to take a photo of the bar in your town. It'd be a wideshot, kind of Hopper-esque, daylight tungsten clashing with the dusky sky, a desert sunset wrapped around the stucco building, a single lightbulb hung inside...

Have you ever read *The Blue of Noon* by Georges Bataille? He keeps talking about chasing, missing, the Bluebird of Happiness... Oh Dick, I'm so saaaad.

Chris

Dear Dick,

I may be leaving the scene of the crime, but I can't let it fade out into nothingness.

Sylvère

Dear Dick,

I'm not sure I still want to fuck you. At least, not in the same way. Sylvère keeps talking about us disturbing your "fragility" but I'm not sure I agree. There's nothing so remarkable in one more woman adoring you. It's a "problem" you're confronting all the time. I'm just a particularly annoying one, one who refuses to behave. That makes the picture less appealing, and I just can't desire you anymore in that straight-up, Saturday night *Some Girls* kind of way. And yet I feel this tenderness towards you, after all we've been through. All I want's a photo of your favorite bar. Today I phoned your colleague Marvin Dietrichson, to find out what you did today. What you said in seminar. What you were wearing. I'm finding new ways to be close to you. It's okay, Dick, we can do the relationship your way.

Chris

Tuesday, December 13, 1994
Crestline, California

Dear Dick,

Call me persistent if you want but if you're an artist you can't rely on other people to do the work for you. Tomorrow night Chris is coming out to Antelope Valley.

Sylvère

And now it's nearly 10 o'clock at night and Chris is heartbroken and Dick still hasn't called. She knows she really won't drive out to Dick's house, she'll just drive away, and she hates Sylvère for pushing her to play the fool. But thanks to Dick, Sylvère and Chris have spent the four most intense days of their lives together. Sylvère wonders if the only way that he can feel close to her is when someone else is threatening to tear them apart.

The telephone rings. Chris jumps a mile. But it wasn't Dick, only the Dart Canyon Storage Man worrying because they'd left the locks to their storage bin open.

Should Chris call Dick? Should she rehearse it? After all, the last time she'd been taken by surprise. A single idea drifts across her mind, based on something she'd heard from Marvin Dietrichson the day before. Dick was struggling to finish writing some grant proposals for his Department before the Christmas break. That was a possible "in." Did Dick know Chris had once been a professional grantwriter? That she could whip out a proposal faster than Dick could whip it out? Should she offer to help, in compensation for all this trouble? But where would they meet? In his office? In his house? In the Antelope Valley bar?

Dear Sylvère,

There has to be something to look forward to, otherwise I just can't go on living.

Love,
Chris

Dear Chris,

From now on we'll have Dick's memory to cherish in everything we do. All through your trip across America we'll exchange faxes about him. He'll be our bridge between the Café Flores and the Texas oilfields…

⊱⋆⋅⋆⊰

Wednesday, December 14, 1994

Sylvère looked sad and tired when Chris left him with his overcoat and bags at the Palm Springs Airport. He'd fly to LAX, then JFK, then Paris while Chris finished packing up the house in Crestline. Chris stopped and bought *The Best of the Ramones* CD. When she got back to the house around lunchtime there were no messages from Dick but Sylvère had left one changing planes. "Hi Sweetie, I'm just calling to say goodbye again. We had a wonderful time together, it just keeps getting better and better."

His message touched her. But later that day, talking to her neighbor's kids, she was shocked to learn that Lori and her family were certain Sylvère was her father. Was it that obvious, even to the most casual observer, they were no longer having sex? Or did it mean that Lori, a confident assertive Black woman from LA, couldn't fathom someone her and Chris' age hooking up with an old wreck? Lori's younger boyfriend was handsome, silent, mean; he was a kind of ghetto-Dick.

"Dear Dick," Chris typed into her Toshiba laptop, "This morning the sun was coming up over the mountains as I drove Sylvère to the airport. It was another glorious California day and I thought about how different it is here from New York. A land of golden opportunity, freedom and the leisure to do—what? Become a serial killer, a Buddhist, swing, write letters to you?

December 15, 1994

Sylvère gets off the plane in Paris, France. Seven thousand miles and 15 hours later he's lost the drift of what it was in California that made writing love letters to his colleague seem like a good idea. He's experiencing Virillian free-fall. His plastic hip is killing him. He carries Percoset and Darvon, searching everyday for the magic mix that'll cut the pain without completely numbing him. Sylvère limps from his mother's tenement apartment near the Bourse across the right bank to Bastille. Of course he hasn't slept. At noon, it's dark and freezing. He feels like an ancient animal. His first meeting is with Isabelle, an old acquaintance, sometime-lover from New York who's acquired an important work of dubious provenance by Antonin Artaud. Nominally, Isabelle's an independent film producer, though in reality she's an ex-cokehead on a trustfund now in four-day-a-week analysis. Sylvère had always thought of Isabelle as one of the wildest and most reckless girls. Therefore, he can't wait to sound her on the Dick adventure. Isabelle listens carefully. "But Sylvère!" she says. "You're crazy. You put yourself in danger."

Back in Crestline, Chris sits hunched over her Toshiba. The truck is packed. She has a vague belief she'll write to Dick throughout the trip. She has a vague belief that writing is the only possible escape to freedom. She doesn't want to lose the drift. She types this story:

EXHIBIT I: "LAST NIGHT AT DICK'S"

I wake up wired, tired, but still running on nervous energy. The sunlight hurts my eyes, my mouth's still fuzzy from last night's booze and cigarettes. The day's not slowing down for me and I'm not ready.

Did we fuck? Yes…but the fuck seems insignificant beside the lengths we went to to get there. The daze I'm in right now seems realer. What's there to say? It was sensationless, pro-forma.

When I got to Dick's around 8 he was expecting me. 'Date' arrangements had been made: dimmed lights, reggae music on the stereo, vodka, condoms waiting by the bed though of course I didn't see them until later. Dick's place suddenly seemed like a cut-rate banquet hall or funeral parlor—generic props waiting to be cleared away for the arrival of the next corpse, bride, girl. Was I entering the same setting of seduction as poor Kyla?

I started out embarrassed and conciliatory, quite willing to admit I was a fly caught in the web of your enormous sex appeal, charisma. But then you deviated from the seducer's role by freely voicing the contempt that lies beneath it. You asked me questions, held up my desire to the light as if it were a strange and mutant thing. As if it were a symptom of my uniquely troubled character. And how was I to answer? I wouldn't be here if I didn't want to fuck. Your questions made me feel ashamed. When I turned them back on you, you answered bored and noncommittally.

Because you patronize me and refuse to see the possible reversibility of our situations it is impossible for me to state my love for you as totally as I feel it. You make me backtrack, hesitate. Then later, confused and psychically dismantled, I fall into your arms. A last resort. We kiss. The obligatory first contact before fucking.

Months later, parts of Chris' story would turn out to be remarkably prophetic.

Flagstaff, Arizona
December 16, 1994
The Hidden Village Motel

Dear Dick,

I got here around 10, 11 last night depending on which time zone you figure, wondering if I can really drive another 3000 miles. The town is wall-to-wall motels, and the billboards advertise a race war between the local rednecks ("American Owned and Operated") and the Indian immigrant majority who offer "British Hospitality." Competition keeps the prices down to 18 bucks a night.

This morning I woke up early and outside it was brilliantly cold and clear, that bright almost-weatherless mountain kind of cold with frosty ground. I made coffee and took Mimi for a walk back behind the train tracks through a scabby mix of low-rent complexes and trailer parks. 200 Dollars Moves You In to Blackbird Roost.

Walking, I thought about you or about the "project." How I'm realizing that even though the movie "failed" I'm left with a wider net of freedom than I've ever had before.

For two years I was shackled to *Gravity & Grace* everyday; every stage of it an avalanche of impossibility that I dismantled into finite goals. It didn't matter, finally, that the film was good or that I wrote 10 upbeat faxes every day, that I was accountable, available, no matter how I felt.

Anyway Dick, I tried my best but it still failed. No Rotterdam, no Sundance, no Berlin...just neg cut problems in New Zealand that drag on. For two years I was sober and asexual every day, every ounce of psychic anima was channeled into the movie. And now it's over; amazingly, and with your help, I almost feel okay.

(Last night I woke up in bed with cold feet, forgetting where I was, curled up and afraid.)

(And sometimes I feel ashamed of this whole episode, how it must look to you or anyone outside. But just by doing it I'm giving myself the freedom of seeing from the inside out. I'm not driven anymore by other people's voices. From now on it's the world according to me.)

I want to go to Guatemala City. Dick, you and Guatemala are both vehicles of escape. Because you're both disasters of history? I want to move outside the limits of myself (a quirky failure in the artworld), to exercize mobility.

I don't have to topless dance or be a secretary anymore. I don't even have to think that much about money. Through the last five years of building Sylvère's career and real estate I've bought myself a very long leash. So why not use it?

This morning I called a New York magazine about my article on Penny Arcade's *Bitch!Dyke!Faghag!Whore!* The assistant maybe did, maybe didn't know who we were, but at any rate she was discouraging and snippy. Is there any greater freedom than not caring anymore what certain people in New York think of me?

It's time to pack and call Sylvère. It's just fine here, being on the road.

Love,
Chris .

Sweetie,

I woke up in the middle of the night last night and wrote you a letter.

Things seem a little rough…

> Santa Rosa, New Mexico
> December 17, 1994: around midnight
> The Budget 10 Motel

Dear Dick, Sylvère, Anyone—

I wouldn't be writing anything tonight if it weren't that I'd left my books out in the car. Now I'm too tired to get dressed again just to read another few pages from the life of Guillaume Apollinaire.

There were some low moments out there on the road tonight—abandonment and what's the point?—but then I pulled in a radio station from Albuquerque playing historical rap and breakdance circa 1982. Kurtis Blow and disco synthesizers made me feel like I could drive all night.

I didn't write anything last night in Gallup and I got a late start after that terrible phone call with Sylvère. Since when're you so impressed with Isabelle that her opinion counts for what we do? And then I got an oil change, had lunch and it was noon…

…but I detoured anyway off the Interstate at Holborn to see the Petrified Forest, which wasn't a forest at all but a museum of boulders and stones. There were very few of us, walking aimless on the mesa, exposed.

Back in the car I started thinking about the Orphan Plan, how what you "want" (our life in East Hampton) can suddenly seem repugnant. What a torture for someone from the Central American rain forest to have to live in East Hampton and attend Springs School.

Somewhere on the drive the whole sex/Dick thing disappeared. I guess I'm ready to go back to asexuality for another year. I don't know what I'm driving towards...

And later thinking about John Weiner's *Poem for Vipers*—

Soon I know the fuzz will
interrupt, will arrest Jimmy and I
shall be placed on probation. The poem
does not lie to us. We lie
under its law, the glamour of this hour...

What were his career strategies? Hah. Pessimism's what Lindsay Shelton liked so much about *Gravity & Grace* and now it's clear the film has no chance in movie terms. I may as well own it but ohhh, I thought there'd be more movies after *G & G*. If there are no movies I need to figure out what it's gonna be.

And now Sylvère's confused and ready to disown this whole escapade, and he's mad at Jean-Jacques Lebel for his depiction of Félix and he's mad at Josephine's boyfriend for writing a book about the pair. But Sylvère, Félix and Josephine were French theory's Sid and Nancy...

Tomorrow's another time zone (Central) and the Texas panhandle. Then Oklahoma, then the South. I bought three pairs of earrings yesterday in Gallup.

Dick, it's hard for me to access you tonight. All your cowboy/loner stuff seems silly.

Chris

❦

As Chris drove East she felt herself being sucked forward into a time tunnel. Christmas was getting closer. There were more Christmas songs on the radio, more Christmas decorations in every little town, as if Christmas was a cloud that descended on New York and feathered out across the West in broken strands. She was literally losing time by crossing time zones to the east and driving pulled her farther away from what she knew. It was like that spatial/optical illusion, being in a car stalled in a single lane of traffic. You panic 'cause you think your car is moving by itself and then you realize it's the other cars that're moving. Yours is standing still.

> **Shawnee, Oklahoma**
> **December 18, 1994: 11:30 Central Standard Time**
> **The American Motel ($25 a night)**

Well Dick,

I got lost in Oklahoma City, nearly out of gas and couldn't find a room. The motel in the AAA book turned out to be a fuck palace by a topless bar and everything else was full. It took another hour driving to find a vacancy here in Shawnee. There's a meat works right across the road.

By the time I realized I was on the wrong Oklahoma City bypass there was construction and it was too late to get off. I had to drive the 50 miles of loop. Panic flashed me back to when I was travelling between New York, Columbus and Los Angeles last year.

Panic. Late winter 1993: Getting off the plane from LA in Columbus around midnight, suddenly and brutally ejected from the tube of business travel into the reality that Radisson and Hyatt, airline platinum cards and Hertz Preferred all insulate you from. The car I'd driven from New York was being fixed at the Columbus Subaru dealership under warranty. I caught a taxi to the auto mall industrial park zone 15 miles outside the city. The duplicate car key was ready. But when we got there the car was nowhere to be found. Suddenly after seven hours in the tube, motel-taxi-plane-to-taxi I'm left at 1 a.m. standing under car yard klieg lights in the snow, guard dogs howling. The driver took me to the city, all barriers between us broken down, and he's ranting about wogs and how reading William Burroughs made him different from all the other cab drivers in Columbus and could I tell him how to make a living as an artist? Well, no.

And then the next day, driving through northeast blizzards, West Virginia, Pennsylvania, torn inside out. It was that Piscean time of year. I thought the snow would never melt—white everywhere and skinny shaken stakes of Northeast trees. Insulation makes us increasingly unable to respond to weather. All that month I was seized by this unnameable emotion. Nature's vengeance. The week I spent doing post-production at the Wexner Center in Columbus I was sick with Crohn's Disease, as if my body was negating the illusion of momentum. Functioning over waves of pain by day, throwing up at night, it's like a hysteria of the organs, walls of the intestine swollen so it's impossible to eat or even drink a glass of water.

The week before on the plane ride from Columbus to Dallas the entire business cabin's filled with salesmen from the Pepsi-Cola Corporation. The one beside me's drunk and wants to talk about his reading habits, his passion for Len Deighton, let me out oh no. And then we're stuck in Dallas because a blizzard grounded the connection from Chicago…and it was there in the Garden Room of the DFW Hilton that I met David Drewelow, the Jesuit priest.

That night I felt like something had been sucked out of me and meeting David Drewelow replaced it. Making eye contact in the restaurant line I mistook him for oh, a software engineer from Amherst, good for forty minute's chat about restoring country houses. But he turned out to be a genius who read Latin, Spanish, French and Mayan and believed that Chrissy Hynde and Jimi Hendrix were avatars of Christ. David Drewelow lived out of a storage bin in Santa Fe, New Mexico and travelled round the country raising money for a Jesuit mission on the Guatemalan coast. More than a liberationist, he saw the church as the only force still capable of preserving vestiges of Mayan life. Of course Drewelow had read Simone Weil's *Gravity & Grace*. He owned Plon's first edition of it, recalled the thrill of finding it in Paris. For several hours we talked about Weil's life, activism and mysticism, France and trade unions, Judaism and the Bhagavad Gita. I told him all about the title sequence I'd been making in Columbus for my movie, named after Weil's book…pans across medieval battle maps and scenes superimposed with static WW2 aerial surveillance target maps…history moving constantly and sometimes visibly underneath the skin of the present. Meeting David Drewelow was like a miracle, an affirmation that some good still existed in the world.

Back in Columbus, Bill Horrigan, Media Curator at the Wexner, asked me how I "really" managed to support myself. I was picking up the restaurant check and driving a new car and obviously this cover story about an art school teaching job fooled no one. "It's simple," I told him. "I take money from Sylvère." Was Bill bothered that such a marginal sexless hag as me wasn't living in the street? Unlike his favorites, Leslie Thornton and Beth B, I was difficult and unadorable and a Bad Feminist to boot.

Oh Bill, you should've seen me in New York in 1983, vomiting in the street. I was bruised with malnutrition on the Bellevue Welfare Ward and hooked up to IV not knowing what was wrong because the City's mandatory catastrophic care plan doesn't cover diagnostic tests.

"Sylvère and I are Marxists," I told Bill Horrigan. "He takes money from the people who won't give me money and gives it to me." Money's abstract and our culture's distribution of it is based on values I reject and it occurred to me that I was suffering from the dizziness of contradictions: the only pleasure that remains once you've decided you know better than the world.

Accepting contradictions means not believing anymore in the primacy of "true feeling." Everything is true and simultaneously. It's why I hate Sam Shepard and all your True West stuff—it's like analysis, as if the riddle could be solved by digging up the buried child.

Dear Dick, today I drove across the panhandle of North Texas. I was incredibly excited when I hit the flatland west of Amarillo knowing that the Buried Cadillac piece would come up soon. Ten of them—a pop art monument to your car, fins flapping, heads buried in the dust. I passed it on the highway, turned back and took two photos of it for you.

Dick, you may be wondering, if I'm so wary of the mythology you embrace, why'd my blood start pumping 15 miles west of Amarillo? Why'd I used to get dressed up to go meet JD Austin in the Night Birds Bar? So he could fuck me up the ass, then say he didn't love me? Tight jeans, red lips and nails this morning, feeling really femme and like time for this isn't on my side. It's a cultural study. To be part of something else. Sylvère and I are twinned in our analytic bent, content with "scrambling the codes." Oh Dick, you eroticize what you're not, secretly hoping that the other person knows what you're performing and that they're performing too.

Love,
Chris

Dear Dick,

Tonight I actually felt like reading as much as writing you. Talking on the phone to Ann, my family, took the edge off.

Everything felt so dismal earlier today in Oklahoma I gave up trying to make good time. I needed to adjust to Northeast landscape. By 2 o'clock the green started looking pretty, and I got off the Interstate in Ozark and walked in a park beside the river. Golden green and blue. In the car I started thinking, once I accept the failure of *Gravity & Grace* it won't matter anymore what I do—once you've accepted total obscurity you may as well do what you want. The landscape in the park reminded me of Ken Kobland's films...that bit of video that The Wooster Group used in *LSD*...camera stumbling around the woods, end of winter, stark blue sky, patches of snow still left on the scabby ground...as evocative as anything of that moment when you're starting to Get Off. Ken really is a genius. His work is pure intentionality, everything is effortless and loaded and I learned how to make films by watching his.

And now the femme trip's over. Everything's different being back in the Northeast. I'm back to basic camouflage. Good country & western song on the radio today: *I Like My Women A Little On The Trashy Side*.

Since this is such a dead-letter night, Dick, perhaps I'll transcribe a few notes that I made in the car:

"12:30 Central Time, Saturday, now in Texas. Looks just like New Mexico. Thinking about Dick's video—the sentiment, Sam Sheppard cowboy stuff, is a cypher. The video was shown in response to my criticism of Sylvère's sentimentality when he writes fiction. I said, you have to do what you're smartest at, i.e., where you're most alive. Then Dick pulled the video out as a manifesto or defense of sentiment."

LATER THAT DAY—

"I'm in Shamrock now—great emptiness. It feels like a resting point or destination. I forgot to mention, D., the menorah on your refrigerator—that impressed us."

THE NEXT MORNING—

"I guess the Northeast hit overnight. When I got out of the motel this morning I was no longer West but East in Shawnee, Oklahoma— there're hills and clumps of skinny trees and lakes and rivers. It'll be the same now 'til I hit New York—a landscape full of dreary childhood memories I have no use for. There's a teariness about the worn-down hills and shivering trees, like in Jane Bowles' story *Going to Massachusetts*, emotion overwhelms this landscape 'cause it's so unmonumental. It elicits little fugues of feeling I'm not ready for. The desert overwhelms you with its own emotion but this landscape brings up feelings that're far too personal. That come inside out, from me. The West is Best, right? I'm nauseous and asleep and the coffeepot is buried underneath the washstand I bought in Shamrock. But all will change. I miss you—

Love,

Chris

"The Wicked Witch of the East"

Chris reached Tennessee and Eastern Standard Time on December 20. She needed to stop driving and stayed two nights in Sevierville. She went hiking through wild mountain laurels in the national park and bought an antique bed for 50 dollars. On the morning of the 22nd she reached Sylvère in Paris. Peaceful and contented, she pictured them returning to Sevierville together for a vacation but Sylvère didn't understand. "We never have any *fun* together," she sighed into the phone. Sylvère replied gruffly: "Oh. Fun. Is that what it's supposed to be about?"

Chris wrote Dick two letters from Sevierville.

"Dear Dick," she wrote, "I guess in a sense I've killed you. You've become Dear Diary…"

She'd begun to realize something, though she didn't think much about it at the time.

Frackville, Pennsylvania

December 22, 1994: 10:30 p.m.

Central Motel

Dear Dick,

All day and into this evening I've been feeling lonely, panicky, afraid. Tonight I didn't see the moon at all until about 8:30 but suddenly, driving north on 81, THERE IT WAS, deep & huge like it'd just risen, nearly full and red orange like a blood tangerine. It felt ominous, and I'm wondering if you feel as I do—this incredible urge TO BE HEARD. Who do you talk to?

On the road today I thought a little bit about the possibility of creating great dramatic scenes out of material that's diaristic, vérité. Remembering Ken Kobland's video *Landscape/Desire*—all those motels, everything flattened to a point where you don't expect a story and so just settle in for the ride. But there has to be a point, to give some point to this shifting landscape of flapping laundry, motel bathroom tiles. Perhaps the aftermath of something? But aftermath rarely is that way. You never sense the "aftermath" because always, something else starts up along the way.

To initiate something is to play the fool. I really came off the fool with you, sending the fax, etcetera. Oh well. I feel so sorry we were never able to communicate, Dick. Signals through the flames. Not waving but drowning—

Chris

December 23 was the brightest clearest winter day on the road across the Poconos into upstate New York. Dark red barns against the snow and winter birds, Cooperstown and Binghamton, colonial houses with front porches, kids with sleds. Her heart soared. It was the image of American childhood, not hers of course, but the childhood she'd watched as a child on TV.

Four thousand miles away Sylvère Lotringer sits reminiscing about the Holocaust with his mother on rue de Trevise. She serves him gefilte fish, kasha, sauteed vegetables and rugelach in the tiny dining room. There's something comical about a 56-year-old man being waited on like a child by his 85-year-old mother, but

Sylvère doesn't see it this way. He's started taping their conversations because details of the War remain so hazy. The Paris roundup following the German Occupation, the escape, false papers, letters coming back from all the relatives in Poland stamped "Deportee."

"Deportee," "Deportee," she intones, her voice like steel, rage keeping her so vibrantly alive. But for himself, Sylvère feels only numbness. Was he there at all? He was just a child. Yet all these years he's been unable to think about the War without tears springing to his eyes.

And now he's 56 years old, and soon he'll need another plastic hip. He'll be 63 before his next sabbatical. The young Parisians in the street belong to a bright impenetrable world.

Chris arrived to an empty house in Thurman, the Southern Adirondack town she and Sylvère discovered when they were looking for an "affordable estate" seven years ago. They'd come upon it one November driving down from a Bataille Boy's Festival in Montreal that co-starred Sylvère and John Giorno. Leaving Montreal they started screaming about which bridge to take, and hadn't spoken since. Chris' own gig at the Festival had been furtively arranged, a Bataille Boy's favor to Sylvère, but when they arrived her name was not on the program. Liza Martin took her clothes off to an enthusiastic prime-time crowd; they put Chris on at 2 a.m. to read to 20 drunken hecklers. Still, Sylvère didn't understand why she was unconsolable. Hadn't both of them been paid? On the Northway near Elizabethtown a pair of falcons flew across the road: a fragile link between themselves and Liza Martin's g-string and *The Falconer's Tale* of medieval France. They stopped to walk, and Sylvère was eager to share something, so he shared her enthusiasm for the Adirondacks and two days later they bought a ten room farmhouse in the Town of Thurman just west of Warrensburg, New York.

Thurman, New York
December 23, 1994
Friday, 11:30 p.m.

Dear Dick,

I got here before dark in time to see Hickory Hill and the two humpbacked mountains west of Warrensburg come into view.

Warrensburg looked as timelessly rundown as ever—Potter's Diner, Stuart's Store, LeCount Real Estate lined up along Route 9… that total absence of New England charm that we find so appealing. I drove 12 miles along the river, past Thurman Station to the house to find Tad, a friend who stays with us there. But he wasn't in, so I went down to the bar in Stony Creek to find him.

The O'Malley's trashed the house before leaving, as I expected. The entire Town of Thurman looked just as bad. The new zoning gives everyone the freedom to do anything. Now there's an ugly little homemade subdivision right next door. No one's crazy enough to waste money gentrifying the Southern Adirondacks. It's a diorama of A Hundred Years of Rural Poverty, each generation leaving relics of its failed attempts to make a living from this land. Tad and I had drinks and then came back to unload the truck. He's been living here since the O'Malley's left.

But I wanted to tell you how exhilarating it felt to step out of the truck and feel the cold dark air around Stony Creek's four corners. There's just one streetlight so you can see every single star. Five hundred people 15 miles away in all directions from anything. Unlike California, upstate New York doesn't lend itself to spiritual retreats or communes. People like Tad who moved here 20 years ago found out the only way they could make it through eight months of winter was by turning into locals themselves.

But that was earlier. My hands are dry and dirty and I'm tired. So Dick, I guess we'll pick this up later.

xxxxo,

Chris

Thurman, New York

December 24, 1994

Saturday, 10:30 p.m.

Dear Dick,

Right now I'm sitting up against some pillows on the floor of the front-north bedroom looking up at the bed I bought in Tennessee—this stupendously beautiful thing I've been working on tonight, massaging with rags dipped in walnut oil, then shining. It's made of poplar, "the pauper's hardwood," and Tad says you can tell it's old because the curves were made without electric tools. There was a lot of pleasure in this, rubbing in the oil and feeling with my hands how it was made. I've always wanted something like it.

Tonight I said to Tad we're starting a Shaker commune here: no sex and we work without ceasing. I've been enjoying the comfortableness of the time here with him very much. Tonight I felt tremendous admiration for Tad, his brave cheerfulness. It's Christmas Eve and here we are alone, he much more so than me: no tree no families no plans. And Tad is such a sentimentalist. Last year his ex-wife ran away with their three children to Australia. Now he's downstairs finishing a woodwork project, not feeling sorry for himself at all.

I realize I haven't told you anything about this place—will I be able to make you understand? It's so different here from California. At the hardware store this morning Earl Rounds asked me where I was living. I said, across the road from Baker's. Oh, Earl said, the old Gideon place.

No matter who else comes and goes this house will *always* be "the old Gideon place" to the locals. The Gideons were an older couple from Ohio who bought the house when it was the Great Dartmouth Tract, a farmhouse/dude ranch on 125 acres. This was in the 1970s and people must've still taken "family vacations" though of course the place was closed eight months a year. One night in January Mrs. Gideon ran screaming, naked across High Street and pounded on Vern Baker's door for several freezing minutes 'til he woke up and let her in. Exposure. Two days later the Gideons packed up and drove away never to be seen again. Did they go back to Ohio?

Last New Year's Eve a New Jersey oil company executive walked off into the woods at Harrisburg wearing nothing but a cashmere cardigan, slacks and loafers. He died quickly of exposure.

Down the road from Baker's there's Chuck and Brenda. I loved Brenda, she was my Hick Correlative—a manic depressive chain talker who threw her energy into buying up distressed slum houses. Chuck, an otherwise unemployable alcoholic, renovated them. She owned about 15 of them, even got a HUD grant to build apartments in Minerva, but everything collapsed when she refinanced them. She and Chuck began a 1500 foot addition to their house to accommodate her four children. But it's five years later and the two kids by her first marriage have long since moved out, back to Warrensburg with their father, because they couldn't stand Chuck and Brenda's screaming. Now she's working as a chambermaid and selling Amway products. All that's left of Brenda's empire is a pink Jacuzzi with brass faucets gleaming in an unheated shell of plywood nailed to 2x4's. If you live here long enough everything becomes a story.

Sylvère and I bought this house from a young couple of Jehovah's Witnesses. He'd inherited it from his parents, Long Islanders who bought it as a hunting camp. No one here remembers them and I doubt Sylvère and I will leave much imprint either.

Dick, I've never been much of a journal writer, but it's been so easy to write to you. All I want is that you should know me, or know a little about what I'm thinking, seeing. "And the moon of my heart is shining forth," a Japanese courtesan named Lady Nijo wrote at the end of her confessions. I've never thought writing could be such a direct communication but you're a perfect listener. My silent partner, listening so long as I stay on track and tell you what is really on my mind. I don't need any encouragement, approval or response as long as you are listening.

Tonight I read a strange and creepy book about Elaine and Willem de Kooning. Really it's a portrait of a period that believed in the utter worthlessness of women—"art tarts" and a few "girl artists" all orbiting around the big Dicks. Put it together with *Odd Girls and Twilight Lovers: A Secret History of Lesbian Life in Twentieth-Century America* and it's impossible to understand how we got from there to here. Stranger than the fall of the Gang of Four after the Chinese Cultural Revolution.

I'll close for now,

> Love,
> Chris

For Christmas, Tad gave Chris a diary: a blank book with Edward Hopper's picture of a tough young woman in a straw hat and flimsy dress leaning up against a pillar on the cover. Looking for trouble?

Chris walked along Mud Street Christmas morning past Josh Baker's trailer wondering if she could describe this place to Dick as well as David Rattray wrote about East Hampton. Could Dick even understand her feelings about Thurman? It was different from his Wild West adventure because she'd lived here, taught school, knew half the town and could never float above the surface of it.

That night she was invited to spend Christmas with her friend Shawna's family in New Jersey. She drove down alone, experiencing every blurry alteration in the landscape with a chill. That night she sat up late in the living room writing her first diary entry. Impossible to write alone. The diary begins: Dear Dick.

Somewhere on the trip across America she'd made a promise (to herself? to Dick?) to write him every day whether she felt like it or not. In the vast scheme of human effort, this wasn't much to do. (As a teenager she'd gotten through rough visits to the dentist by thinking about the bravery of China's poor and lower middle peasants.)

William, Shawna's dad had just come back from Guatemala with a Quaker group. After Christmas dinner the family gathered round to hear highlights of the torture testimonies he'd recorded. These tapes got her thinking. The testimonies, though they recounted incredible atrocity, were uniformly clear and undigressive—as if each speaker were somehow part of a larger person. Was it the unifying force of narrative? Was it because all the speakers belonged to the same rural Indian community? Chris was not a torture victim, not a peasant. She was an American artist, and for the first time it occurred to her that perhaps the only thing she had to offer was her specificity. By writing Dick she was offering her life as Case Study.

Shawna's husband Jack was such an asshole. William was recounting his brief meeting with the American activist Jennifer Harbury, who'd gone on a hunger strike and chained herself to the steps of the American embassy in Guatemala City. Shawna and Chris were awestruck. "Excuse me, Bill," Jack oozed. "Correct me if I'm wrong but isn't Jennifer a Harvard educated lawyer?" He was speaking in the same seductive gravelly voice, reeking of sincerity, that he used on frightened actresses. "I mean, she comes from bucks. And don't you think if Jennifer really cared about her husband she would've found a quarter million to throw at El Capitano? Isn't that how it works down there? If she wanted him released she wouldn't've made this public scene…" Jack Berman obviously was an expert on what constitutes a Virtuous Woman. Someone who keeps her mouth shut and respects the rules of "privacy." Jack's five ex-wives were all paragons of virtue. Bill was stumped and Chris, for once, was virtuous because she didn't want to ruin Christmas.

✧✦✧✦✧

December 26, 1994

On Monday Chris drives to JFK to meet Sylvère's plane from Paris. Their plan is to go from JFK to their other (rented) house in East Hampton, deal with a basement flooding problem, pick up some books Sylvère needs for the semester and then drive back to Thurman where they'll spend the rest of Christmas Break. The plane's due in at 7:30 but they don't leave the airport 'til much later because Chris arrives 10 minutes late, Sylvère wanders off to find her and they circle around the terminal looking for each other for two hours. They fight about this all the way to Riverhead. Exhausted around midnight they settle into the Greenport Waterfront Inn motel (off season rates). For the first time since leaving California Chris fails to write to Dick. She and Sylvère still seem 4,000 miles apart; the distance drains her. But finally when Sylvère takes off his clothes they're back on common ground: he's wearing a homemade moneybelt stuffed with hundred dollar bills that his mother, a retired furrier, sewed on the eve of his departure. By June they hoped to pay down their most expensive mortgage. They count out the money on the bed—25 fresh one hundreds—they're thrilled! They'd only been expecting 20.

And then they made love twice, Chris told Dick the next morning when she finally wrote her letter. Sylvère wanted to collaborate on details but Chris wanted to tell Dick about other stuff, about her visits with her girlfriends Ann and Shawna.

"Dick," she wrote after sending Sylvère out for coffee, "this house business is so absorbing I wonder when I'm ever going to get back to the tedium and humiliation of the movie. I guess I will. Would it be enough to write to you? Yes, I don't know, maybe—"

Maybe she told Sylvère how estranged she felt or maybe he sensed it. Because the next day, December 28, against his better judgment, Sylvère found a way of inserting himself back into the story.

EXHIBIT L: A VISIT TO SYLVÈRE AND DICK'S
                MUTUAL FRIENDS BRUCE AND BETSEY

> Bruce & Betsey's Guest Room
> Mount Tremper, New York
> Wednesday, December 28, 1994: 12 a.m.

Dear Dick,

Well the house was a disaster and I was too tired to write to you after 12 hours siphoning floodwater out of the cellar, then packing-shopping-driving. We'd meant to drive straight through to Thurman but we started talking about you in the car and Sylvère had this idea that maybe we could stop and visit your friends Bruce and Betsey in Mt. Tremper. I mean, they're sort of his friends too (though if they find out about these letters, they won't be). It seemed so outrageous and farfetched, but when Sylvère called Bruce from a pay phone he said, "Of course! You'll spend the night!"

Next Morning:

It's 7:45, Sylvère's gone to get some coffee and I'm writing here in bed under a pile of wooly blankets. In fact it's beautiful: a maple tree, a frozen river, woods and winter chickadees seen through warpy glass French windows. Twenty years ago the place would've been an ideal setting for group acid trips.

Sylvère tried so hard last night to bring you into a final gasping conversation. The visit up 'til then had been so bourgeois and impersonal…shared platitudes about country houses, academic life, the advantages and disadvantages of commuting. Just as we were heading up to bed Sylvère had the nerve to pop the question: What did Bruce and Betsey think of you? Betsey remembered something smart you'd said: I don't believe in the evil of banality but I believe in the banality of evil. What's Dick got to do with Hannah Arendt? I wondered, while Betsey and Sylvère speculated on the banality you've embraced since moving to California. Sylvère gave the usual rap about America's mythic hold on Europeans—why doesn't he extend himself to you? He sounds so glib. "All my life," you said, "I've thought about moving to the desert"; and "The nihilism beneath things here is terrifying." Anyway Dick I like you so much better than these people. Bruce asks questions but never listens to the answers. Betsey blathers on to fill the void. She looks a little like the model Rachel Hunter: thin and busty, flat ass and masses of great hair, she's read everything Bruce's read but he has the career. Do you find these people charming Dick? Bruce looks even older than Sylvère, the two of them remind me of the kind of aging rock & roller/supermodel couple you see around East Hampton—kind of dumb and self-absorbed. I don't know why I dislike them so much, Dick. But I do. I guess I'm disappointed? After all, Sylvère and I came here on a mission, and that mission was to be close to you.

I never told you about last night at Claire and David's. David said the most subtle and intelligent thing about Arnold Schoenberg: When the form's in place, everything within it can be pure feeling. It's true of them as much as of atonal music. They are the perfect hosts from a world I've only read about, where having dinner is a kind of temporal art. They're so cultured and intelligent, not nasty-smart but still provocative, drawing people out so that by the time the coffee's served you feel like something has—occurred.

But now it's time to get up and make one last effort here with Bruce and Betsey.

Love,

Chris

Thurman, NY
Friday, December 30, 1994: 10 a.m.

Dear Dick,

Sylvère has taken Mimi to the vet & I'm alone & want to bring you up to date on what happened yesterday at Bruce and Betsey's.

Things got better. Betsey and I made pancakes while Sylvère and Bruce talked Marcel Mauss and Durkheim. Betsey's studying to be a curator and we talked about her work. She's already quite professional because she was careful not to commit herself by expressing any interest in my work. And then we ate and took a walk along the river. Outside the house Betsey and Bruce seemed more relaxed. Four deer ran across the towpath. We froze. I started liking them.

Then we walked over to another, 19th-century house that Bruce and Betsey bought at auction after it'd been repossessed. They joked about the pathetic former owner, a chainsmoking 50-year-old spinster who lived alone and made a living as a "commercial writer." Of course I identified immediately. Betsey'd more or less cleared out the mess except for a few crateloads of trashy paperback romances. How odd. Perhaps these were books the "commercial writer" wrote? At any rate, Sylvère and I were ecstatic. Didn't their titles perfectly describe my feelings? We'd found the missing clue.

Here are the titles of some books we took from Bruce and Betsey's:

Second Chance At Love—Halfway There
Second Chance At Love—Passion's Song
Second Chance At Love—A Reckless Longing
Research Into Marriage
Wife In Exchange
Beyond Her Control
All Else Confusion

Bruce and Betsey seemed puzzled and bemused but I don't think they connected it with you. On the car ride home I started reading *Research Into Marriage*, then underlining, footnoting and annotating all the passages that could relate to me and you. It's an exercise both adolescent (me!) and academic (you!)…my first art object, which I'll give you as a present.

Later when I asked Sylvère why we like you so much better than Bruce and Betsey, he said: Because Dick is sensitive. I think that's true. Bruce and Betsey are undeserving of your loyalty.

Dick, all the work in the house is going to start this afternoon, so I'd better get ready for it. But I keep you in my heart, it keeps me going.

Love,
Chris

～☆◝☆ ☆◜☆～

December 31, 1994

On New Year's Eve Sylvère and Chris had dinner at Bernardo's with Tad and Pam, his ex-biker girlfriend. Chris had always liked, admired, Pam—her life story, her interests and her art aspirations. Over drinks Pam told them how much she "hated" Chris' movie, "although," she said "I'm still thinking about it." Chris wondered what it was in her appearance or her character that made people think they could say these things. As if she had no feelings. Earlier that day she'd felt awful, haggling with David about the price of windows that she'd offered to buy upstate and transport to a Bridgehampton barn he was renovating. David offered her 500 bucks. Well, no—that was way too little—would she spend two days on someone else's windows if she didn't need the money? In five minutes David called back, offering to pay double and Chris was stunned. Buy cheap sell dear. She didn't expect these laws to apply between two friends. She felt the same as when she'd let some guy feel her tits for 50 bucks at the Wild West Topless Bar, then learned Brandi always held out for 100.

That night Sylvère and Chris had faltering sex. He was upset, confused, not knowing where or who he was. Crestline-Paris-East Hampton and now Thurman. In three weeks he'd be in New York again: a new semester, another seven years of teaching. Considering Thurman as their "home" was a provisional delusion like everything else in his life with Chris. The house wasn't Leonard Woolf's estate in southern England—it was a woodframe rural slum, trashed by a family of deadbeat hicks who they'd evicted before Christmas. Now they were painting, cleaning, and in three weeks they'd be gone again. What kind of life could they believe in? What kind of life could they afford?

In the early hours of the New Year Chris wrote to Dick:

"I don't know where I am and the only reality is moving. Soon I'll have to deal with the reality of this expensive, unlikeable movie, the fact I don't have a job. You moved to California because Europe was so claustrophobic. You cleared the junk out of your life…is it possible for you to understand this kind of freefall? Virilio's right—speed and transience negate themselves, become inertia.

You're shrunk and bottled in a glass jar, you're a portable saint. Knowing you's like knowing Jesus. There are billions of us and only one of you so I don't expect much from you personally. There are no answers to my life. But I'm touched by you and fulfilled just by believing."

Love,
Chris

New Year's Sunday was another sad and melancholy day. Gray-black fog hung around all afternoon 'til finally darkness crept in around 4:30. Sylvère and Chris stayed in bed 'til noon, talking, drinking coffee, then finally got up to take a drive. A flock of crows perched on the bare trees beside the farm on River Road. The countryside seemed dismal. For once, Chris understood the world of Edith Wharton's *Ethan Frome*. She was chilled by all this "charming" ancient squalor. Driving past the cabins, logging stumps and farmhouses, Chris felt the claustrophobia of a life among people who lived here 50 years ago, several to a room, afraid of freezing, starving, afraid that one of them will catch a contagious and incurable disease. People who'd never been to Albany let alone New York or Montreal. An Incredible String Band cassette was playing in the car—a traditional ballad called *Job's Tears* about winter, death and heaven.

We'll understand it better in the sweet bye and bye
You won't need to worry and you won't need to cry
Over in the old Golden Land

Don't you see why the people here actually looked forward to dying? A fellow schoolteacher'd told her once how all the gingerbread on the houses here—the stars, the crescent moons—were patterned on Masonic symbols. Clearly the people felt themselves in need of some protection. And how did The Incredible String Band, four attractive hippies in their 20s, ever manage to locate the desperation behind rural folk religion? Maybe they just thought the songs were pretty.

Chris considered using her studio visits at Art Center to testify about Dick, exhorting all the students there to write to him. "It will change your life!" She'd write a crazy tract called *I Love Dick* and publish it in Sylvère's school magazine. Hadn't her entire art career been this unprofessional?

Sylvère and Chris walked a little way towards Pharaoh Lake, got cold, went home, had tea and sex and took a nap. Then they got up and started the long job of unpacking boxes.

They spent the next week at the house with Tad and Pam, installing new old windows, cherry floors and tearing down partitions.

EXHIBIT M: SCENES OF PROVINCIAL LIFE

Thurman, New York
Thursday, January 5, 1995: 10:45 p.m.

Dear Dick,

Tonight we went to the Thurman Town Court as plaintiffs against our former tenants, the O'Malley's, sandwiched in between the bad check writers and drunk drivers. This should pretty much evoke for you the world we live in. We can't imagine you in that position. Actually we can hardly imagine ourselves there. When it was all over and we won, we both agreed we couldn't care less about material possessions. We were just sick of being had all the time by everyone, even these stupid hicks who we sued for non-payment of rent, and who will eventually get the better of us. Oh Dick, I wish you were here to save us from life in the provinces.

Signed,
Charles and Emma Bovary

The next day, Friday January 6, (Epiphany) Chris drove to Corinth to replace some broken glass in a medicine chest. She felt totally attuned to this upstate January day…dazzling ice and snow turned scrunchy from the cold, Corinth's army of welfare clients, former mental patients and the semi-self-employed walking around town, settling into four more months of winter. She loved the way the clouds turned pink in the afternoon and noticed how the season changed, the subtle shifts that made January different from December. She worried a bit about running into her ex-boyfriend Marshall Blonsky at Joseph Kosuth's birthday party two weeks from Saturday, though really she was looking forward to it. "My first party in New York where I don't give a shit," she confided to Dick. "I'm looking forward to the future so long as you are in it." Does this mean she was happy?

Sylvère and Chris bumbled around the construction site that was their house "helping" Tad and Pam, non-Jews who mistook their constant screaming at each other for hostility. Maija, their apartment subletter in New York phoned to say she'd decided to stop paying rent.

Both of them assumed Dick was out of town for the holidays. They were trying to figure out their next move. One afternoon Sylvère called his friend Marvin Dietrichson in LA to try and get a read on Dick's reaction. And yes, before the Christmas break, Marvin'd run into Dick in the school hall and said: "I heard you saw Sylvère and Chris—How'd it go?" "I don't know," Marvin recalled Dick saying, "it was some strange scene."

Some strange scene. When Chris heard this her stomach contracted and she vomited. Was this really all it was? "Some strange scene?" Was there any way of reaching Dick beyond the filters of Sylvère and Marvin?

Crohn's Disease is a hereditary chronic inflammation of the small intestine. Like any chronic ailment its triggers can be physical, psychic or environmental. For Chris the trigger was despair, which she saw as very different from depression. Despair was being backed into a corner without a single move. Despair began with a contracting, swelling of the small intestine which in turn created an obstruction which in turn caused vomiting beyond bile. This obstruction was accompanied by abdominal pain so overwhelming she could only lie beneath it, waiting for the onset of high fevers, dehydration. The pain was like a roller coaster: once it reached a certain point she was strapped in for a ride which inevitably took her to the hospital for sedation, intravenous drugs and fluids.

Sylvère'd become an expert at tricking the disease. All it took to stop the rollercoaster was to calm Chris down and make her sleep. Cups of tea with liquid opium, fluffy dogs and stories.

That afternoon Sylvère brought Chris a pen and writing pad. "Here," he said. "Let's write to Dick." This made her sicker. So then he stroked her hair and made some tea and told a story about their dead dog Lily, the one they'd loved who'd died a year ago of cancer, his words tracing a perimeter around a sadness so unspeakable and huge that they both cried.

Chris fell asleep and Sylvère retreated back into "his" room, the master bedroom. Since arriving from Long Island they stayed in separate rooms for the first time in ten years. "A very democratic arrangement," Sylvère noted resentfully. Chris had said something about needing privacy...the better to share her thoughts with Dick? But even with Chris occupying the northwest room with the sloping saltbox roof and tiny windows and Sylvère in the big east bedroom that overlooked the pond there were still four others empty. Room for the orphan, room for the pony trainer/caretaker, room for the nanny...an entire cast of characters who'd never quite arrived to share this Edwardian fantasy.

Chris' sickness was what had originally ensnared him twelve or thirteen years ago. Not the physical signs of it—dull hair, strange bruises, blue marks on her legs and thighs. He'd found these quite repulsive. "Usually the girls that I go out with are better dressed and better looking," Bataille'd reported of his meetings with the philosopher Simone Weil. And truly, unlike Sylvère's many other girlfriends, Chris' body didn't offer any pleasure. It wasn't blonde or opulent; dark, voluptuous—it was thin and nervous, bony. And while Chris was obviously intelligent, even unusually cultivated, Sylvère knew plenty of smart men. And at that time he had all New York to choose from. All through the year that they met, Sylvère kept her at a distance, rarely asking her to spend the night. What he liked was lunch-time sex followed by some disembodied philosophic talk…this always helped to get her out the door.

It wasn't 'til that summer when David Rattray called him to report that Chris was in a Minneapolis hospital that Sylvère realized Chris' sickness could have anything to do with him: that by accepting her he could save her life. The rest was history, or, Chris had gotten one thing right: beneath his reputation at the Mudd Club as the philosopher of kinky sex, Sylvère was a closet humanist. Guilt and duty more than S&M propelled his life.

But now in her infatuation, Chris' body had filled out, become so sexual. She was attenuated and available. Curled up in bed in a floral satin robe, staring through ruffled curtains across the snowy road to Baker's Garage and junkyard, she looked a little like Eliza-beth Barrett Browning without the spaniel in Virginia Woolf's *Flush*, a book Sylvère'd talked about in England thirty years ago with Vita Sackville-West.

Early in the evening Chris got up and went to Sylvère's room. "I'm not going to get sick. You stopped it." And then she took a bath and Sylvère sat beside her near the tub the way they used to do. Sitting there, Sylvère watched glimpses of her body melting in the water, one elbow raised, tips of breasts piercing the surface of the water, the dense net of pubic hair. Piles of snow outside matched the paleness of her body. As she reaches for a towel white curves meshed against the snowbanks on the hill beyond the window. Hot water steamed over the bathtub and the wind outside lifted up the snow as if in steamy clouds. As if there was no difference now between cold and hot, in and out.

Then they lay down on the mattress in Sylvère's room and started fucking. This time it's real, a spontaneous rush of tenderness and desire, and when it's over they rest and start again and neither of them talk.

EXHIBIT N: SYLVÈRE THANKS DICK FOR HIS
            NEW-FOUND SEXUALITY

Thurman, New York
Thursday, January 12, 1995

Dear Dick,

This is Charles Bovary. Emma and I have been living together for some nine years. Everyone knows what this entails. Passion becomes tenderness, tenderness turns soft. Sex collapses into warm intimacy. We could spend months without, and whenever we did it became short and interrupted. Was it desire that had left me? Or maybe the fragility that comes with closeness, I don't know. The main result was that I never had anymore those glorious hard-ons of yore.

Emma often suggested I should see a sex therapist. You could tell there was something pleasing to her about this idea, sending the old white male to the repair shop after years of gradually dismantling his most instinctive habits.

Over the years, Emma had become very keen on transforming my sexuality, which had been so celebrated in New York, into something less Foucauldian and controlling into a more restrained submissive dick-dwindling kind of thing. And I concurred. Emma and I set out to challenge centuries of male supremacy and dick-dom. I lay there, more passive than women were supposed to be, waiting for Emma to overwhelm me with her hard dick of desire. But soon she grew dissatisfied. I wasn't responding. (I never found her advances heartfelt enough.) And so began the gradual detumescence of my once glorious erections.

Sex became short and somewhat wobbly. Emma, at first thrilled by the project, grew impatient with my bumbling impulses. We had sex rarely, pretended it didn't matter. Our friendship strengthened, our love increased and sex was sublimated to more worthy social endeavors: art, careers, property. Still, occasionally the troubling thought surfaced that a couple without sex is hardly a couple at all. It's at this point, Dick, after we'd convinced ourselves that a life without sex was a better life, that you entered our lives like an angel of mercy.

At first Emma's crush on you was a blow to what remained of my self-esteem (and it's thanks to you that I am willing to admit that self-esteem exists and matters; can one be American without it?). Our sexuality invested itself in a new erotic activity: writing to you, Dick. And isn't every letter a love letter? Since I was writing to you, Dick, I was writing love letters. What I didn't know was that by writing love letters I was writing letters to love, and timidly reawakening all the dormant powers in my rather repressed emotions.

This is a long story, Dick, and you're the only one who I can tell it to. Emma's love for you was the final blow to my sexuality. I always knew that however much we denied sex it would one day show its ugly head again, like a snake, and in a sense you were that snake,

Dick. Here was a time, my friend, of tabula rasa: no desire, no future, no sex. But paradoxically this defeat opened up a new set of possibilities—that Emma, who for so long had been disinterested in sex, was now fantasizing about your prick, Dick, raised the possibility of renewal. If there are Dicks somewhere, there might be dick for us.

This is not mere sex therapy. I'm confiding in you, not in the position of a penitent with his tail between his legs, ready to assume the position of abject sinner. No, the Renaissance has come, and whether you have anything to do with it's debatable. Emma's desiring elsewhere enabled me to regain desire. How it happened remains a miracle. It returned suddenly about a week ago—the spirit of sex, like one of these little Roman gods, touching every part of my body, arousing them to the sacredness of pleasure. As if the veil was lifted and a new field of human possibility revealed.

I can assure you, Dick, that it was not a mere attempt to match your fabulous sexual powers that produced this change in me. You can call it denial, and take pride in the healing you've accomplished in our favor. But for this, Dick, you would've had to be in some kind of contact with us, which you've carefully managed to make impossible. So don't be too fast to attribute yourself with miraculous sexual powers, The Christ of Love. Emma and I created you out of nothing, or very little, and in all fairness, You owe us everything. While you flounder in your daily life we have built you up as a truly poweful icon of erotic integrity.

I dedicate this letter to you, Dick, with all my

Love,
Charles

But sex with Charles did not replace Dick for Emma. While Sylvère sorted through his manuscripts and boxes, Chris settled into a dreamy delirium that could only last another week or so. Next Monday she'd agreed to drive the windows to East Hampton; from there she and Sylvère would fly back to LA for his studio visits at Art Center. And then Sylvère's job started in New York and they'd live in the East Village until May.

She read Harlequin Romances, wrote her diary and scribbled margin notes about her love for Dick in Sylvère's treasured copy of Heidegger's *La question de la technique*. The book was evidence of the intellectual roots of German fascism. She called it *La technique de Dick*.

Time was short. She needed answers and so like Emma Bovary in Yonville she found solace in religion. Loving Dick helped her understand the difference between Jesus and the saints. "You love the saints for what they do," she wrote him. "They're self-invented people who've worked hard to attain some state of grace. George Mosher, the horse logger on Bowen Hill, is a kind of saint. But Jesus is like a girl. He doesn't have to do anything. You love him 'cause he's beautiful."

On Friday January 13 Chris' friends Carol Irving and Jim Fletcher drove up to visit them in Thurman. They stayed up late reading Paul Blackburn's translations of the Troubadour poems out loud. Jim's deep midwestern twang soared over the one by Aimerac de Beleno—

When I set her graceful body within my heart
the soft thought there is so agreeable I
sicken, I burn for joy—

And it occurred to them that love's like dying, how Ron Padgett had once called death "the time the person moves inside." Sylvère the specialist abstained, finding their earnest conversation too jejune.

And then Ann called to read a passage from the new book she was writing. The night was perfect.

⌁⌁⌁⌁⌁

January 19, 1995

Sylvère and Chris checked in to The Regal Inn Motel in Pasadena Wednesday night. On Thursday afternoon Sylvère called Dick expecting to get his answerphone, but unexpectedly reached him. Mick and Rachel Tausig, two friends from New York, were visiting. Would Sylvère and Chris like to join them all for dinner Sunday at his house?

"By the way, Sylvère," Dick added before hanging up, "I didn't get Chris' fax the day she sent it. It got mixed up with the Christmas mail so I only read it two weeks later."

"Ah—a little Christmas present," Sylvère chuckled.

"Well, it's been some time now," Dick replied. "I expect the temperature's dropped."

"Yessss," Sylvère said uneasily.

⌁⌁⌁⌁⌁

On Sunday, January 22 Sylvère and Chris drove out to Antelope Valley in their rental car. She was carrying a xerox of the letters—90 pages, single-spaced. Sylvère doubted she'd be mad enough to give them to him. But the way that Dick embraced her at the door, a contact that was more than social, that might be even sexual, made her stumble. That was sign enough.

Dinner with Dick and Mick and Rachel, two curators from the Getty, an art critic and Sylvère was very hard. The atmosphere was countercultural-casual. Chris felt like a cockroach beside the poised and glamorous Rachel, who was the only other woman in the room. Dick sat next to Chris, across from Rachel. Perhaps Dick noticed Chris was silent and she hadn't touched the food. At any rate he turned to her with a slight, complicitous smile to ask: "How's the... ah,...project going?" Rachel, also smiling, was all ears. Chris gave up trying to find the right pitch for her reply. "Actually it's changed. It's turned into an epistolary novel, really." Rachel rose to it. "Ah, that's so bourgeois." "Huh?" "Didn't Habermas say once that the epistolary genre marked the advent of the bourgeois novel?" Chris flashed back to a breakfast she and Sylvère had once with Andrew Ross and Constance Penley at a conference in Montreal. Constance brilliantly corrected Chris' bumbling appreciation of Henry James, touching every intellectual base. How articulate this woman was at 8:30 in the morning! But still she wondered to herself: Rachel, didn't Lukács say it first?

At any rate the other guests were gone by midnight. She and Sylvère stayed for one last drink. It seemed Sylvère and Dick would never finish talking about new media technology. Chris reached into her purse. "Here," she said. "What I was talking about."

Well. Dick was gobstruck and Sylvère for once was speechless. But Dick was generous and kind. He took the 90 pages. "Chris," he said, "I promise you I'll read them."

<hr>

January 26, 1995

Back in New York winter, Sylvère and Chris drove up to Thurman one last time. On Saturday they'd close the house in time to drive down again for Joseph Kosuth's birthday party.

On Sunday morning, January 29, they woke up woozy and hung-over, happy to be back in New York. Joseph's party had been perfect, intimate and large. So many of Sylvère's old friends from the Mudd Club days had been there. They got up slowly and had brunch at Rattner's, heading for the Lower East Side. Sylvère'd be attending his first dinner soon with trustees from the MOMA to discuss the Artaud catalogue: surely he should dress the part.

The proprietor of the store on Orchard Street where Sylvère spent several hundred dollars on Italian clothes was a remarkable person, a true light. He lived in Crown Heights and studied Kabbala. Customers drifted in and out as he and Sylvère exchanged ideas about 17th-century Jewish mysticism, Jakob Franck and Lévinas.

It was late afternoon when they left Orchard Street, mild and sunny. They walked with shopping bags back through the freshly landscaped, newly curfewed Tompkins Square Park. Suddenly it hit Chris she was a stranger here and the East Village used to be her home. Her name last night had been missing from the list at Joseph's party and yes, she'd never been part of any glamour-scene in '70s New York. But she'd had friends here...friends who'd mostly either died or given up trying to be artists and disappeared into other lives and jobs. Before she met Sylvère, she'd been a strange and lonely girl but now she wasn't anyone.

"Who's Chris Kraus?" she screamed. "She's no one! She's Sylvère Lotringer's wife! She's his 'Plus-One'!" No matter how many films she made or books she edited, she'd always keep being seen as no one by anyone who mattered so long as she was living with Sylvère. "It's not my fault!" Sylvère yelled back.

But she remembered all the times they'd worked together when her name had been omitted, how equivocal Sylvère'd been, how reluctant to offend anyone who paid them. She remembered the abortions, all the holidays she'd been told to leave the house so Sylvère could be alone with his daughter. In ten years, she'd erased herself. No matter how affectionate Sylvère'd been, he'd never been in love with her.

(The first night they ever stayed together in Sylvère's loft, Chris asked him if he ever thought about history. At that time Chris saw history like the New York Public Library, a place to meet dead friends. "All the time," Sylvère replied, thinking about the Holocaust. It was then she fell in love with him.)

"Nothing is irrevocable," Sylvère said. "No," she screamed, "you're wrong!" By this time she was crying. "History isn't dialectical, it's essential! Some things will never go away!"

And the next day, Monday, January 30, she left him.

PART 2: EVERY LETTER IS A LOVE LETTER

EVERY LETTER IS A LOVE LETTER

Love has led me to a point
where I now live badly
'cause I'm dying of desire
I therefore can't feel sorry for myself
and —

—Anonymous, 14th-century French Provençal

Thurman, New York
Wednesday, February 1, 1995

Dear Dick,

I'm writing to you from the country, the Town of Thurman in upstate New York. Yesterday I drove up here without stopping except for gas in Catskill at the Stewart's store. Tad's moved back to Pam's in Warrensburg. The house is empty and it's the first time I've been up here alone. It's funny how I don't feel lonely, though. Maybe it's the ghost of Mrs. Gideon. Or maybe 'cause I know the whole Thurman cast of characters from buying wood and fixing up the house and working at the school. The *Adirondack Times* reports on local happenings like Evie Cox's visit to the podiatrist in

Glens Falls. Somehow this redneck town allows the possibility of a middle-aged New York City woman bouncing round a house alone more generously than Woodstock or East Hampton. It's a community of exiles anyway. No one asks me any questions 'cause there's no frame of reference to put the answers in.

For several days now I've been wanting to tell you about an installation I saw last week in New York. It was called *Minetta Lane —A Ghost Story*, by Eleanor Antin, an artist/filmmaker who I don't know very much about. The installation was pure magic. I sat in it for about an hour and felt I could have stayed all day. It was at Ronald Feldman Gallery on Mercer Street. You entered it through a sharply cornered narrow corridor—the white sheet rock of the gallery abruptly changed to crumbling plaster, rotting slats and boards, rolls of chicken-wire and other prewar tenement debris. You stumbled over this stuff the way you stumbled up the stairs, maybe, if you were lucky enough to've lived in NYC in the '50s when people still lived this way, on your way to a party or to visit friends. And as you rounded the last corner you came to a kind of foyer, a semi-circular wall with two large windows mounted on one side and a single window mounted, slightly higher, on the other.

There was a single wooden chair in front of the two windows and you sat down in it uneasily, not wanting to get your feet covered in plaster dust (I can't remember if the dust beside the chair was real or not). Three films played simultaneously in each of the three windows, rear-projected against the window panes. The corridor'd led you to this point so you could attend a kind of seance, becoming a voyeur.

Through the far-left window a middle-aged woman was painting on a large canvas. We saw her from behind, rumpled shirt and rumpled body, curly rumpled hair, painting, looking, thinking, drawing on a cigarette, reaching down onto the floor to take a few drinks from a bottle of Jim Beam here and there. It was an ordinary scene (though it's very ordinariness made it subversively utopian: how many pictures from the '50s do we have of nameless women painting late into the night and living lives?). And this ordinariness unleashed a flood of historical nostalgia, a warmth and closeness to a past I've never known—the same nostalgia that I felt from seeing a photo exhibition at St. Mark's Church a few years ago. There were maybe a hundred photos gathered by the Photographic/Oral History Project of the Lower East Side of artists living, drinking, working, in their habitat between the years 1948 and 1972. The photos were meticulously captioned with the artists' names and disciplines, but 98% of them were names I didn't know. The photos tapped into that same unwritten moment as Antin's show—it was the first time in American art history, thanks to allowances provided by the GI Bill, that lower-middle class Americans had a chance to live as artists, given time to kill. Antin recalls: "There was enough money around from the GI Bill to live and work in a low-rent district… Studios were cheap, so were paints and canvases, booze and cigarettes. All over the Village young people were writing, painting, getting psychoanalyzed and fucking the bourgeoisie." Where are they now? The Photographic/Oral History Project show transformed the streets of the East Village into tribal ground. I felt a rush of empathetic curiosity about the lives of the unfamous, the unrecorded desires and ambitions of artists who had been here too. What's the ratio of working artists to the sum total of art stars? A hundred or a thousand? The first window did the job of shamanistic art, drawing together hundreds of disparate thoughts, associations (photos in the exhibition; lives; the fact that some of them were female too) into a single image. A rumpled woman paints and smokes a cigarette. And don't you think a "sacred space" is sacred only because of the collectivity it distills?

And then there was strange magic in this window too: a magic that would connect this window with the very different states depicted in the other two. After several minutes a little girl wearing a velvet dress and a large bow walks into the frame, the painter's "room." Is this girl the woman's daughter? Is she the daughter of a friend? It's certain right away that the little girl lives in an entirely different metabolic and perceptual universe than her mother/caretaker/older friend. The canvas holds no particular appeal, though she's not pointedly disinterested in it either. She looks at it, then drifts away to look at something (us?) outside the window. Then this gets boring too, (She's got so much energy!) So she starts jumping up and down. Up 'til now the painter has been just peripherally aware of the little girl. But now she puts her brush down, lets herself glide into the game. The woman and the little girl jump up and down together. Then that moment passes too and the woman's drawn back into her work again.

(This installation grounds the structuralist fascination with the minutiae of varied states of concentration, passing moments, in the only thing that gives these moments any meaning: history and time passing through other people's lives…)

Through the second window on the right-side of the painter, a young couple cavort in a tenement kitchen bathtub. The girl's pale blonde, maybe 16, laughing, splashing water on her partner, a tall Black man in his 20s. They slip and slide, arm wrestling in and out of soggy embraces. It's not clear which one of them lives here (perhaps they both do, or maybe it's an apartment that they borrow?). At one point the little girl wanders out of the painter's window in this apartment chomping on a sandwich. She sits and eats, watching them from a ledge above the tub.

Her entry is a strange twist of voyeurism: we're watching her watching them. But of course there's no pornography in real-time. There isn't any story, either. Who these people are or where they're coming from is not what makes us want to watch them. It's a fact that's hinted at, that may or may not be revealed. We're outsiders, choosing just how much of this alternately awkward and cinematic slice of life we'll watch before shifting our gaze to another window. The couple are oblivious to us and continuous. They exist much more forcefully than we do.

After a while the little girl leaves and the young woman gets out of the bath, leaves the frame and returns wearing a big wool skirt and cotton camisole. She pulls on a white blouse (Catholic school uniform or standard boho-wear? Either way the intimacy of the scene is very casual and untransgressive) as her partner grabs a towel and climbs out of the bath.

In the third window, the one you have to turn your head or move the chair to see, an old European man gazes, quietly trans-fixed, into an empty ornamental bird cage in the foreground of his elaborately decorated prewar apartment. The walls behind him are deep green. Obviously he's lived in them for many years. There's a crystal chandelier above the bird cage and a warm light cuts across his face. The scene is timeless, concentrated, existing someplace outside ambivalence or emotion. We don't see any of what the man is seeing or pretends to, but we see shadows of it across his face. It's the most compelling, least definable of all three windows. Looking through it we're watching someone totally absorbed by something we can't see: a missing bird, a stranger's past, the mysteries of aging.

Later on (maybe segueing with an erotic highpoint in Window #2 and the little girl's arrival in the painter's room) a woman's face with golden Jean Harlow hair, lit '30s style by the chandelier, leans above the bird cage that the man so intently watches. The woman is an angel or a gift that the man doesn't seem to react to. Was she there all this time? Is his expression numbness, is it bliss? The man just keeps looking into the birdcage.

"The form of a city changes faster than the human heart," Eleanor Antin quoting Baudelaire. The installation was a magic Cornell box, a tiny epic: all ages, modes of life, existing equally and together through the keyhole of this lost time. The installation was troubling and ecstatic.

Dick, its 10:30 at night, I broke off this morning after describing to you the first window and I'm too tired to continue now. This afternoon I went out for a walk feeling very light and clear—"Bright days," I thought, thinking about an old movie idea I'd once had depicting the suicide of Lew Welch, the San Francisco poet, another beneficiary of the GI Bill, who walked off into the Sierra Mountains one winter in the mid-'70s never to be seen again... How perfectly this upstate winter landscape fits such a scene. I was even debating the kind of camera I would use, the kind of film, where I'd get it and the tripod, would there be another story, any actors?...when the logging road trailed off.

But I kept walking, thinking how I like winter best, along a deer trail, over ice, across a beaver fort 'til I was lost. The ground's all frozen but there's hardly any snow so it was impossible to follow tracks. I came up against an old chainlink fence, then left it walking what felt like south, over a stream then into a clearing, thinking High Street would be very close. But it wasn't—there were just more woods everywhere, scraggly trees grown up over land that's been logged and raped a dozen times in the past 150 years, deer tracks disappearing into bramble, and I realized I was walking erratically in jagged circles.

Up hill and down, I saw a partridge strut out from under a tree trunk. It took my breath away 'til I remembered I was lost. I went back and found the fence. It was mid-afternoon, a cloudy day though not too cold. Finding the fence'd taken nearly half an hour and now it was 3:30. I didn't know where the fence would go but maybe I should follow it? But maybe not. I tried one more time to walk back the way I came but nothing looked familiar. Woods-woods-woods and frozen ground. I saw no way out, no animal markings, which in any case I don't know how to read. So carefully I traced my way back again to the chainlink fence. I felt as though my eyes had moved outside my body. By now I'd left so many boot marks on the scattered snow I didn't know which tracks to follow home.

I looked out in the woods and felt alone and panicky. Anything could happen. In another 90 minutes it'd be pitch dark. If I didn't find the road by then what would happen? I thought of stories about people lost in winter woods and realized that I hadn't paid enough attention. At fifteen degrees on a stormless winter night, was death by hypothermia a done deal? Was it better to rest under some bramble or keep walking?

Just then I heard the distant sound of a chainsaw coming from what might've been the north side of the woods: should I follow it? The woods were thick, the sound was muted and sporadic. Should I try to find the stream and follow it, hoping it would lead back to the creekbed behind my house? But last year's logging'd left so many ruts it was impossible to tell which ice was streambed, which was frozen drainage. Then what about the fence? I didn't know how far or where it led, but neighbors said the fence marks off the property of the North Country Beagle Club which owns several hundred acres of this unwanted land.

Three springs ago my friend George Mosher and the State EnCon man stood out the back of my place trading stories about fools who'd gotten turned around walking through the woods back here and gotten lost. (None of these stories as I recalled took place in winter.) George, who's lived here his entire 80 years, says: *To find your way out of the woods look at the top tips of hemlock trees because they point North.* But I couldn't tell a hemlock from a balsam tree and I didn't know which direction the street is in, and anyway the woods were full of treetops pointing everywhere: north? east? south?

It occurred to me that there was only enough daylight left to act on one decision. If I chose wrong and was still here after dark, would Sylvère call the cops after finding me not home when he phoned from New York? Fat chance, because Sylvère says he is committed to supporting my independence, my new life. So if nobody would miss me until midnight or even tomorrow morning, what then? I had a wool scarf, my long black coat and vinyl gloves, though no matches or warm socks. Could I run in place from nightfall until 8 tomorrow morning to stay warm?

I chose the fence: walked to the left, because I knew the Beagle Club stretched down the right ending up several miles down Lanfear Road in Stony Creek. I ripped a forked branch from a tree to mark the spot. The fence didn't follow a straight line. In order not to lose it I jumped over fallen trees, crawled through piled up branches, thorny frozen weeds.

I started running through the woods, profoundly grateful for having started taking an aerobics class. The sound of the chainsaw got fainter, further. I ran for 10 or 20 minutes, not thinking so much about death or deals with God as how many hours there'd be of night, and how it's possible to survive it. Finally through the trees I saw a clear snow-covered slope, then farther on, a trailer.

I came out on Elmer Woods Road, a one house lane that cuts off Mud Street and walked a couple of miles down Mud Street to Smith Road. There weren't any cars. I thought about a story told by 9 year old Josh Baker, who lives here in a trailer, about his mother walking alone down Mud Street one winter night when a demon-ghost leapt into her throat. This story, always colorful, now seemed not at all improbable.

xxo,

Chris

PS—Dick, Now it's Wednesday night and all week I've been thinking about calling you: knowing that if I'm going to do it I will have to do it soon. By now you'll have my note express mailed Tuesday and you're leaving, what?—tomorrow, Friday?— for ten days overseas. I can't remember what I wrote but Ann Rower promised it wasn't too drippy when I read it on the phone. I think I said I was embarrassed about the ninety single-spaced pages of letters. Then something like, "The idea of seeing you alone is a vision of pure happiness and plea-sure." God now I'm really cringing. Anyhow I know I lied about "having" to be in LA at Art Center alone on February 23. Sylvère and I are going there tomorrow to do studio visits Friday. And I want to make it casual but the telephone's so brutal. What if I reach you when your head's a million miles away? Could I handle that as well as being lost in the woods at dark? No. Well, maybe. I'm torn between maintaining you as an entity to write to and talking with you as a person. Perhaps I'll let it go.

Love,
Chris

New York City
Thursday, February 2, 1995

DD,

I'm sitting here at the West End Bar on Broadway having a coffee & a cigarette before going over to meet Sylvère. Have already been travelling most of the day: left home around 10:15, drove down to Albany through snow squalls, and then the endless train.

After talking to you last night I didn't fall asleep 'til 3 a.m. Heart & sex chakras pounding, mixing themselves up 'til sex feelings are overwhelmed by heart. Or perhaps it's more like sex feelings pumping out of heart. Anyway it was a kind of excited bliss, & I haven't felt this way for 10 years, since I fell in love with Sylvère. At that time it went so badly—those feelings were barely expressed and never accepted. I had to resort to other stratagems, like being the most intelligent and useful girl.

My personal goal here—apart from anything else that may happen—is to express myself as clearly and honestly as I can. So in a sense love is just like writing: living in such a heightened state that accuracy and awareness are vital. And of course this can extend to everything. The risk is that these feelings'll be ridiculed or rejected,

& I think I'm *understanding* risk for the first time: being fully prepared to lose and accept the consequences if you gamble.

I think our telephone call went well last night, despite the ambiguous archness of your question: "And you only want to talk, right?" I can't remember what I answered, the answer just flowed out, but I think we understood that we were talking about the same thing.

Chris

Fillmore, California
(The Condor Preserve—
late afternoon, 94 degrees)
Friday, February 3, 1995

DD,

Art, like God or The People, is fine for as long as you can believe in it.

Things To Do With The Person You're Having An Affair With:

1. Take photobooth pictures of yourselves
(Note: finish this list later.)

What I was thinking about in the car:

That I don't want be the person who always knows anymore, who has the vision for two people and makes the plans. I never understood before people who would do this (i.e., turn their whole lives around)— I thought it was idle, self indulgent, another way of just avoiding doing things in the world. But will, belief, breaks down...& now I do.

Here's the formulation: I got together with Sylvère because I saw how I could help him get his life together. I'm drawn to you 'cause I see how you can help me take my life apart...

⚜

Pasadena, California

Saturday, February 4, 1995

"Maktub" in Arabic means "it is written."

Write a narrative in which the speaker starts to understand that events, as they happen in her/his life, can be seen not as surprises but as an uncovering—the systematic revelation of fate.

⚜

DD,

I am sitting in the Art Center library and starting, systematically, to read your essay on *The Media and Magic Time* in the Zurich Kunstmuseum catalog that I'd come across here last trip. I think that I am your ideal reader—or that, the ideal reader is one who is in love with the writer & combs the text for clues about that person & how they think—

(Through love I am teaching myself how to think)—Looking at the text as *the way in*. Given that disposition no text is too difficult or obscure and everything becomes an object of study. (Study's good, because it microcosms everything—if you understand everything within the walls of what you study you can identify other walls too, other areas of study. Everything's separate and discrete and there is no macrocosm, really. When there are no walls there is no study, only chaos. And so you break it *down*.)

I think that in that essay you (perhaps a lot of other people too, but since I'm in love with you I'll pretend that you're unique) were on the brink of a very important discovery: how to bring some politics to bear on the visionary ecstacy of Levi-Strauss, the ecstatic nihilism of Baudrillard, without becoming an old stodge. Politics means accepting that things happen for a reason. There's a causality behind the flow and if we study hard enough it's possible to understand it. Can politics be articulated in a way that's structural, electric, instead of being dug up again, the boring bit at the bottom of the barrel? I think the clue to this is simultaneity, a sense of wonder at it: that the political can be a PARALLEL SOURCE OF INFORMATION, & more is more: adding an awareness of politics, how things happen, to the mix can just enhance our sense of how the present is exploding into Now Time. I'm thinking of the quote you cite from Levi-Strauss—"a universe of information where the laws of savage thought reign once more." As if the instantaneous transmission of information can return us to the time-based, finite and deliberate magic of the medieval world. "The Middle Ages were built on seven centuries of ecstacy extending from the hierarchy of angels down into the muck" (Hugo Ball). So when you introduce political information to your texts, it shouldn't be a matter of "And yet—" "But still—", as if politics could be the final countervailing word. (I'm thinking of the essay on postmodern retro camp in your book *The Ministry Of Fear*.) Politics should be introduced: "And and." Breathless, keeping it afloat—how much information about one subject can you juggle in two hands?

You write about art so well.

I disagree with you, obviously, about the frame. You argue that the frame provides coherence only through repression and exclusion. But the trick is to discover *Everything* within the frame.

"Think Harder" as Richard Foreman used to blast out over the PA in his early plays. Or just Look Closer.

⋆⋇⋆⋇⋆

New York City
Tuesday, February 7, 1995

The sweetest tongue has the sharpest tooth.

DD,

I woke up with a start last night after maybe 20 minutes of cramped airplane sleep with a very vivid dream.

I was out for the night with Laura Paddock, my best (only really) friend among the Art Center Students. We were at someone's place (a student's?); a bunch of people having dinner, & Laura & I'd planned to leave early so I could hook up with you. I was supposed to call you to confirm, & I did that from the party, & when I reached you you cryptically called the whole thing off. And I hung up the phone, & in front of this roomful of art students in their 20s let out a huge & uncontrollable sob. No one looked at me but Laura, who instantly knew, & I collapsed into her arms.

⋆⋇⋆⋇⋆

Laura and I met Saturday morning in Pasadena for coffee, sat in a courtyard off Colorado pretending we were in Mexico or Ibiza, continuing a dialogue we'd started months ago circling around mysticism, love, obsession. Our conversations are not so much about the theories of love & desire, as its manifestations in our favorite books & poems. Study as a Fan Club meeting—the only kind.

There's an implicit understanding between us that we accept it (love, extremity, desire) & can share some personal information/vision best by swapping favorite epigrams and poems. It was Laura who told me about this proverb about tooth & tongue—"That means, I guess," she said, looking straight at me with wide and ice-blue eyes, "that the one you love the best has the most power to hurt you." And we both nodded, smiling slightly, like we knew. But since this's school, not girltalk, we both work hard to keep our conversations on a referential but ever so suggestive plane. Meeting Laura's always like inhaling ether; like ladies in the Heian Court, we're always conscious of 'the form.'

When I first met Laura Paddock I was impressed by the fat notebooks she was keeping, full of favorite quotes and drawings & her own lines. Remembered how I used to do that years ago. And now—

⋇✵※⋇

Thurman, New York
February 9, 1995

—All yesterday on the train and today I've been reading your last book, *The Ministry Of Fear*, which I checked out from the Art Center library. It's so amazing that the book came out in 1988 because even though the title comes from Orwell it took four more years for fear to drive everybody back into the fold. 1988 was the year when *Seven Days*, a magazine about real estate and restaurants swept New York and ending up living in the park no longer seemed impossible.

Famous-Artist dinner party talk included stories about former colleagues seen scavenging in dumpsters. Money rewrote mythology and the lives of people I'd admired now seemed like cautionary tales. Paul Thek died of AIDS in 1986 and David Wojnarowicz was dying and there was all this academic shit out there about The Body as if it were a thing apart. And in the midst of this you wrote the most amazing thing about the need to bring things DOWN:

"The biological," you wrote (quoting Emanuel Levinas) "with the notion of inevitability it implies, becomes more than an object of spiritual life. It becomes its heart. The mysterious urgings of the blood…lose the character of problems to be solved by a sovereignly free Self. Because the self is made of just these elements. Our essences no longer lie in freedom but in a kind of chaining. To be truly oneself means accepting this ineluctable original chain that is unique to our bodies, and above all in accepting this chaining."

And then in *Aliens & Anorexia* you wrote about your own physical experience, being slightly anorexic—how anorexia arises not from narcissism, a fixation with your body, but a sense of its aloneness:

"If I'm not touched it becomes impossible to eat. Intersubjectivity occurs at the moment of orgasm: when things break down. If I'm not touched my skin feels the flip side of a magnet. It's only after sex sometimes that I can eat a little."

And that by recognizing the aloneness of your body it's possible to reach outside, become an Alien, escape the predetermined world:

"Anorexia is an active stance. The creation of an involuted body. How to abstract oneself from food fluxes and the mechanical sign of the meal? Synchronicity shudders faster than the speed of light around the world. Distant memories of food: strawberry shortcake, mashed potatoes…"

This's one of the most incredible things I've read in years.

It's now 2 o'clock in the afternoon and as I copied these lines out from your book by hand I felt a shudder of connection with myself when I was 24, 25. It was as if I was right back there in the room on East 11th Street, all those pages of notes that I was writing then, tiny ballpoint letters on wrinkly onion paper about George Eliot, diagrams of molecular movement and attraction, Ulrike Meinhof and Merleau-Ponty. I believed I was inventing a new genre and it was secret because there was nobody to tell it to. Lonely Girl Phenomenology. Living totally alone for the first time, and everything I'd been before (a journalist, New Zealander, a Marxist) was breaking down. And all that writing eventually cohered or was manipulated (the mind's revenge over dumb emotion!) into *Disparate Action/Desperate Action*, my first real play.

The arteries of the hand & arm that write lead straight into the heart, I was thinking last week in California, not seeing then that through writing it's also possible to re-visit a ghost of your past self, as if at least the shell of who you were fifteen years ago can somehow be re-called.

When I got here yesterday the house was banked in snowdrifts three feet high. The pipes are frozen so I'm shitting in the yard and making coffee out of boiled snow. As I was writing this Tom Clayfield and his wife Renee pulled up with a load of firewood. Quick cut to winter coat and gloves, icy breath, hurling logs onto the ground. And suddenly it's Survival Time in the Great Northwoods—the inescapable part of living here, not good or bad, just takes you someplace else... But even though this winter's real it doesn't seem as real as this... At least not for a little while.

What I was about to start writing before this poor Tom Clayfield (32 years old, a torn-up face and his few remaining teeth completely rotted) came by was The 1st Person. The difference between now and fifteen years ago is I don't think I was able, ever, to write any of those notebooks then in the 1st Person. I had to find these ciphers for myself because whenever I tried writing in the 1st Person it sounded like some other person, or else the tritest most neurotic parts of myself that I wanted so badly to get beyond. Now I can't stop writing in the 1st Person, it feels like it's the last chance I'll ever have to figure some of this stuff out.

Sylvère keeps socializing what I'm going through with you. Labeling it through other people's eyes—Adultery in Academe, John Updike meets Marivaux...Faculty Wife Throws Herself At Husband's Colleague. This presumes that there's something inherently grotesque, unspeakable, about femaleness, desire. But what I'm going through with you is real and happening for the first time.

(Is there a place in this to talk about how wet I've been, constantly, since talking on the phone to you 8 days ago? Talking, writing, teaching, working out and dealing with this house, this part of me is melting & unfolding.)

Back to the 1st Person: I'd even made up art theories about my inability to use it. That I'd chosen film and theater, two artforms built entirely on collisions, that only reach their meanings through collision, because I couldn't ever believe in the integrity/supremacy of the 1st Person (my own). That in order to write 1st Person narrative there needs to be a fixed self or persona and by refusing to believe in this I was merging with the fragmented reality of the time. But now I think okay, that's right, there's no fixed point of self but it exists & by writing you can somehow chart that movement. That maybe 1st Person writing's just as fragmentary as more a-personal collage, it's just more serious: bringing change & fragmentation closer, bringing it down to where you really are.

I don't know what I'll do with this writing, & I don't know what I'll do if because of circumstances of your own, Dick, it proves impossible to connect with you. Before I started writing I flashed forward briefly to a scene two weeks from now when I visit you: alone in bed the next day at the Pear Blossom Best Western with a bottle of scotch & two fresh percoset refills. But when I'm feeling (rarely) suicidal it's 'cause I'm stuck and right now I feel very much alive.

But all I want right now, if nothing else, is for you to read this, so you'll know at least some of what you've done for me.

Love,
Chris

ROUTE 126

And then everything came to pass almost exactly like I thought it would. The preset lights and music, the smokey kiss, the bed. Stumbling sunblind round the driveway the next morning. The motel scotch, the percoset. But that was just a story. Reality is in the details and even if you can predict what's going to happen you can't imagine how you'll feel.

It's taken me eleven months to write this letter since our visit. Here's how it began:

Pear Blossom Best Western
February 24, 1995

Dear Dick,

Yesterday afternoon I was driving towards Lake Casitas in sheets of grief and rage. I hadn't started crying yet, just a little welling up of tears around the eyes. But shaking, shaken, so much I couldn't see the road in front of me or stay in the right lane...

Ann Rower says "When you're writing in real time you have to revise a lot." By this I think she means that every time you try and write the truth it changes. More happens. Information constantly expands.

Dear Dick,

Three weeks before I met you I caught a Sun Charter Jet Vacation plane to Cancun, Mexico alone en route to Guatemala. I was wrapped in blankets with laryngitis and a temperature of 102. When the plane landed I was crying: low concrete molds of airport seen through a veil of misty tears. All fall I'd been living in Crestline, California with Sylvère, my husband, pretty much against my will. I thought I'd spend September in Wellington putting *Gravity & Grace* through the lab, then on to festivals in Rotterdam, Berlin and France. But in August Jan Bieringa, my contact in New Zealand, stopped returning calls. Finally in October she called me from an airport to say the plug was pulled. The funders hated it. The major European festivals hated it. I was sitting up in Crestline broke and 14,000 dollars short of finishing the film. Michelle at Fine Cut faxed from Auckland to say that 10,000 numbers on the Canadian EDL were fucked. Would I rather she just throw away the film?

For three weeks I'd been bursting into tears so often it became a phenomenological question: at what point should we still say "crying" or instead describe the moments of "not-crying" as punctuation marks in a constant state of tears? I'd completely lost my voice and my eyes were swollen closed. The doctor at the Crestline clinic looked at me like I was crazy when I asked him for a "sleeping cure."

I was going to Guatemala because I'd heard Jennifer Harbury talk about her hunger strike on NPR. Jennifer Harbury, briefly married to the captured Mayan rebel leader Efraim Bamaca, said:

"It's my last chance to save his life." It's unlikely at that moment—three years after Bamaca's disappearance and 17 days into the hunger strike—that Harbury, a life-long activist, had much illusion Bamaca was alive. But the human interest story she created let her speak against the Guatemalan army in *Time* and *People* magazine. "The only thing unusual about this case," Harbury told the press, "is that if a Guatemalan spoke as I do, they would be dead. They would be immediately dead." Harbury's voice was quick and light but formidably informed. Her heroic savvy Marxism evoked a world of women that I love—communists with tea roses and steel-trap minds. Hearing her that November in the car made me reflect, however briefly, that perhaps the genocide of the Guatemalan Indians (150,000 people, in a country of six million, disappeared and tortured in ten years) was an injustice of a higher order than my art career.

I caught a taxi to a bus station outside the tourist zone and bought a one-way ticket to Chetumal. Blasts of radio and diesel fumes. I liked the bus's springy orange seats, the broken windows. I imagined it being driven someplace in America maybe thirty years before. Tulsa, Cincinnati, sometime before the sectoring of cities, a time when not just derelicts rode buses and people in bars and streets crossed between different modes and walks of life. Sex and commerce, transience and mystery. The dozen other riders on the bus to Chetumal all seemed employed. It was six weeks before the peso crashed and Mexico seemed like an actual country, not just a free-world satellite. When the diesel engine finally kicked over I wasn't crying anymore. Radio music blared. A lead blanket lifted off my chest as we drove south through towns and villages. Banana trees and palms, people passing food and money through the windows everytime we hit another town. It didn't matter who

I was. Cypress yielded to bamboo as the amperage of the sun faded slowly down.

At that moment (November 9, 1994) Jennifer Harbury was on the 29th day of her hunger strike outside the Guatemala City government buildings in the Parque Nacional. She was sleeping in a garbage bag because tents were not allowed.

"I learned that if you see stars," she told the journalist Jane Slaughter later, "which after day 20 was every ten minutes, you bend down and tie your shoelaces. After awhile you know you're starting to die. I didn't want to lie down. They were going to drag me to a hospital, strap me down and put me on IV so I didn't want anyone to think that I'd passed out."

At that moment Bamaca had already been reported 'killed in action' by the Guatemalan army for three years. But when Harbury legally forced the exhumation of his body it turned out to be another man's. In 1992 Bamaca's friend Cabrero Lopez escaped from a military prison with the news he'd seen Bamaca being tortured by some soldiers trained at a US army base. Two years later was there any chance that he was still alive?

In a photo taken just before the hunger strike Jennifer Harbury looked like Hillary Clinton on a budget: a well-proportioned face with good WASP bones, blonde tousled bubble-cut, a cheap tweed coat, clear gaze and and heavy knowing eyes. But four weeks later, starving, Jennifer looks more like Sandy Dennis after five martinis in *Who's Afraid Of Virginia Woolf?* The resolution in her face has broken down, she's running now on something we can't see beyond the openness, confusion. Jennifer Harbury was a zealot with a Harvard law degree camped out in a park in Guatemala City on a garbage bag. Passersbys look at her with fear and wonder, a strange animal like Coco Fusco's native on display in *Two Undiscovered*

AmerIndians Visit... Yet Jennifer is not a saint because she never loses her intelligence.

⚬⚬⚬⚬

This letter's taken almost a year to write and therefore it's become a story. Call it *Route 126*. On Thursday night I got off a plane from JFK to LAX. I was going to your house, if not by invitation, at least with your consent. "I don't feel so sunny and terrific or able to pull things off," I wrote somewhere over Kansas. "I'm ragged, tired and unsure. But WWBWB. On the other side of sleep I could feel different—" And then I dozed but still I didn't.

This visit would be my first time ever seeing you alone. Eleven weeks ago I fell in love with you and started writing letters that were turning into—what? I hadn't told you how three weeks ago I'd left my husband and moved upstate alone. But two days before I'd Fed-Ex'd *Every Letter Is A Love Letter*, the manifesto I'd addressed to you about snowy woods and female art and finding the 1st Person, so I thought you'd know. You never read it. And if you had, you told me later, you might've been less cruel. You were a rock & roller from the English Midlands. Whatever made me think these subjects would interest you?

My love for you was absolutely groundless, as you'd pointed out that night in January in the company of my husband. It was about the only time you ventured an opinion past your sexy cryptic silence, the silence that I'd written on. But what does "groundless" really mean? My love for you was based upon a single meeting in December which you finally described in an exasperated letter to my husband as "genial but not particularly intimate or remarkable." Yet this meeting had driven me to write more words to you than there were numbers on that EDL, 250 pages and still counting.

Which in turn led to the rental car, this rainy drive along Route 126, this plan to visit you.

At that time in your life, you said, you were experimenting with never saying No.

I got off the plane at 7 buzzed with warm air, palms and jetlag serotonin, picked up a rental car and started north on 405. But I was nervous too, like walking through a script you know's already been written except the outcome's been withheld. Not giddy nervous. Nervous as in dark with dread. My outfit's dreadful. I watch the road, smoke and fiddle with the radio. I'm wearing black Guess jeans, black boots, an iridescent silver shirt, the black bolero leather jacket that I bought in France. It's what I planned but now it's making me feel gaunt and middle-aged.

Eleven weeks ago I'd tailed your gorgeous car along 5 North en route to that "genial but not particularly intimate or remarkable meeting" at your house between my husband, you and I. And everything then seemed different: delicious, charged. The three of us got very drunk and there was all this strange coincidence. There were just three books in your living room. One was *Gravity & Grace*, the title of my film. I was wearing the snake pendant that I'd bought in Echo Park; you told a story about shooting a video outside your house when a snake magically appeared. All night I was playing Academic Wife, helping you and Sylvère Lotringer exchange ideas and then you mentioned David Rattray's book and that was very weird. Because all night long I'd felt his ghost beside me and David had been dead almost two years. You looked at me and said: "You seem different than the last time that we met. As if you're ready to come out." And then I did—

What touched me most that night was how freely you admitted being lonely. That seemed so brave. Like you'd accepted it as the price for clearing all the garbage from your life. You told us how you stayed alone most nights, drinking, thinking, listening to tapes. If you're prepared to do something anyway it doesn't matter if you're afraid. You were the greatest Cowboy. And Sylvère and me, with our two-bit artworld hustles, projects, conversation skills—well, we were Kikes. You made me ready to recant on 15 years spent studying wit and difficulty in New York. I'd become a hag. And you were beautiful. Let the desert burn it out.

And now I'm heading out to visit you again alone along Route 126 but something's wrong. Nothing takes me past my body, plain-faced thin and serious, crammed into this rental car. I'm a schoolteacher in flashy clothes. The jeans are tight. I have to pee. I'm sensing that the farthest point of synchronicity is fear and dread.

It was nearly dark when the bus arrived in Chetumal. Friday night —a shopping night in this five block city of appliance stores. A city founded so Belizeans and Guatemalans who weren't rich enough to shop in Dallas or Miami could still buy duty-free TVs. The benefits of civil war? I took a taxi to the Guatemalan embassy but it was closed. Fittingly, there's a huge new glass and steel Museum of the Mayan Indian with very little in it at the edge of Chetumal. On the bus all afternoon I'd been reading the autobiography of Guatemalan rebel leader Rigoberta Menchú and thinking about Jane Bowles. Two different kinds of misery, alertness. After that, I checked in to a twenty dollar a night hotel.

The next morning I got up early to take a walk around Chetumal. According to the map it was a coastal town. The bus to Guatemala didn't leave 'til later on that afternoon. I caught a local city bus and time slowed down. Suburban Chetumal looked kind of like Mar Vista—stucco bungalows and tiny yards—except there were no bus stops, the bus stopped for anyone who flagged it down. And then seven miles and 60 minutes later the bungalows thinned out and the bay leapt out of nowhere when the road curved round. Sleepy dullness opening up to startlingly blue water, every particle of air locked into a glistening frame. The coastal land was jungly. I got off and walked along a jungly path to a waterfront cafe at the end of a round peninsula but it was closed. I gasped when I saw a tree monkey tethered to a pole. Finally a man came out and said in English that he'd bought the cafe and the beachfront and the monkey after working in a car shop in America. The monkey didn't seem to mind. I watched it, squatting, tracing circles on the ground. Its fur was dusty, cream smudged with cinders. It had ten perfectly articulated fingers, scrunched up toes.

Jennifer Harbury was 39 years old when she met Efraim Bamaca in a rebel training camp in the Guatemalan highland jungle. Until that time her life had been one dry and dusty road. From Baltimore to Cornell. From Cornell to North Africa, then to Afghanistan, backpacking around the outer reaches of these countries without any special plans. She met exiled Palestinians. She saw a lot of poverty and was moved to ask: Must people starve so that we can live the way we do? It's a question that can drive you crazy. Asking it sent Jennifer to Harvard Law School at a time when being a feminist meant refusing to be a co-dependent fuck-up. Lots of women were finding self-empowerment through careers in corporate law. But Jennifer-the-bad-feminist took a job defending immigrants in East Texas at a Legal Aid storefront. Many of the clients were Guatemalan Mayans facing deportation. People of another timescape who sat patiently on plastic chairs radiating thick and strange charisma. Jennifer wanted to know more. Unlike, perhaps, her colleagues, or the Texas lawyer she'd been married to for just a little while, "Mayan people have an ability to be completely communal. They are very humble, very sweet, very giving." Her work took her to Guatemala to substantiate theft claims for asylum from the war. In Guatemala City she met members of the underground and she became involved. 1989 saw her reaping the career rewards for twenty years of impassioned brilliant activism during the Bush and Reagan years: a battered pickup truck, a cheap apartment paid for by loans or gifts from old friends, a contract with an obscure small press in Maine for a book of oral histories she'd made with Guatemalan activists and peasants. Since Jennifer's a girl, we can't help measuring the distance between her burning vision and her sad and scrappy days when we think about her life. Even the article lionizing her in the *New York Times* calls her "quirky." "Really," an old school friend told the *Times* the week Ted Turner bought the character rights to her life, "she was a *tank*."

The story of Route 126 reads like a secret history of southern California. It runs west into Ventura County from Valencia, a former Indian burial ground. In the 1940s, Val Verde and Stevenson's Ranch were Black upper middle class resorts. Before the gated subdivisions of "northern LA county" were built here in the '80s, corpses were often dumped around the desert near Valencia. These facts inspired the horror movie *Poltergeist*. Of course Valencia is also the location of the Disney-funded art and animation school, CalArts. "Valencia is Smiles, Not Miles Away," a downtown billboard of a happy lion boasts. The locals like to call Route 126 "Blood Alley" for its freakily high number of fatal car accidents.

The geography and land-use blurs as you drive west from orange groves to onion fields to flower farms. But who does the work is clear: small produce stands owned by second generation Chicanos "banking on America" line the road; undocumented Mexican and Central Americans still work six or seven days a week in the fields. They live in rented propane-heated shacks. Several years ago a virtual slave-trade was discovered operating out of Camarillo. Shades of Rigoberta Menchú's childhood on plantations along the Guatemalan coast: desperate people rounded up in villages, packed standing into the airless backs of trucks—just an introduction to the horrors that await them. Dachau South.

Route 126 is a trucker's detour to Ventura around the weigh-station on Highway 101. It's a good place to buy speed. The road behind the town of Fillmore running to what used to be the National Condor Preserve is the venue for illegal drag races. When the Condor population dropped to three, they were rounded up and moved. The artist Nancy Barton recalls a project made in 1982 by Nan Border: she located the unsolved murder sites of eight female hitchhikers and prostitutes along Route 126 and mounted plaques beside their shallow graves.

In 1972 the artist Miriam Shapiro began a Feminist Art Program at CalArts. Mostly, the Program happened because her husband was then President of the School. But CalArts was a Jeffersonian democracy, so Shapiro had to spend six months playing Scheherazade: inviting every male department head, separately, to dinner, to coax and charm and guarantee their votes.

Artists in the program wanted, according to Faith Wilding, to "represent our sexuality in different, more assertive ways... 'Cunt' signified to us an awakened consciousness about our bodies... [We made] drawings and constructions of bleeding slits, holes and gashes..." The program lasted for one year. "Our art...which was meant to contest formalist standards," Wilding continues, "was subjected to scathing criticism by many in the school."

That spring everyone in Judy Chicago's class collaborated on a 24 hour performance called *Route 126*. The curator Moira Roth recalls: "the group created a sequence of events throughout the day along the highway. The day began with Suzanne Lacy's *Car Renovation* in which the group decorated an abandoned car...and ended with the women standing on a beach watching Nancy Youdelman, wrapped in yards of gossamer silk, slowly wade out to sea until she drowned, apparently..." There's a fabulous photo taken by Faith Wilding of the car—a Kotex-pink jalopy washed up on desert rocks. The trunk's flung open and underneath it's painted cuntblood red. Strands of desert grass spill from the crumpled hood like Rapunzel's fucked-up hair. According to *Performance Anthology—Source Book For A Decade Of California Art*, this remarkable event received no critical coverage at the time though contemporaneous work by Baldessari, Burden, Terry Fox boasts bibliographies several pages long. Dear Dick, I'm wondering why every act that narrated female lived experience in the '70s has been read only as "collaborative" and "feminist." The Zurich Dadaists worked together too but they were geniuses and they had names.

⚕ ⚕ ⚕ ⚕

By the time I turned off Route 126 onto Antelope Valley Road I really had to piss. You were expecting me at 8 and it was already 8:05 and pissing suddenly became so problematic. I didn't want to have to do it the moment I walked into your house, how gauche, a telltale sign of female nervousness. And yet considering everything I knew about Route 126 I was afraid to take a slash outside. Every 20 seconds the headlights of another car clipped by: marauding rednecks, cops, angry migrant workers? I pulled over at the Antelope Valley turnoff, turned off the headlights, stopped the car. Outside the grass was wet with rain. Who was it, Marx or Wittgenstein, who said that "every question, problem, contains the seeds of its own answer or solution through negation"? There was a half-drunk styrofoam cup of coffee in the car. I rolled down the window, dumped it, slid my jeans down past my knees and pissed into the empty cup. The cup was full before my bladder emptied but what the hell, I'd hold the rest. With shaking hands I tipped the brimming cup of urine in the grass.

That left the evidence. Several large drops still clung to the styrofoam, what if it smelled? I was afraid to litter. Dear Dick, sometimes there just isn't a right answer. I scrunched the cup up, tossed it under the back seat and wiped my hands. By this time I was feeling very drawn.

It was after midnight when our bus finally crossed the border into Guatemala. Klieg lights, a guard shack, barricades and the start of seventy miles of unpaved rutted road where Belize's National Highway ended. We were separated into groups by nationality and questioned while soldiers searched the luggage on the bus. The visa officer, a suave middle-aged mestizo with a handlebar mustache, scrutinized my passport, deep in thought, pretending not to recognize my picture. Finally he smiled and said: Welcome to Guatemala, Christina. When I got back to the bus the Rigoberta Menchú book was gone.

⚜

Hundreds of little colored Christmas lights were draped around the cactus plants outside your house. And there you were: sitting by the picture window in the living room, grading papers or pretending to, deep in thought. You got up and at the door we kissed hello kind of brusquely without lingering. The last time I was at your house for dinner back in January you kissed me when my husband, Mick and Rachel and the two men from the Getty were seven feet away. That kiss radiated such intensity I stumbled past you through the door.

Later on that night in January, when all the other guests had gone and the three of us were drinking vodka, Sylvère and I confessed to twelve years of fidelity. And suddenly that concept seemed so high-school and absurd we started laughing. "Ah but what," Sylvère said, "is fidelity?" That night the *Some Girls* album cover with the chicks in pointy bras was still propped up against your wall. I'd spent eleven weeks deliberating whether your display of it was camp or real and decided I agreed with Kierkegaard, that the sign will always triumph through the screen of an ironic signifier.

But tonight you were expecting me alone. I looked around the living room and saw the *Some Girls* album cover missing. Were you responding to my second letter, questioning your taste?

After the kiss, you invited me to sit down in the living room. Right away we started drinking wine. After half a glass I told you how I'd left my husband.

"Hmmm," you said compassionately, "I could've seen it coming."

And then I wanted you to understand the reasons. "It's like last night," I said, "I met Sylvère in New York for a French department dinner. Régis Debray, the guest of honor, never showed and everyone was kind of tense and uneasy. I was bored and spacing out but Sylvère thought I was suffering from a linguistic disability. He took my hand and said in English to the Beckett specialist Tom Bishop, 'Chris is an avid reader.' I mean, C'MON. Does Denis Hollier say this about Rosalind Krauss? I may have no credentials or career but I'm way too old to be an academic groupie."

You sympathized and said, "Well, I guess now the game is over."

How could I make you understand the letters were the realest thing I'd ever done? By calling it a game you were negating all my feelings. Even if this love for you could never be returned I wanted recognition. And so I started ranting on about Guatemala. The femme seduction trip seemed so corrupt and I was clueless how to do it. The only way I knew of reaching you apart from fucking was through ideas and words.

So I started trying to legitimize the "game" by telling you my thoughts about Case Studies. I was using Henry Frundt's book about the Guatemalan Coca-Cola strike as a model.

"'Cause don't you see?" I said. "It's more a project than a game. I meant every word I wrote you in those letters. But at the same time I started seeing it as a chance to finally learn something about romance, infatuation. Because you reminded me of so many people I'd loved back in New Zealand. Don't you think it's possible to do something and simultaneously study it? If the project had a name it'd be *I Love Dick: A Case Study*."

"Oh," you said, not too enthusiastically.

"Look," I said. "I started having this idea when I read Frundt's book after getting back from Guatemala. He's a sociologist specializing in Third World agribusiness. Frundt's a structural Marxist—instead of ranting on about imperialism and injustice he wants to find the reasons. And reasons aren't global. So Frundt researched every aspect of the Guatemalan Coca-Cola strike during the 1970s and '80s.

"He recorded everything. The only way to understand the large is through the small. It's like American first-person fiction."

You were listening, eyes moving up and down between me and your wine glass on the table. I saw what I was saying register across your face...cryptically, ambiguously, shifting between curiosity and incredulity. Your face was like the faces of the lawyers in the topless bars when I started telling Buddhist fairy tales with my legs spread wide across the table. *Some Strange Scene.* Were they amused? Were they assessing their capacity for cruelty? Your eyes were slightly crinkled, your fingers wrapped around glass. All this encouraged me to continue.

(Dear Dick, I always thought that both of us became political for the same reason. Reading constantly and wanting something else so fiercely that you want it for the world. God I'm such a Pollyanna. Perhaps enthusiasm's the only thing I have to offer you.)

"The more particular the information, the more likely it will be a paradigm. The Coca-Cola strike's a paradigm for the relationship between multinational franchises and host governments. And since Guatemala is so small and all the facets of its history can be studied, it's a paradigm for many Third World countries. If we can understand what happened there, we can get a sense of everything. And don't you think the most important question is, *How does evil happen*?

"At the height of the Coca-Cola strike in 1982, the army killed all the leaders of the strike and all their families. They killed the lawyers too, Guatemalan and American. The one they missed—her name was Marta Torres—they found her teenage daughter on a city street, disappeared and blinded her."

Did it cross my mind that torture was not a sexy topic of conversation for this, our first, our only date? No, never. "'Cause don't you see? By recording every single memo, phone call, letter, meeting that took place around the strike, Frundt describes how *casually* terror happens. If Mary Fleming hadn't sold her Coca-Cola franchise to John Trotter, an ultra-rightist friend of Bush, the strike might not have happened. All acts of genocidal horror may be nauseatingly similar but they arise through singularity."

I still hadn't gotten round to explaining what Guatemalan genocide had to do with the 180 pages of love letters that I'd written with my husband and then given you, like a timebomb or a cesspool or a manuscript. But I would, I would. I felt like we were facing each other from the edges of a very dark and scary crater. Truth and difficulty. Truth and sex. I was talking, you were listening. You were witnessing me become this crazy and cerebral girl, the kind of girl that you and your entire generation vilified. But doesn't witnessing contain complicity? "You think too much," is what they always said when their curiosity ran out.

"I want to own everything that happens to me now," I told you. "Because if the only material we have to work with in America is our own lives, shouldn't we be making case studies?"

OH EGYPT I AM WASHING MY HAIR TO GAIN KNOWLEDGE OF YOU, and by this time we were eating dinner. It was packaged fresh linguini, packaged sauce and salad. I couldn't eat a bite. "That's fine," you said. "Just don't take me down along with you."

≈≈≈

"He took me by the shoulders and shook me out." That's how Jennifer Harbury described meeting Efraim Bamaca.

Jennifer was interviewing rebel fighters in the Tajumulco combat zone in 1990. She felt so pale and large. "Compared to everyone else I'm huge, I'm 5'3. A giant." Bamaca was a Mayan peasant educated by the rebel army. At 35 he was notorious, a leader. Meeting him surprised her. "He looked almost like a fawn," she said. "He was so quiet and discreet. He never gave orders but somehow everything got done." And when she interviewed him for her oral history book, that most self-erasing lefty genre, he turned the questions back on her and listened.

They fell in love. When Jennifer left Tajumulco, Bamaca promised not to write. "There's no such thing as a fantasy relationship." But then he did, notes smuggled from the highlands to a safehouse, mailed from Mexico. A year later they met again and married. "It was a side of Jennifer I'd never seen," another law school friend told the *New York Times*. "She seemed so happy."

≈≈≈

After dinner, then, you leaned back in your chair and fixed me with your gaze and asked: "What do you want?" A direct question tinged with irony. Your mouth was twisted, wry, like you already knew the answer. "What did you expect by coming here?"

Well I'd come this far, I was ready for all kinds of trials. So I said, out loud, the obvious: "I want to stay here tonight with you." And you just kept staring at me, quizzically, wanting more. (Even though I hadn't slept with anyone but my husband for 12 years, I couldn't remember sexual negotiations ever being this humiliatingly explicit. But maybe this was good? A jumpcut from the cryptic to the literal?) So finally I said: "I want to sleep with you." And then: "I want us to have sex together."

You asked me: "Why?"

(The psychiatrist H.F. Searles lists six ways to drive another person crazy in *The Etiology of Schizophrenia*. Method Number Four: Control the conversation, then abruptly shift its modes.)

The night Sylvère and I slept over at your house I'd dreamt vividly about having different kinds of sex with you. While Sylvère and I slept on the sofabed I dreamt I'd slipped into your bedroom through the wall. What struck me most about the sex we had was, it was so intentional and deliberate. The dream occurred in two separate scenes. In Scene One we're naked on your bed, viewed frontal-horizontally, foreshortened like Egyptian hieroglyphics. I'm squatting, neck and shoulders curved to reach your cock. Tendrils of my hair brush back and forth across your groin and thighs. It was the most subtle, psycho-scientific kind of blowjob. The perspective changes in Scene Two to vertical. I sit on top of you, you're lying flat, head slightly arched, I'm sinking up and down your cock, each time I'm learning something new, we gasp at different times.

"What do you want?" you asked again. "I want to sleep with you." Two weeks ago I'd written you that note saying the idea of spending time alone with you was a vision of pure happiness and pleasure. On the phone you'd said, "I won't say no" when I asked you what you thought, but all the reasons, factors, desire splintered in a hundred hues like sunlight through a psychedelic prism came crashing with a thud when you asked me: "Why?"

I just said, "I think we could have a good time together."

"We were in love," Jennifer Harbury told the *New York Times* about her life with Efraim Bamaca.

"We hardly ever fought—"

⁂

And then you said, "But you don't even know me."

⁂

Route 126 runs west along the base of the San Padre mountains. The landscape changes when it hits the Antelope Valley from rounded rolling hills to something craggier, more Biblical. The night (December 3) Sylvère and I stayed at your house because, as you said in a letter to him later, "weather reports had indicated that you might not be able to make it back to San Bernardino," we were amazed by where you lived. It was an existential dream, a Zen metaphor for everything you'd said about yourself…living, "all alone," you kept repeating, at the end of a dead-end road on the edge of town opposite a cemetery. A roadsign outside your place said, No Exit. And all night long as the three of us got drunker you found so many ways to talk about yourself, so many ways of making loneliness seem like a direct line to all the sadness in the world. If seduction is a highball, unhappiness has got to be the booze.

You said, "There's no such thing as a good time. It always ends in tears and disappointment." And when I blundered on about blind love, infatuation, you said, "It's not that simple." We had totally reversed positions. I was the Cowboy, you were the Kike. But still I rode it.

"Can't things just be fabulous?" I said, staring out the window. Things were getting dreamy, elongated, metaphysical. Moments passed. "Well then," you asked, "have you got any drugs?"

I was prepared for this. I was carrying a vial of liquid opium, two hits of acid, 30 Percoset and a lid of killer pot. "Relax, you've got a date!" Ann Rower'd said when she counted out her gift of Burmese flowerheads. Somehow this wasn't going how either of us had planned. But I rolled a joint and we toasted Ann.

The record ended and you got up to make some coffee. In the kitchen we stood fumbling accidentally-on-purpose brushing hands but this was so embarrassing and clunky we both withdrew. Then we talked some more about the desert, books and movies. Finally I said: "Look, it's getting late. What do you want to do?"

"I'm a gentleman," you answered coyly. "I would hate to be inhospitable. If you don't feel you can drive…"

"It's not *about* that," I said brusquely.

"Ah then… Do you want to share my bed? I won't say no."

Oh come on, had mores changed this much while I'd been married?

"Do you want us to have sex or don't you?"

You said: "I'm not uncomfortable with that idea."

This neutrality was not erotic. I asked you for enthusiasm but you said you couldn't give it. I made one final stab within this register: "Look, if you're not into this, it'd be more—gentlemanly— just to say so and I'll go."

But you repeated, "I'm not…uncomfortable…with the…idea."

Well. We were electrons swimming round and round inside of a closed circuit. No exit. *Huis clos*. I'd thought and dreamt about you daily since December. Loving you had made it possible to admit the failure of my film and marriage and ambitions. Route 126, the Highway to Damascus. Like Saint Paul and Buddha who'd experienced their great conversions as they hit 40, I was Born Again in Dick. But was this good for you?

This is how I understood the rules:

If you want something very badly it's okay to keep pursuing it until the other person tells you No.

You said: *I won't say no.*

So when you got up to change the record I bent down and started to untie my bootlace. And then things changed. The room stood still.

You came back, sat on the floor and took my boots off. I reached for you, we started dancing to the record. You picked me up and now we're standing in the living room, my legs are braced around your waist. You tell me "you're so light" and now we're swaying, hair and faces brushing. Who'll be the first to kiss? And then we do…

Here are some uses of ellipses:

• …fade to black after ten seconds of a kiss in a Hayes Commission censored film.

• …Celine separates his phrases in *Journey to the End of Night* to blast the metaphor out of language. Ellipses shoot across the page like bullets. Automatic language as a weapon, total war. If the coyote is the last surviving animal, hatred's got to be the last emotion in the world.

You put me down and gesture to the bedroom. And then the record changes to *Pat Garrett and Billy the Kid* by Bob Dylan. How perfect. How many times have each of us had sex in the foreground of this record? Six or seven tracks of banjo strum and whine that culminate around Minute 25 (a Kinsey national average) in *Knocking At Heaven's Door*. A heterosexual anthem.

And then you're laid out on the bed, head propped on pillows and we take our shirts off. The blue lamp beside the bed is on. I'm still wearing the black Guess jeans, a bra. I watch you feel my tits and we both watch my nipples as they get hard. Later on you run your index finger across the outside of my cunt, not into it. It's very wet, a Thing Observed, and later still I think about the act of witnessing and the Kierkegaardian third remove. Sex with you is so phenomenally...sexual, and I haven't had sex with *anyone* for about two years. And I'm scared to talk and I'm wanting to sink down on you and then words come out, the way they do.

"I want to be your lapdog."

You're floating like you haven't really heard so I repeat it: "Will you let me be your lapdog?"

"Okay," you say. "C'mere."

And then you ease me, small and Pekinese, 'til my hands are braced above your shoulders. My hair's all over.

"If you want to be my lapdog let me tell you what to do. Don't move," you say. "Be very quiet."

I nod and maybe whimper and then your cock, which until now'd been very still, comes rushing up, waves pulsing outward through my fingers. Sound comes out. You put your fingers on my lips.

"Come on little lapdog. You have to be real quiet. Stay right here."

And I do, and this goes on for maybe hours. We have sex 'til breathing feels like fucking. And I sleep fitfully in your turquoise room.

I wake up around six and you're still sleeping.

Rain's made the weeds outside your window very green. I find a book and settle on the living room sofa. I'm scared about the morning part, don't want to make my presence too invasive or demanding. But soon enough you're leaning in the doorway.

"What're you doing out there?"

"Resting."

"Well rest in here."

So we had fuzzy halting morning sex, the sheets, bright daylight, everything more real, but still that flood, the rushing of endorphins and for a long time after it was over neither of us said a word.

And this's when things get pretty weird.

"*Get* weird?" Scott B. said on the phone tonight when I was telling him the story. "What did you expect? The *whole thing* was completely weird."

Well yeah, I see his point. But still—

"So," I said as we sort of shifted out of sex, "what's the program?"

"What program do you mean? *The Brady Bunch*?"

"Noooo…I mean, I'll be in town 'til Tuesday and I was wondering if you think we should see each other again."

You turned and said, "Do you want to?"

"Yes," I said. "Definitely. Absolutely."

"Definitely… absolutely" you repeated with an ironic curl.

"Yes. I do."

"Well, actually I have a Friend (you somehow feminized the word) arriving for the weekend."

"Oh" I said, this information dropping like a stone.

"What's the matter?" you asked, seizing an idea. "Did I burst your balloon—destroy the fantasy?"

I struggled for a way to answer this without my clothes.

"I guess you were right about the disappointment. Probably if I'd known I wouldn't've stayed."

"What?" you laughed. "You think I'm *cheating* on you?"

Well this was very cruel, but loving you'd become a full-time job and I wasn't ready to be unemployed. "No," I said. "I don't. You just have to help me find a way to make this more acceptable."

"Acceptable?" you mimicked. "I don't have to do *anything* for you."

You were assuming a position, mockery heightening your face into a mask. Ultra-violence. Attack and kill.

"I don't owe you anything. You barged in here, this was your game, your agenda, now it's yours to deal with."

I wasn't anything at that moment except shock and disappointment.

Changing gears, you added archly: "I guess now you'll start sending me hate letters. You'll add me to your Demonology of Men."

"No," I said. "No more letters."

I had no right to be angry and I didn't want to cry. "You don't have to be so militantly callous."

You shrugged and made a point of looking at your hands.

"So militantly mean?" And then, appealing to your Marxist past, "So militantly against mystification?"

This brought a smile.

"Look," I said, "I'll admit that eighty percent of this was fantasy, projection. But it had to start with something real. Don't you believe in empathy, in intuition?"

"What?" you said. "Are you telling me you're schizophrenic?"

"No..., I just—" and then I lapsed into the pathetic. "I just—felt something for you. This strange connection. I felt it in your work, but before that too. That dinner we had three years ago with you and Jane, you flirted with me, you must've felt it—"

"But you don't know me! We've had two or three evenings! Talked on the phone once or twice! And you project this shit all over me, you kidnap me, you stalk me, invade me with your games, and I don't want it! I never asked for it! I think you're evil and psychotic!"

"But what about my letter? When I left Sylvère I wrote it trying to break through this thing with you. No matter what I do you think it's just a game but I was trying to be honest."

("Honesty of this order threatens order," David Rattray'd written once about René Crevel and I was trying then to reach that point.)

I continued: "Do you have any idea how hard it was for me to call you? It was the hardest thing I've ever done. Harder than calling William Morris. You said to come. You must've known then what I wanted."

"I didn't need the sex," you barked. And then a gentlemanly afterthought: "Though it was nice."

By now the sun was very bright. We were still naked on the bed.

I said, "I'm sorry."

But how could I explain? "It's just—" I started, foraging through fifteen years of living in New York, the arbitrariness of art careers, or were they really arbitrary? Who gets to speak and why? David Rattray's book sold only about 500 copies and now he's dead. Penny Arcade's original and real and Karen Finley's fake and who's more famous? Ted Berrigan died of poverty and Jim Brodey was evicted, started living in the park before he died of AIDS. Artists without medical insurance who'd killed themselves at the beginning of the onset so they wouldn't be a burden to their friends…the ones who moved me most mostly lived and died like dogs unless like me they compromised.

"I hate ninety percent of everything around me!" I told you. "But then, the rest I really love. Perhaps too strongly."

"I'd rethink that, if I were you," you said. You were leaning up against a dusky wall. "I *like* 90 percent of everything I see, the rest I leave alone." And I listened. You seemed so wise and radiant, and all the systems that I used to understand the world dissolved.

Of course the truth was messier. It was only Friday morning. The drive to Lake Casitas, the motel room, the percoset, the scotch were still to come. I lost my wallet, drove 50 miles to find it on 1/8 a tank of gas. There was still the phone call Sunday, meeting you for dinner and then the bar together Monday night. A production-number medley of all the highlights of the show. It wasn't 'til I reached Ann Rower on Saturday on the phone that I stopped crying long enough to start shifting things around. Ann said: "Maybe Dick was right." This seemed so radically profound. Could I accept your cruelty as a gift of truth? Could I even learn to thank you for it? (Though when I showed Ann the outline of this story, she said she never said that. Not even close.)

On Saturday I spent the night on Daniel Marlos' couch. José made beans and carne asada. Daniel was working three jobs seven days a week to make money for an experimental film and not complaining. Sunday morning I walked through Eagle Rock down Lincoln Avenue to Occidental College. "Even here," I sat writing in my notebook, "in this bunched together neighborhood, people are taking Sunday morning walks. The air smells like flowers."

At the library I looked up *Gravity & Grace* by Simone Weil:

"It is impossible," she wrote, "to forgive whoever has done us harm if that harm has lowered us. We have to think that it has not lowered us but revealed to us our true level."

In the Guatemalan rainforest I saw wild monkeys and Toucan parrots. I stayed at a hotel attached to a villa owned by the environmentalist Oscar Pallermo. Oscar was the black sheep of one of the Guatemalan oligarchy's leading families...though not so black he didn't have the villa, a house in Guatemala City and an apartment in New York. Oscar included me in a routine with his extended family straight out of *Stealing Beauty*—two hour lunches, trips along the river. Three years ago a farmhouse on his land was torched by Mayan rebels.

On the 29th day of Jennifer Harbury's hunger strike *60 Minutes* aired a segment about her plight. On Day 32 her lawyer flew down from Washington with the news: "People in the White House will talk to you now." On March 22, New Jersey Congressman Robert Toricelli unveiled the findings of a House Intelligence Committee investigation of the CIA in Guatemala. The three years and ten days that Harbury spent trying to find the truth behind Bamaca's disappearance had led her—or rather, led the media and government—to discover what she'd surely always known: her husband's killer had been hired by the CIA. Colonel Julio Alberto Alpirez, Guatemala's answer to Mengele, also kidnapped, tortured, killed Michael Devine, an American innkeeper.

Didn't Alexander Cockburn say, for every dead American we read about there's always 30,000 nameless peasants? Alpirez's CIA-funded outfit, the Archivo, killed and tortured countless Guatemalan priests, nurses, trade unionists, journalists and farmers. They raped and tortured the American nun Diana Ortiz and stabbed the anthropologist Myrna Mack to death on the streets of Guatemala City at 3 o'clock in the afternoon. On March 24 the US government withdrew all military aid to Guatemala. Several CIA section chiefs were fired. Jennifer Harbury was off her garbage bag and testifying before Congress. (Though just last month in Washington on the eve of Guatemala's first elections, a bomb exploded in her lawyer's car.)

For months I thought this story would be something about how love can change the world. But that's probably too corny.

Fassbinder said once, "I detest the idea that love between two persons can lead to salvation. All my life I have fought against this oppressive type of relationship. Instead, I believe in searching for a kind of love that somehow involves all of humanity."

I got my voice back several days after leaving Guatemala.

Love,
Chris

THE EXEGESIS

> *"Entry 52 shows that Fat at this point in his life reached out for any wild hope which would shore up his confidence that some good existed somewhere."*

> — Philip K. Dick, *Valis*

Thurman, New York
March 4, 1995

Dear Dick,

1. Some Incidents In The Life of a Slave Girl

How do you continue when the connection to the other person is broken (when the connection is broken to yourself)? To be in love with someone means believing that to be in someone else's presence is the only means of being, completely, yourself.

And now it's Saturday morning and tomorrow I'll be 40 which makes this the last *Saturday Morning In Her 30s* to quote the title of an Eileen Myles and Alice Notley poem that I've thought of with a smile maybe 60 times while making phone calls, running errands during scattered Saturday mornings over the last ten years.

Yesterday afternoon I drove back here from New York. I was

disoriented and confused (and I'm confused now, too, whether to address you in the declarative or narrative; that is, who'm I talking to?). I got back to New York on Tuesday night after spending those five days in LA "with" you. And then Sylvère and I spent Wednesday, Thursday, moving all our stuff from Second Avenue to Seventh Street. All through the move I was regretful, and I'm trying not to be regretful still.

In the late '70s when I was working in the New York City topless bars there was this disco song that stayed around forever called *Shame* by Evelyn Champagne King. It was perfect for that time and place, evoking the emotion without owning it—

Shame!
What you do to me is a shame
I'm only tryna ease the pain…,
Deep in your arms
Is where I want to be

'Cause shame was what we always felt, me and all my girlfriends, for expecting sex to breed complicity. ("Complicity is like a girl's name," writes Dodie Bellamy.)

"Is that what you wanted?" you asked me Friday morning. It was nearly 10. We'd been arguing in bed without our clothes for hours. And you'd just charitably, generously, told me a sad story from your life to make amends for calling me psychotic. To try and make things right. "Is that what you wanted? A ragged kind of intimacy?"

Well yes and no. "I'm just trying to be honest," I'd confessed to you that morning, and it sounded oh so lame. "Whenever someone makes a breakthrough into honesty," David Rattray'd said in an interview I'd arranged for him with the editor Ken Jordan, "that means not just self-knowledge but knowledge of what others can't see. To be honest in a real absolute way is to be almost prophetic, to upset the applecart." I was just trying to promote his book and he was ranting in a way that made me cringe about his hatred for everyone who'd kept him down, who were out to silence "every bright young person who comes along with something original to say." The interview was made just three days before he collapsed on Avenue A with a massive and inoperable brain tumor.

"Because after all," I typed, following his deep and unmistakable patrician voice, "the applecart is just an endless series of indigestible meals and social commitments that are useless and probably shouldn't even be honored, and futile pointless conversations, gestures, just to finally die abandoned, treated like a piece of garbage by people in white coats who are no more civilized than sanitation workers…that's what the applecart means to me."

Shame is what you feel after being fucked on quaaludes by some artworld cohort who'll pretend it never happened, shame is what you feel after giving blowjobs in the bathroom at Max's Kansas City because Liza Martin wants free coke. Shame is what you feel after letting someone take you someplace past control—then feeling torn up three days later between desire, paranoia, etiquette wondering if they'll call. Dear Dick, you told me twice last weekend how much you love John Rechy's books and you wish your writing could include more sex. Because I love you and you can't or you're embarrassed, maybe this is something I can do for you?

At any rate in order not to feel this hopelessness, regret, I've set myself the job of solving heterosexuality (i.e., finishing this writing project) before turning 40. And that's tomorrow.

Because suddenly it seemed, after arriving from LA, jetlagged and moving boxes between apartments, that there was so much more to understand and say. Was this the bottom of the snakepit? In the restaurant Monday night we talked about our favorite Fassbinder movie, *The Bitter Tears of Petra Von Kant.* I was wearing a white long-sleeved tailored shirt, looking pointedly demure, the whore's curveball, and I felt like suddenly I'd understood something. "Fassbinder was such an ugly man," I said. "That's the real subject of his films: an ugly man who was wanting, looking to be loved."

The subtext rested on the table in between us like the sushi. Because of course I was ugly too. And the way you took this in, understanding it without any explication, made me realize how everything that's passed between us all came back to sex and ugliness and identity.

"You were so wet," Dick _____'d said to me in the bar that Monday night about the sex we'd had on Thursday. My heart opened and I fell beneath the polite detente that we'd established in the restaurant, your black Italian jacket, my long-sleeved buttoned shirt. Were you seducing me again or just alluding to things I'd written in my manifesto *Every Letter Is A Love Letter* which you'd finally read that afternoon? I didn't quite know how to take this. But then Dick glanced brusquely at his watch and turned to look at someone else across the room. And then I knew you never wanted to have sex with me again.

I came back devastated by the weekend, begging Sylvère to give me some advice. Even though his theoretical side is fascinated by how this correspondence, love affair, has sexualized and changed me, all his other sides are angry and confused. So can I blame him when he responded like a cut-rate therapist? "You'll never learn!" he said. "You keep looking for rejection! It's the same problem that you've always had with men!" But I believe this problem's bigger and more cultural.

We looked great together Monday night walking into the Ace of Diamonds Bar. Both of us tall and anorexic and our jackets matched. "Here comes the Mod Squad," the barman said. All the regulars looked up from their beers. How hilarious. You're a mod and I'm a modernist. "Buy you a drink?" "Sure." And then suddenly I'm back in 1978 at the Nightbirds Bar, drinking smoking flirting, shooting sloppy pool with my then-boyfriend Ray Johannson. Ha ha ha. "You can't sit on the pool table! You've gotta keep both legs on the floor!" Within minutes of arriving we trashed the whole agreement of mature neutrality we'd worked out in the sushi bar. You were flirting with me, anything seemed possible. Back to English rules.

Later, legs pressed close under one of those tiny barroom tables, we were talking one more time about our favorite ghost, David Rattray. And I wanted to explain how I made allowances for David's bad behavior, all those years on alcohol and heroin, how he got bigger while his wife who'd been on the scene with him shrank until she nearly disappeared. "He was part of the generation that ruined women's lives," I told you. "It's not just that generation," you replied. "Men still do ruin women's lives." And at the time I didn't answer, had no opinion, took it in.

But at 3 a.m. last Wednesday night I bolted up in bed, reaching for my laptop. I realized you were right.

"J'ACCUSE," (I started typing) "Richard Schechner."

Richard Schechner is a Professor of Performance Studies at New York University, author of *Environmental Theater* and several other books on anthropology and theater and editor of *The Drama Review*. He was once my acting teacher. And at 3 a.m. last Wednesday night it occurred to me that Richard Schechner had ruined my life.

And so I'd write this broadside rant and wheatpaste it all around Richard's neighborhood and NYU. I'd dedicate it to the artist Hannah Wilke. Because while Hannah's tremendous will to turn the things that bothered her into subjects for her art seemed so embarrassing in her lifetime, at 3 a.m. it dawned on me that Hannah Wilke is a model for everything I hope to do.

"J'ACCUSE RICHARD SCHECHNER who through sleep deprivation amateur GESTALT THERAPY and SEXUAL MANIPULATION attempted to exert MIND CONTROL over a group of 10 students in Washington, D.C."

Well, it was a plan. And at that moment I believed in it as strongly as the plan Sylvère and I made one night on 7th Street when I was so depressed and he joined me in my suicide attempt. We each drank some wine and took two percosets and decided to read Chapter 73 of Julio Cortazar's book *Hopscotch* out loud into your answerphone. "Yes but who will cure us of the dull fire, the colorless fire that at nightfall runs along the rue de la Huchette…" At the time it seemed so daring, apropos and brilliant but Dick, like most conceptual art, delirium can get so referential—

At Richard Schechner's Aboriginal Dream Time Workshop in Washington, D.C., he and I were the only people in the group who got up before the crack of noon. We drank coffee, shared the *Post* and *New York Times* and talked about politics and world events. Like us, Richard had some kind of politics and in that group I was the only other person interested in the news. I was a Serious Young Woman, hunched and introspective, running to the library to check out books about the Aborigines—too dumb to realize in that situation that the Aborigines were totally beside the point.

Richard seemed to like our morning conversations about Brecht and Althusser and Andre Gorz, but later on he turned the group against me for being too cerebral and acting like a boy. And weren't all these passionate interests and convictions just evasions of a greater truth, my cunt? I was an innocent, a de-gendered freak, 'cause unlike Liza Martin, who was such a babe she refused to take her platforms off for Kundalini Yoga, I hadn't learned the trick of throwing sex into the mix.

And so on Perilous Journey Night, I went downtown and took my clothes off in a topless bar. Shake shake shake. That same night Marsha Peabody, an overweight suburban schizophrenic who Richard'd let into the group because schizophrenia, like Aboriginal Dream Time, breaks down the continuum between space and time, decided to go off her medication. Richard spent Perilous Journey Night on the football field behind the changing sheds getting a blowjob from Maria Calloway. Maria wasn't in our group. She'd come all the way from NYC to study with Richard Schechner but she'd been shunted into Leah's workshop on Body/Sound because she wasn't a "good enough" performer. The next day Marsha disappeared and no one asked or heard from her again. Richard encouraged me and Liza Martin to work together in New York. I gave up my cheap apartment and moved into Liza's Tribeca loft, topless dancing several nights a week to pay her rent. I was investigating the rift between thought and sex or so I thought, letting lawyers smell my pussy while I talked. This went on for several years and Dick, on Wednesday night I woke up realizing you were right. Men still *do* ruin women's lives. As I turn 40 can I avenge the ghost of my young self?

To see yourself as who you were ten years ago can be very strange indeed.

On Thursday afternoon I walked over to Film/Video Arts on Broadway to make a copy of the videotape of *Readings From The Diaries of Hugo Ball,* a performance piece I'd staged in 1983.

Though he's remembered as the person who "invented" Dada

at Zurich's Cabaret Voltaire in 1917, Ball's art activities lasted only about two years. All the other years were fractured, restless. He was a theater student, factory worker, circus attendant, journalist for a leftist weekly and amateur theologian chronicling the "hierarchy of angels" before his death of stomach cancer at age 41. Ball and his companion Emmy Hennings, a cabaret performer, puppet maker, novelist and poet, zigzagged across Switzerland and Germany for 20 years recanting and revising their beliefs. They had no steady source of income. They moved around Europe looking for the perfect low-rent base where they could live cheap and work in peace. They broke with Tristan Tzara because they couldn't understand his careerism—why spend your life promoting one idea?—and were it not for the publication of Ball's diaries, *Flight Out of Time*, all traces of their lives probably would've disappeared.

Morphine

What we are waiting for is one last fling
At the dizzy height of each passing day
We dread the sleepless dark and cannot pray.
Sunshine we hate, it doesn't mean a thing.

We never pay attention to the mail.
The pillow we sometimes favor with a silent
All-knowing smile, between fits of violent
Activity to shake the fever chill.

Let others join the struggle to survive
We rush helplessly forward through this life,
Dead to the world, dreaming on our feet.
The blackness just keeps coming down in sheets.

Emmy Hennings wrote this poem in 1916 and Dick, it was just so thrilling to discover there were people in the past like Ball and Hennings, making art without any validation or career plans when my friends and I were living in the East Village, New York City in 1983.

Reading about them saved my life, and so to stage the diaries I invited the nine most interesting people that I knew to comb through Ball and Henning's writings for the parts that best described themselves. There were the poets Bruce Andrews, Danny Krakauer, Steve Levine and David Rattray. There were the performers Leonora Champagne and Linda Hartinian, the actress Karen Young, the art critic Gert Schiff and me.

And since three of these nine people are dead now, and since I'd recently read Mick Tausig's account of Ball in his book *The Nervous System* (who regrets the historical absence of Dadaist women, but doesn't look too hard to find them—Dear Dick, Dear Mick, I'm just an amateur but I found three: Emmy Hennings, Hannah Hoch and Sophie Tauber), I wanted to take another look at the play.

As instigator of the piece I played the role of hostess/tour guide, giving my friends a chance to speak and filling in the expository holes. To do this I stole the character of Gabi Teisch, a German high school history teacher created by Alexandra Kluge for her brother's film *The Patriot*. Because she is unhappy in the present, Gabi Teisch decides to excavate the whole of German history to find out what went wrong. I was unhappy too. And until we own our history, she thought, I thought, there can be no change.

To get into the role I found a sensible tweed skirt flecked with tiny rhinestones and a long-sleeved lacy blouse: a costume that reminded me of an arcane archetype, the Hippie Intellectual High-school Teacher, of her, of me.

So on Thursday afternoon I stood around the Film/Video Arts dub room watching myself at 28 as Gabi Teisch: a scarecrow with bad hair, bad skin, bad teeth, slouched underneath the weight of all this information, every word an effort but one worth making because there was just so much to say.

To perform yourself inside a role is very strange. The clothes, the words, prod you into nameless areas and then you stretch them out in front of other people, live.

Chris/Gabi was a mess, persona-less, trying to lose herself in talking. Her eyes were open but afraid, locked in neutral, not knowing whether to look in or out. While she was in rehearsal for the play, Chris had started having sadomasochistic sex with the downtown Manhattan luminary Sylvère Lotringer. This happened about twice a week at lunchtime and it was very confusing. Chris would arrive at Sylvère's Front Street loft after doing errands on Canal Street. She'd be ushered into Sylvère's bedroom, walls lined with books and African water bags and whips and he'd push her down onto the bed with all her clothes on. He held her, squeezed her tits until she came. He never let her touch him, often he wouldn't even fuck her and after awhile she stopped wondering who this person even was, revolving on his bed deeper through time tunnels into memories of childhood. Love and fear and glamour. Browsing through his books she realized she was up against some pretty stiff competition, reading some of the inscriptions: "To Sylvère, The Best Fuck In The World (At Least To My Knowledge) Love, Kathy Acker." Afterwards they'd eat clam soup and talk about the Frankfurt School. Then he showed her to the door...

So what was Chris performing? At that moment she was a picture of the Serious Young Woman thrown off the rails, exposed, alone, androgynous and hovering onstage between the poet-men, presenters of ideas, and actress-women, presenters of themselves. She wasn't beautiful like the women; unlike the men, she had no authority. Watching Chris/Gabi I hated her and wanted to protect her. Why couldn't the world I'd moved around in since my teens, the underground, just let this person be?

"You are not beautiful but you are very intelligent," the Mexican gigolo says to the 38-year-old New York Jewish heroine of the film *A Winter Tan*. And of course it's at that moment that you know he's going to kill her.

All acts of sex were forms of degradation. Some random recollections: East 11th Street, on the bed with Murray Groman: "Swallow this mother 'til you choke." East 11th Street, in the bed with Gary Becker: "The trouble with you is, you're such a shallow person." East 11th Street, up against the wall with Peter Baumann: "The only thing that turns me on about you is pretending you're a whore." Second Avenue, the kitchen, Michael Wainwright: "Quite frankly, I deserve a better-looking, better-educated girlfriend." What do you do with the Serious Young Woman (short hair, flat shoes, body slightly hunched, head drifting back and forth between the books she's read)? You slap her, fuck her up the ass and treat her like a boy. The Serious Young Woman looked everywhere for sex but when she got it it became an exercise in disintegration. What was the motivation of these men? Was it hatred she evoked? Was it some kind of challenge, trying to make the Serious Young Woman femme?

2. The Birthday Party

Inside out
Boy you turn me

Upside down and
Inside out
　　　—late '70s disco song

Joseph Kosuth's 50th birthday party last January was reported the next day on *Page 6* of the *New York Post*. And everything was just as perfect as they said: about 100 guests, a number large enough to fill the room but small enough for each of us to feel among the intimates, the chosen. Joseph and Cornelia and their child had just arrived from Belgium; Marshall Blonsky, one of Joseph's closest friends and Joseph's staff had been planning it for weeks.

Sylvère and I drove down from Thurman. I dropped him off outside the loft, parked the car and arrived at Joseph's door at the same moment as another woman, also entering alone. Each of us gave our names to Joseph's doorman. Each of us had names that weren't there. "Check Lotringer," I said. "Sylvère." And sure enough, I was Sylvère Lotringer's "Plus One" and she was someone else's. Riding up the elevator, checking makeup, collars, hair, she whispered, "The last thing you want to feel before walking into one of these things is that you're not invited," and we smiled and wished each other luck and parted at the coat-check. But luck was something that I didn't feel much need of because I had no expectations: this was Joseph's party, Joseph's friends, people, (mostly men, except for female art dealers and us plus-ones) from the early '80s art world, so I expected to be patronized and ignored.

Drinks were at one end of the loft; dinner at the other. David Byrne was wandering across the room as tall as a Moorish king in a magnificent fur hat. I stood next to Kenneth Broomfield at the bar and said a tentative hello; he hissed and turned away. A tighter grip around the scotch-glass, standing there in my dark-green

Japanese wool dress, high heels and makeup... But look! There's Marshall Blonsky! Marshall greets me at the bar and says that seeing me reminds me of the party we attended some 11 years ago when I was Marshall's date. And of course he would remember because the party was given by Xavier Fourcade to celebrate the publication of Marshall's first book, *On Signs,* at Xavier's Sutton Place townhouse. It was late winter, early spring, Aquarius or Pisces and I remember guests tripping past the caterers and staff to walk around the green expanse of daffodils and bunny lawn that separated us from the river. David Salle was there, Umberto Eco was there, together with a stable-load of Fourcade's models and a reviewer from the *New York Times.*

At that time I was living in a tenement on Second Avenue and studying charm as a possible escape. Could I be Marshall Blonsky's perfect date? I'd given up trying to be as sexual as Liza Martin but I was small-boned, thin, with a New Zealand accent trailing off to something that sounded vaguely mid-Atlantic. Perhaps something could be done with this? By then I'd read enough that no one guessed I'd never been to school. Marshall and I'd been introduced by our mutual friend Louise Bourgeois. I loved her and he was fascinated by her iron will and growing fame. "It is the ability to sublimate that makes an artist," she told me once. And: "The only hope for you is marrying a critic or an academic. Otherwise you'll starve." And in the interest of saving me from poverty, Louise had given me, for this occasion, the perfect dress: a straight wool-boucle pumpkin-colored shift, historically important, the dress she'd worn accompanying Robert Rauschenberg to his first opening on East 10th... Most of Marshall's friends were men—critics, psychoanalysts, semioticians—and he liked that he could walk me round the room and I'd perform for them, listening, cracking jokes in their own special languages, guiding the conversation back to Marshall's book. So French New Wave… Being weightless and gamine, spitting prettily at rules and institutions, a talking dog without the dreariness of a position to defend.

Dear Dick, It hurts me that you think I'm "insincere." Nick Zedd and I were both interviewed once about our films for English television. Everyone in New Zealand who saw the show told me how they liked Nick better 'cause he was more sincere. Nick was just one thing, a straight clear line: *Whoregasm*, East Village gore 'n porn, and I was several. And-and-and. And isn't sincerity just the denial of complexity? You as Johnny Cash driving your Thunderbird into the Heart of Light. What put me off experimental film world feminism, besides all it's boring study groups on Jacques Lacan, was its sincere investigation into the dilemma of the Pretty Girl. As an Ugly Girl it didn't matter much to me. And didn't Donna Haraway finally solve this by saying all female lived experience is a bunch of riffs, completely fake, so we should recognize ourselves as Cyborgs? But still the fact remains: You moved out to the desert on your own to clear the junk out of your life. You're skeptical of irony. You are trying to find some way of living you believe in. I envy this.

Jane Bowles described this problem of sincerity in a letter to her husband Paul, the "better" writer:

August 1947:

Dearest Bupple,
        …The more I get into it…the more isolated I feel vis-à-
vis the writers whom I consider to be of any serious mind…I
am enclosing this article entitled New Heroes *by Simone de*

Beauvoir... Read the sides that are marked pages 121 and
123. It is what I have been thinking at the bottom of my mind
all this time and God knows it is difficult to write the way I
do and yet think their way. This problem you will never have
to face because you have always been a truly isolated person so
that whatever you write will be good because it will be true
which is not so in my case... You immediately receive recog-
nition because what you write is in true relation to yourself
which is always recognizable to the world outside... With me
who knows? When you are capable only of a serious approach
to writing as I am it is almost more than one can bear to be
continually doubting one's sincerity...

Reading Jane Bowle's letters makes me angrier and sadder than anything to do with you. Because she was just so brilliant and she was willing to take a crack at it—telling the truth about her difficult and contradictory life. And because she got it right. Even though, like the artist Hannah Wilke, in her own lifetime she hardly found anybody to agree with her. You're the Cowboy, I'm the Kike. Steadfast and true, slippery and devious. We aren't anything but our circumstances. Why is it men become essentialists, especially in middle age?

And at Joseph's party time stands still and we can do it all again. Marshall walks me over to two men in suits, a Lacanian and a world banker from the UN. We talk about Microsoft and Bill Gates and Timothy Leary's brunches in LA until a tall and immaculately gorgeous WASP woman joins us and the conversation parts away from jokes about interest rates and transference to make room for Her...

(As I write this I feel very hopeless and afraid.)

Later Marshall made an academic birthday speech for Joseph that he'd been scribbling on all night. And Glenn O'Brien, looking like Steve Allen at the piano, performed a funny scat-singing recitative about Joseph's legendary womanizing, wealth and art. Everybody clapping, laughing, camp but serious and boozy like in the film *The Girl Can't Help It*, men in suits playing TV beatniks but where's Jayne Mansfield as the fall girl? Then David Byrne and John Cale played piano and guitar and people danced.

Sylvère got drunk and teased Diego, something about politics, and Diego got mad and tossed his drink in Sylvère's face. And Warren Niesluchowski was there, and John and Anya. Later Marshall marshalled a gang of little men, the banker, the Lacanian and Sylvère, to the cardroom to drink scotch and talk about the Holocaust. The four looked like the famous velvet painting of card-playing dogs.

And it got late and someone turned on some vintage disco, and all the people young enough never to've heard these songs the first time round got up and danced. *Funky Town*, *Le Freak*, *c'est Chic* and *Upside Down*...the songs that played in topless clubs and bars in the late '70s while these men were getting famous. While me and all my friends, the girls, were paying for our rent and shows and exploring "issues of our sexuality" by shaking to them all night long in topless bars.

Gabi Teisch's life was very hard.

She hardly slept or ate, she forgot to comb her hair. The more she studied, the harder it became to speak or know anything with certainty. People were afraid of her; she forgot how to teach her classes. She became that word that people use to render difficult and driven women weightless: Gabi Teisch was "quirky."

On New Year's Eve in Germany, 1977 it was snowing very hard. Gabi Teisch invited several of her women friends around to celebrate the holiday. The camera keeps its distance, circling round the table of drinking smoking laughing talking women. It's happiness. A bright island in the snowy night. A real cabal.

This morning it's my birthday and I drove out to Garnet Lake. Upstate March is the moodiest, most desolate time of year. February's glistening cold becomes unsettled. Water in the streams and brooks begins to move under melting ice: stand outside and you can hear it rushing. *The Torrents of Spring*. But the sky's completely gray and everybody knows the snow'll be around at least until the end of April. The weather's dull, resentful. I drove out through Thurman, Kenyontown, past the "burnt-down store" (a landmark and epistemological joke—in order for it to mean anything you would've had to be here 20 years ago when the store was standing), the Methodist church and schoolhouse where as recently as 30 years ago local kids between the ages of 5 and 17 arrived by foot and horse from within an 8 mile radius. "What do you consider to be the greatest achievement of your life?" a teenager from the Thurman Youth Group asked George Mosher, a 72-year-old trapper, farmer, handyman and logger. "Staying here," George said. "Within two miles of where I was born." Dear Dick, The Southern Adirondacks make it possible to understand the Middle Ages.

There were two guys out ice fishing on Garnet Lake, skinny speckled fish, pickering or mackerel. My long black coat open, dragging through the snow as I walked around the lake's perimeter. When I was 12 it occurred to me for the first time it might be possible to have an interesting life. Yesterday when I phoned Renee up over at her trailer to find out if her brother Chet might be able to come over and unfreeze the kitchen pipes she said Yeah, but I don't want to put a time on it because I'm high.

In all the books about the 19th century New England Transcendentalist Margaret Fuller, they tell this story about her and the English critic George Carlyle. When she was 45 she ran away to join the Italian liberal revolution of 1853 and fell in love with Garibaldi. "I accept the universe," Margaret Fuller wrote in a letter postmarked out of Italy. "Well she'd better," Carlyle replied. She was drifting further and further on a raft out into the Caspian Sea. Today I'm going to New York,

Love,
Chris

KIKE ART

3/14/95

East Village

DD,

This afternoon I went to see the R.B. Kitaj exhibition at the Met. He's a painter you're probably familiar with because he lived so many years in London.

I went to see the show because my friend Romy Ashby told me to. She liked the charcoal drawing of two black cats fucking (*My Cat and Her Husband*, 1977). The show, which opened last year in London, was panned by all the critics there on weirdly specious grounds. Kitaj has followed Arnold Schoenberg in proclaiming "I have long since resolved to be a Jew... I regard that as more important than my art." And his work's been called a lot of things that Jews are called: "abstruse, pretentious"; "shallow, fake and narcissistic"; "hermetic, dry and bookish"; "difficult, obscure, slick and grade f." Too much in dialogue with writing and ideas to be a painter, he's been called "a quirky bibliophile... altogether too poetic and allusive... a little too literary for his own good."

It's hard to figure out just why Kitaj's been criticized this way. His paintings are a little bit Francis Bacon, a little bit Degas, a little bit Pop Art, but mostly they are studies. Thought accelerates to a pitch where it becomes pure feeling. Unlike the Abstract Expressionists or the Pop artists who he's been unfavorably compared to, his paintings never are one single statement or one transcendental thing. It's like he's conscious he's the Last Remaining Humanist, using painting as a field for juggling ideals that don't quite hold. Unlike painters of the '50s whose works celebrate disjunction, Kitaj's paintings recognize disjunction while in a certain sense lamenting it. Melodies floating across a cafe patio that evoke another world. Walter Benjamin smoking hashish in Marseilles to enjoy the subtle pleasures of his own company. An intellectual rigor that allows the possibility of nostalgia.

In Paris in the '50s, upwardly mobile ghetto Jews like Sylvère Lotringer suffered a terrible dinner party dilemma: whether to announce the fact that they were Jews to offset possible racial slurs and jokes and be accused of arrogantly 'flaunting it;' or say nothing and be accused of deviously "hiding it." Kitaj the slippery Kike is never just one thing and so people think he's tricking them.

It amused me that Kitaj has wrapped himself around the idea of creating "exegesis" for his art, writing texts to parallel each painting. "Exegesis": the crazy person's search for proof that they're not crazy. "Exegesis" is the word I used in trying to explain myself to you. Did I tell you, Dick, I'm thinking of calling all these letters *The Cowboy and the Kike*? Anyhow, I felt I had to see the show.

The exhibition was presented by the Met with a huge amount of explication that served to distance Kitaj further from his viewers and his peers. Curatorial excitement mixed with apprehension: how to make this "difficult" work accessible? By introducing us to the artist as an admirable freak.

Entering the exhibition, the viewer encounters the first in a series of large-scale placards explaining Kitaj's strange career. A sentimental pen-and-ink portrait of the not-yet-dead artist is displayed beside a text describing biographic landmarks. Kitaj grew up in Troy, New York and ran away at age 16 to be a merchant seaman. He enlisted in the Army, then attended art school in Oxford on the GI Bill. After school he moved to London, painted, showed. After the unexpected death of his first wife in 1969, Kitaj stopped painting for several years. This fact is disclosed in a tone of awed surprise. (Why has every single life that deviates from the corporate norm—from high school to an east coast BA, followed by a California art school MFA, followed by a cheerful steady flow of art-production—become so oddly singular?)

The placards in the second room continue amplifying Kitaj's oddness. He is "a voracious reader of literature and philosophy" "a bibliophile." The facts of Kitaj's life are sketched so bare that he becomes exotic, mythic. The text is telling us that while it may be impossible to love the artist or his work we must admire him. Although his work is "difficult," it has a substance and a presence; it can't be entirely dismissed; it holds its own. And so at 62, in his first major retrospective, Kitaj becomes revered/reviled. All the rightness of his work is undermined by singularity. He's a talking dog domesticated into myth.

(Am I being too sensitive? Perhaps, but I'm a kike. And isn't it well-documented that those kikes who don't devote themselves to power-mongering and money-grubbing are hopelessly highstrung?)

The placards go on to apologize/explain Kitaj's prose. After years of fucked-up readings of his work, he was forced to write his own. The placard suggests you spend some money to access Kitaj's texts (buy the catalogue, rent the audiocassette) but in reality you don't have to. Because in the middle of the second room there're multiple copies of the catalog displayed on two long library tables complete with shaded reading lamps and chairs. How perfect—a tiny architectural slice of the New York Public Library or Amsterdam's grand American Hotel. (You too can be a kike!) This display was so archaic that the catalogs weren't even chained, and I contemplated stealing one, though finally I didn't. Because although Kitaj's friends include some of the greatest poets in the world, I didn't like his texts that much. His texts spoke to someone not quite real, the "perplexed but sympathetic viewer." You either like the paintings or you don't. Kitaj's writing pandered so it was disappointing.

But Kitaj's paintings never pander and they aren't disappointing.

My first favorite, painted in 1964, was called *The Nice Old Man and The Pretty Girl (With Huskies)*. What a terrific painting to own! What a lot it says about your life circa 1964 if you were somebody significant in the art world! It's a painting that's seduced by the frenetic energy and glamour of this time while mocking it.

The colors of this painting—mustard yellow, Chinese red and forest green—were high fashion in their time. The nice old man sits facing us in 3/4 profile from the depths of a mauve Le Corbusier-inspired chair. The Nice Old Man's head has been replaced with a side of ham that makes him look like Santa Claus. Over it, he wears a gas mask. The chair is expediently correct, Roche-Bobois, but not remarkable or beautiful. Perhaps chosen by an uninspired decorator. The Nice Old Man's body extends across almost the entire frame, ending in one of those Nordic fur-trimmed boots that go in, though mostly out, of style. And this boot is pointed squarely at the knee (*Claire's Knee* by Eric Rohmer?) of the Pretty Girl, who is completely headless. Her coat is Chanel red and almost matches the Nice Old Man's seedy Santa outfit. Except it's better cut—tight at the top, then flaring. Her dress is mustard orange.

And then there're *those huskies*, visitors from a David Salle work that's travelled back in time, panting, grinning, moving, even though each is trapped inside a white rectangle, towards a snow-bank rising from the bottom right corner of the frame. Between them there's a red square displaying some of their possessions: a model of a monolith for him, a Gucci scarf for her. What a modish pair. And what could be more modish than Kitaj's acerbic portrait of them? Except that the acerbic-ness seems to go too far, beyond the effervescent skepticism of the period towards a moral irony that lays it bare.

And, perfectly, appropriately to that first adrenaline rush of art & commerce that characterized the art world in 1964, the painting's circle of meaning is completed by its ownership. *Nice Old Man* was loaned to the exhibit by its owners Susan and Alan Patricoff, prominent members of the mid-'60s New York City/East Hampton art and social scene. Alan Patricoff, a venture capitalist, art collector and early owner of *New York* magazine is a great supporter of Kitaj's. According to the writer Erje Ayden, he and Susan Patricoff gave the most amazing parties in East Hampton, where writers, art-world luminaries and miss-outs mixed with famous socialites.

And what an edgy choice this painting must've been: a painting that both disparages and contains the witty effervescence of that scene. As if to say, they're capable of taking an ironic distance from their values and their fame, this scene they made; powerful and secure enough to pat the mouth that bites the hand that feeds it. It's deadpan wit with cynicism at its core. And isn't it cynicism that makes the money, while enthusiasm spends? To buy such cynicism confirms that Patricoff was no consumer, but a highly self-reflexive creator of this scene. *Nice Old Man* draws an outside circle around the giddiness and wit that characterized Pop Art, a movement read by some as the closest thing the art world's come to Sophisticate Utopia. It's a painting, finally, for victors, reminding us that there're winners & losers in every game.

LATER—

Oh D, it's Thursday morning 9 a.m. and I feel so emotional about this writing. Last night I "replaced" you with an orange candle because I felt you weren't listening anymore. But I still need for you to listen. Because—don't you see?—no one is, I'm completely illegitimate.

Right now Sylvère is in Los Angeles at your school making $2500 for talking about James Clifford. Later on tonight you'll have a drink and he'll drive you to the plane, because you're about to speak in Europe. Did anybody ask me my ideas about Kitaj? Does it matter what they are? It's not like I've been invited, paid to speak. There isn't much that I take seriously and since I'm frivolous and female most people think I'm pretty dumb. They don't realize I'm a kike.

WHO GETS TO SPEAK AND WHY?, I wrote last week, IS THE ONLY QUESTION.

Sylvère's in California for a week and I am writing you from 7th Street and Avenue C, where I am living in the independent poverty I've believed since I was 12 to be my birthright. I don't have to spend my days thinking about money, or dream about it multiplying overnight. I don't have to work at menial degrading jobs (if you're a girl menial always turns out to be degrading) or pretend to believe in my career in the third-rate world of experimental film. After building up my husband's academic/cultural career and investing all his money I have enough to live on so long as I don't spend too much. And luckily my husband is a very reasonable man.

And I have brilliant friends to talk to (Eileen, Jim and John, Carol, Ann, Yvonne) about writing and ideas but I don't (will never have?) (this writing is so personal it's hard to picture it) any other kind of audience. But even so I can't stop writing even for a day—I'm doing it to save my life. These letters're the first time I've ever tried to talk about ideas because I need to, not just to amuse or entertain.

And now it's springtime and I want to tell you a little bit about this neighborhood, the world outside: the tiny Spanish gardens with their ramshackle pavilions built on vacant lots, the rutted streets, Adela's, a Puerto Rican nationalist cafe. There's a panaderia and a carniceria, bananas cost 15 cents apiece and the white people who live here do so without too much avarice or display of wealth. The panaderia on C and 9th sells cakes of the most amazing brilliant colors. I've started wearing underwear that's green and pink, like Guatemala. And even though there's sadness wafting through this writing, I'm very happy here.

I want to talk to you about two paintings in the second room of the exhibition hanging side by side: *The Autumn of Central Paris (After Walter Benjamin) 1972/1973* and *If Not, Not*, a painting about the Holocaust painted several years later in 1975/1976. I question the sense of historiography that installing them this way implies. As if there's any correlation between chunks of history, past events. As if somehow if we just looked hard enough we could discern some immanent causality between the Autumn Years of Paris in the 1920s, early '30s and their subsequent annihilation in the War. Wasn't modernism's greatest coup to destroy the notion of progression? And yet it still comes back in history books, in dialectical materialism, in the New Age's recycled Confucianism—the hope that all of us are travelling through concentric rings of knowledge towards some greater truth. And beneath that hope, the biggest lie: that things are *getting better*. Portentousness is only retrospective.

In *Walter Benjamin*:

This painting is a dictionary of everything we know about the brilliant cafe world of Paris and Vienna in the '20s. All the images and tropes we've read about this time are closely flanked, jammed up against each other, sliding down from the top left of the frame to the bottom right. History as a Jumble Sale. At the bottom of the pile Kitaj paints red cut-out silhouetted icons of the Communist Revolution: red hammers and red sickles raised by Red Worker's arms. Right above them, Walter Benjamin sits presiding at a cafe table with a young man turned away from us and a doe-eyed, pretty, serious young woman. She's one of the few attractive female figures in Kitaj's work accorded any dignity—most of the pretty girls are naked curving cat-like creatures without any barriers of resistance to the painter's gaze, and Kitaj's serious women are mostly totally asexual and middle-aged. I guess he likes to characterize us, as male kikes do, as either sisters, mothers, aunts, or whores. The young woman's looking up at Walter and she's listening. Though his mouth is momentarily shut, he's obviously Holding Forth and he looks terrific in his tinted eyeglasses, waving a cigarette beyond his fleshy sculpted face, so poised. And above these two, at the top left of the frame, the painting cuts to EXT SIDEWALK SAME DAY, a small assortment of EDUCATED JEWS, spanning the spectrum of the middle class transplanted from Europe to Long Island, Skokie and Canarsie: there're the middle aged, smoking women in big hats and basic makeup (the well-to-do aunts, the Canasta-killers); a shy and sheepfaced guy in cap and shirt-sleeves (the skilled worker, union organizer brother).

But there's a terrible rupture in this picture, between the world of the cafe, imperfectly protected by its gorgeous gray & mustard zigzagged awning, and the world outside. At the cafe's outdoor tables, and beyond them out along the street leading to a residential suburb, we see people of a different order, a little more attenuated, brink-ish, all poised in some relation to a nameless future that opens at the top right of the frame.

Seated alone, at a sidewalk table there's a rakish, yellow coated punk (that's me!) with shocking bright red hair. This person could be male or female and her/his back is turned towards us, so that s/he can clearly see the future at the top of the frame. And closer to the future there's a young blonde woman in a big black dress (a big sister or a nanny) holding a small child against her chest. She's facing us, of course, in order to protect the child.

And what about this future? Dark green poplars line its streets, met by a bird's-egg blue, cloud strewn sky. This future's purely European: the sky is borrowed from Magritte, the poplars reek of secrets and opacity of the Alain Resnais and Robbe-Grillet kind. And just like in Magritte, there's a man walking straight into this future, a generic European man in a shabby cap and overcoat. And like the future, and unlike the paintings of Magritte, this image is both liberating and extremely scary. He's like the fucked-up heroines in Fassbinder's *Lola* or Bette Gordon's *Variety*, hobbling on high-heeled shoes towards a fate that the audience has long since guessed but they're completely unaware of. But unlike the fucked-up heroines, this man seems to have no expectations.

I think the downward rush of images from inside the cafe—history, our collective popular unconscious—performs ironic sabotage in the same way *Huskies* celebrates, subverts, the atmosphere of Pop Art and the New York School. We're touched by the nostalgia, seeing Walter at the center of our extended European family, but our smarter selves find greater satisfaction knowing history as we understand it is really just an avalanche of garbage toppling down.

CHICKEN MARENGO

I come over to your house with a bag of groceries in the late afternoon. It's beautiful California sunlight. I go into your kitchen and start making Chicken Marengo.

(Sautee garlic in olive oil, then add chicken for 20 minutes while cutting up onions, carrots and potatoes. When chicken's brown, add crushed tomatoes, then the vegetables. Then add bay leaves, pepper…)

It's an easy kind of scene and you walk in and out. When that's all done I put it in a pot to stew. I come out and tell you it needs 45 minutes simmering. We go to bed. What else could fill the time as well? Is this the purpose of slow cooking?)

After we have sex we eat chicken marengo, talk awhile.

And then I go…

Lately I've been imagining other scenes of beauty too. Tearing down 2nd Avenue last night in my truck, plotting the best grid to beat traffic all the way to 8th & 5th I flash suddenly on parties that I've been to in New York, East Hampton: everybody jagged, brilliant, cinematic, all of these personas blurring as the night goes on, drugs, ambition, money, electricity... Do you remember the wretched movie Oliver Stone made about Jim Morrison's life? According to Oliver, Jim was a wholesome California Boy—cute blonde girlfriend, magic mushrooms, milk & freckles—'til he met the Crazed Kike Witches of New York. The Witches dragged him down with their exotic drugs, their wild parties, their mindfuck demonology. They understood his poetry, though. The Witches are why Jim died of an overdose in the bathtub of a Paris hotel.

Realize, D, that I am one of those Crazed Kike Witches and I understand your fear.

And why's Janis Joplin's life read as a downward spiral into self-destruction? Everything she did is filtered through her death. Roger Gilbert-Lecomte, Kurt Cobain, Jimi Hendrix, River Phoenix all suicided too but we see their deaths as aftermaths of lives that went too far. But let a girl choose death—Janis Joplin, Simone Weil—and death becomes her definition, the outcome of her "problems." To be female still means being trapped within the purely psychological. No matter how dispassionate or large a vision of the world a woman formulates, whenever it includes her own experience and emotion, the telescope's turned back on her. Because emotion's just so terrifying the world refuses to believe that it can be pursued as discipline, as form. Dear Dick, I want to make the world more interesting than my problems. Therefore, I have to make my problems social.

The correspondence between Gustave Flaubert and Louise Colet reads like a Punch & Judy show. Louise Colet, female writer of the 19th-century, had rosy cheeks and little ringlet curls. Unlike her enemy George Sand who chose to "live like a man" until age shielded her as a grand matriarch, Louise wanted to write and she wanted to be femme. Louise turned the difficulty of combining those two occupations into a subject of her art. Flaubert thought: "You are a poet shackled to a woman! Do not imagine you can exorcise what oppresses you in life by giving vent to it in art. No! The heart's dross does not find its way on paper." For years they met in Paris at times and places designated by him—sex and dinner once a month whenever Flaubert needed a break from his writing schedule in Rouen. Once, Louise asked to meet his family. And here Flaubert's biographer Francis Steegmuller steps in: "Flaubert's depiction of Emma Bovary's vehemence was doubtless nourished somewhat by Louise's shrill demands." When Flaubert finally broke her heart she wrote a poem about it and he replied: "You have made Art an outlet for the passions, a kind of chamberpot to catch the overflow of I don't know what. It doesn't smell good! It smells of hate!"

To be female in 19th century France was to be denied access to the apersonal. And still—

I found it hard to write about the second painting, the one paired with *Walter Benjamin* that everybody says deals with the Holocaust so I went back on Sunday to take another look. I drove down to New York City after spending Saturday with my old friend Suzan Cooper, a Crazed Kike Witch of the First Order. Suzan's been exiled by her family after many years in New York to Woodstock, where she runs a gallery.

Suzan always has several hustles running. One of them is selling photos taken around Andy Warhol's Factory by Billy Name. I bought a black & white print of John Cale, Gerard Malanga and Nico staring stoned into the distance in their Nehru jackets in a park that looks like the murder scene in *Blow Up*. I don't know if Billy Name's name at the bottom of the photo in silver magic marker was signed by Suzan or by Billy but I didn't care.

There are two groups of three people (men) gathered in *If Not, Not*, the second picture. Each group is joined by one naked woman. The first group is gathered at the bottom left of the frame beside a blackish pool with floating objects. The subconscious is a dark oasis. The men are wounded soldiers. These are the objects in the pool:

—A sheep beneath a bushy olive tree
—Two blue-backed books, discarded
—A girl's face looking straight up at the sky from underwater
—A broken pillar
—A naked man sitting up in bed from sleep
—A black crow perched on parchment writing
—A red cylindrical kitchen garbage can

The second group of men are resting in a palm-grove at top frame right. The palm trees move and bend like people's backs. Between the resting men, a shadow or a cloud rears up from the ground like a wild rat or a pig. Have these men already visited the pool or are they looking towards it? Either way they're exhausted, in a state ("where the river don't bend") that's something like Richard Hell's great cover of Dylan's *Going Going Gone*.

The sky above these people's streaky purple, orange, exploding nuclear Hawaiian from a tangerine funnel in the middle of the painting. But the sky on the left-side of the funnel's very different—black-green thunderclouds drawn around a barn-like institutional building. Dachau, Auschwitz. A gaping double door: a mouth, a port of entry. We can make what we like of the differences between the two sides of this sky—are these skies evoking centuries or geography? Though everybody knows "there is nothing that can change the sky or make anything even approaching a wrinkle in its skin... no scream of terror or despair or hate or the imploring eyes of 60 million saints and innocent children ever moved it." (*The Angel*, David Rattray) The nature of a sky is to be implacable.

A duckshit-colored roadway, leading to an arch against the sky, separates these two sides of the painting. But through it, in an opening where the tangerine-slashed sky ought to continue, we see the painting's single act of superimposition. A blue tree on the roadway just before the arch points towards this archway. It's the door to heaven. And heaven here's some clustered bushy trees and blossoms, a Fra Angelico landscape in green and pink. And this tiny scene itself contains another superimposition: the sky behind the trees has been replaced by an abstracted close-up: a blurry mass of pink and green slammed up behind this almost Biblical landscape.

I didn't like this painting very much. I thought its problem was the same problem many Jews have in wanting to "place" the Holocaust, to find some meaning or redemption. An end to rootless cosmopolitanism. This painting, particularly in relation to *Paris Autumn/Walter Benjamin*, is telling us that extreme suffering may be redeemed because it carries us back or forward into the Land of the Subconscious. *If Not, Not* suggests that the subconscious is what lies behind us and ahead of us. It's the entire Tarot deck compressed into a single card. The subconscious is what history's been reduced to. *If Not, Not* is one of the few paintings of Kitaj's where disjunction's used to unify the frame. The tools of study (rupture) used this time to enact a mystical state or union. All the people (men) inhabit space only in relation to that murky pool: they approach it or avoid it or seek comfort from a naked woman after seeing it. But is the subconscious really irreducible?

I think Kitaj's vision of the subconscious is mushier than both Chicken Marengo reheated on the second day and the little scene I wrote for you about cooking it. Why?

(Because it's been torn away from time).

I didn't really know I was a kike 'til I was 21 and met my relatives when I moved back to New York. Oh, there'd been intimations: that I picked Wendy Winer, one of 6 or 7 Jews, as my best friend out of 2000 kids in our little redneck town. That my only significant New Zealand boyfriends were named Rosenberg and Meltzer. The single out'ed Jew in my grade-school class, Lee Nadel, was taunted by the entire school as "Needle Nose." Perhaps my parents, who both attended Christian church, were just trying to protect me.

The only person I admired among our family's few relatives and friends was Aunt Elsie (surname, Hayman), an elegant self-invented woman with olive skin and long gray hair pulled back in a chignon. Elsie's accent was a fascinating blend of roots and cultivation. She said "ain't" and "COSTUME" instead of "costume," she talked slang straight off the streets of working class New York where she grew up, but she talked about ballet, symphonies and books with the most astonishing precision. Elsie'd married into a family of stockbrokers, and with it, a modest amount of money—which she spent, after her husband's death, with tremendous style—never maintaining a "fancy" place on Central Park like others in that family. Elsie lived in a 3 room flat in the East 70s and spent her money travelling the world—India, Europe, Bali, Indonesia. When she was 67 and a Buddhist she climbed the Himalayas.

Christians believe in the redemptive power of suffering. It's the basis of the whole religion. Jesus was frailty personified, his life the Ur-text of suffering, betrayal and abandoned dreams. The suffering of Jesus teaches us that God understands. I don't see any advantage in believing this. Kikes would rather side-step the whole question of redemption. They think that suffering brings knowledge but knowledge is just a step out into the world. Redemption's meaning-less because there's nowhere else to go, as humans we're all locked into the orbit of a life together.

"Jews don't like images," I said, explaining some of Sylvère's work to you that evening in the restaurant, "because images are charged. They rob people of their power. Believing in the transcen-dental power of the image and its Beauty is like wanting to be an Abstract Expressionist or a Cowboy." And isn't undermining this the basis of Kitaj's most successful work? His best paintings sub-vert the power of their image by tossing them around in a critical, cerebral mix. It's through an act of will—collision, contra-diction, that these paintings attain their power. Kitaj infiltrates the image in the same way certain Jews lived through World War 2 with phony passports. Kitaj the Sneaky Kike bluffs his way into the Host Culture, Painting, and turns it back upon itself. He paints to challenge iconography.

My father's favorite writer is William Burroughs.

This morning, after dreaming about dead turtles, I wrote this in my notebook:

My entire state of being's changed because I've become my sexuality: female, straight, wanting to love men, be fucked. Is there a way of living with this like a gay person, proudly?

※

One painting in this show maybe has the answer. There's a Peter Handke story where a youngish German couple drive around America through the desert looking for the famous Hollywood director John Ford. They've lost the drift of why they were together, have no idea how to continue with their lives. (In Idaho last summer, Sylvère and I felt this way too.) The German couple thought John Ford would have the answer. (Sylvère and I never looked to anybody, though, for answers, except maybe the idea of you.) John Ford figured they were crazy. He didn't want to be anybody's saint, though in this particularly sentimental story he turns out to be.

Peter Handke and Kitaj must've known the same John Ford, likeably garrulous and ugly, the kind of guy who thinks that to be alive is to be in charge.

In this painting, *John Ford on his Deathbed (1983/84)*, John Ford is sitting up presiding over his own deathbed, fully dressed, holding his rosary like a stopwatch and smoking a cigar.

It's a brilliant and theatrical painting, art-directed like a Mexican-shot Western with its deep blue walls and straw-planked floors, color so strong it reconfigures the painting's Euro-American script.

There're several separate scenes within this painting. These scenes are dissonant, but not strategically oppositional. The painting is a chronicle of a life's events, like the Medieval story paintings that prefigured comic books but these events are splayed like life, chaotic and abstracted. All the dissonance is drawn together in a frame that can contain them not through magic but through Ford's formidable self-invented will.

At the bottom of the painting we see a scene from John Ford's past: a man of boundless middle-age talking through a megaphone to actors costumed as poor immigrants in what must've been a Texas western—cobblers making cowboy boots. His legs are crossed, his broad face, oblivious to its own ugliness, is partly covered by dark glasses and a squat black hat. In the middle of the painting a matador, maitre'd or major domo holds an empty frame pierced by a salmon pink pole, the kind you'd see on a restaurant patio or in a dancehall. A dancing couple spread their arms around it, Fred Astaire and Ginger Rogers (sort of) painted by Chagall. And there're lights strung through the painting, extending out into the room, flesh-pink, like the lobster terrace restaurants in La Bufadora, Mexico. The painting frame above Ford's bed is partly Mexican too, its green-red-yellow frame hanging askew, though its subject is decidedly European: a solitary man in black carrying something through the gray-white snow. It's pogrom-land, it's an old television movie.

In this painting dissonance's disappeared and been reborn as elevated schtick. It's a grand finale, the production number, where all the show's motifs come back as jokes. And Kitaj-as-Ford delivers, like movies're supposed to do, a dazzling punchline: at the upframe center of Ford's blue wall there's an Ed Ruscha knock-off framed in black that reads

THE

END

and below it, a tiny painting, window opening out from deep blue walls to deep blue sky. There is no road to immortality but there's a porthole to it. In this painting objects, people, dance and move but still there's flesh and weight. Transcendence isn't only lightness; it's attained by will.

And why do we crave lightness so?

Lightness is a '60s lie, it's Pop Art, early Godard, *The Nice Man and the Pretty Girl (With Huskies)*. Lightness is the ecstacy of communication without the irony, it's the lie of disembodied cyberspace.

Through his medium John Ford, Kitaj is telling us that matter moves but you can't escape its weight. The dead come back to dance not as spirits but as skeletons.

⋆⋆⋆⋆⋆

DD,

On December 3, 1994 I started loving you.
I still do.

Chris

SYLVÈRE AND CHRIS WRITE

IN THEIR DIARIES

EXHIBIT A: SYLVÈRE LOTRINGER

Pasadena, California
March 15, 1995

"Gave Proust seminar and first lecture today at Dick's school. One more to go. Dick was direct and friendly, though in the car I suddenly had flashes of his hand going across Chris' cunt. Images. The whole situation is so weird. In any case, Chris once again has pulled a fast one. Even though Dick's rejected her, she's managed to cover all the bases: She doesn't need him to respond for her love to go on. She can maintain a relationship with me, draw inspiration from Dick for her work, and even put her film into a vault without pushing it any further.

Chris faxed me her piece about Kitaj, the "kike" painter she identifies with. It's very heady, spiralling around his idiosyncratic life, critical rejection, East Hampton in the '60s. I've never heard of him, but she manages to weave everything in, including her own present predicament.

I felt very moved by it, exhilarated. Chris now believes that the failure of *Gravity & Grace* was "destiny," pushing her towards some further explication of all the emotion within her films.

She's writing without any destination or authority, unlike Dick, who's off to give another talk in Amsterdam and never writes unless he's asked to; unlike me, about to give my *Evil* lecture, collect my check and go home.

And yet Chris was feeling very sad, cut off from Dick, and I was sad too after talking to her. The situation was hopeless: she loved him, needed him, couldn't stand the idea of not being close to him or communicating with him. I decided I will talk to Dick tomorrow night on our drive out to the airport. I don't know how he'll take it; after all, he's been quite clear about ending this ambiguous situation. And yet if I happened to be heard by him, that would kill me: the idea of a strong connection between the two of them that excludes me. I ended up sobbing until 2 a.m., unable to fall asleep, feeling pretty down and desperate."

EXHIBIT B: CHRIS KRAUS

Los Angeles, California
March 31, 1997

"I found Sylvère's diary entry last night when I was searching all the backfiles of this computer for some link between *Kike Art* which I wrote that March and the last two essays in the book. Because I'd decided, and everyone agrees, that the only way to make this writing be a novel was to make the throughline very clear. But when I read his diary entry last night I was just so overwhelmed and moved. How much he loves me. How much he's taken all my questions as his own.

On the phone this morning to Sylvère who's in East Hampton I was talking about reading. How I like to dip into other people's books, to catch the rhythm of their thinking, as I try to write my own. Writing around the edges of Philip K. Dick, Ann Rower, Marcel Proust, Eileen Myles and Alice Notley. It's better than sex. Reading delivers on the promise that sex raises but hardly ever can fulfill—getting larger 'cause you're entering another person's language, cadence, heart and mind.

On April 9, 1995 I saw Dick alone in Los Angeles for the last time. We took a walk behind Lake Avenue. On April 20, I phoned him from upstate New York. I was upset and wanted resolution. The conversation was long and messy. He asked me why I made myself so vulnerable. Was I a masochist? I told him No. "'Cause don't you see? Everything that's happened here to me has happened only cause I've willed it." On April 23, I met John Hanhardt, then curator of the Whitney Museum, to talk about my films. I was expecting John to offer me a show; instead, he wanted to engage me in a dialogue about the "failure" of my films.

On June 6, 1995 I moved permanently to Los Angeles.

The philosopher Ludwig Wittgenstein wrote in his diary, "Understand or die."

That summer I was hoping to understand the link between Dick's misapprehension of me as a "masochist" and John Hanhardt's judgement of my films. Both men admitted that though they found my work repugnant, it was "intelligent" and "courageous." I believed that if I could understand this link I could extend it to the critical misreads of a certain kind of female art. "I have just realized that the stakes are myself," Diane di Prima wrote in *Revolutionary Letters* in 1973. "Because we rejected a certain kind of critical language, people just assumed that we were dumb," the genius Alice Notley said when I visited her in Paris. Why is female vulnerability still only acceptable when it's neuroticized and personal;

when it feeds back on itself? Why do people still not get it when we handle vulnerability like philosophy, at some remove?

Today at Barnes & Noble I bought a new book by Steve Erickson. The jacket blurbs, placing him within a new and all-male canon, offended me. "Erikson's a major player," the *Washington Post* crowed, shades of Norman Mailer in the '50s, "up there with his contemporaries Richard Powers and William Vollman, the spokesmen of the chaos generation."

"Dear Dick," I wrote in one of many letters, "what happens between women now is the most interesting thing in the world because it's least described."

MONSTERS

DD,

This letter comes to you from Eagle Rock, Los Angeles—it's 40 miles away from where you're living but it feels very far away. I got to LA two weeks ago, seems like forever. Constant loops from one mood to another, loneliness and optimism, fear, ambition... Do you know the meaning of those roller coaster billboards that you see driving round the city? A black & white slightly blurred photo of some people on a roller coaster, a red circle slash for "No" printed at the center? Don't know if it's some kind of public art. It's a poor attempt at menace if it is one. In New York on 7th Street between Avenues B and C there's a plywood hoarding nailed like a canopy to some scaffolding above the entrance of a crackhouse. Someone's wheat-pasted a poster of two men in loose black clothes leaning with their guns against a high-rise patio balustrade. It's very scary: war-time reality slammed up against the image of a new-wave '60s futuristic movie. This is no movie, the poster seems to say. It's Beirut, these guys are serious, and so is thug business. Walking east towards it your eyes perform a double flip—the image of the patio seems to be protruding from the building, very trompe l'oeil, but by the time you've finally unravelled it you're already walking past the armored door.

God what a hoot. I'm moved to talk to you about art because I think you'll understand and I think I understand art more than you—

—Because I'm moved in writing to be irrepressible. Writing to you seems like some holy cause, 'cause there's not enough female irrepressibility written down. I've fused my silence and repression with the entire female gender's silence and repression. I think the sheer fact of women talking, being, paradoxical, inexplicable, flip, self-destructive but above all else *public* is the most revolutionary thing in the world. I could be 20 years too late but epiphanies don't always synchronize with style.

But really Dick I'm moved to write you differently 'cause everything is different now. I think of you a lot now that crossing socially seems inevitable. Both of us are in the LA artworld and it's small.

The image that I have of you is frozen in a single snapshot: April 19, the opening of the Jeffrey Vallance/Eleanor Antin/Charles Gaines show at the Santa Monica Museum. You're standing in the largest Jeffrey Vallance room, talking, drink-in-hand, to a knot of younger people (students?). Tall, black shirt and Euro-cut black jacket, standard opening wear for artists. You're standing very straight, your face smushed back in against itself; smiling-talking-moving yet imploding somehow backwards towards the immobility of the frame. You're locked. You are a country. A separate state. Visible, unbridgeable. And I'm standing in a tiny cluster next to yours, a trio, Daniel Marlos and Mike Kelley and just like you I'm shaky— my body trembles slightly as it cuts through space. But also very present. The Conquering of Fear is like performance. You recognize your fear and then you move with it.

So far I've told "our" story twice, late at night, as fully as I could, to Fred Dewey and Sabina Ott. It's the story of 250 letters, my "debasement," jumping headlong off a cliff. Why does everybody think that women are debasing themselves when we expose the conditions of our own debasement? Why do women always have to come off clean? The magnificence of Genet's last great work, *The Prisoner of Love*, lies in his willingness to be wrong: a seedy old white guy jerking off on the rippling muscles of the Arabs and Black Panthers. Isn't the greatest freedom in the world the freedom to be wrong? What hooks me on our story is our different readings of it. You think it's personal and private; my neurosis. "The greatest secret in the world is, THERE IS NO SECRET." Claire Parnet and Gilles Deleuze. I think our story is performative philosophy.

The artist Hannah Wilke was born Arlene Butter in 1940 and grew up in Manhattan and Long Island. She died of cancer at the age of 52. Wilke's output was prolific and consistent. Through constant effort she maintained a visible career. At a certain point, perhaps the early '70s, her work began addressing the following question:

If women have failed to make "universal" art because we're trapped within the "personal," why not universalize the "personal" and make it the subject of our art?

To ask this question, to be willing to live it through, is still so bold.

In 1974, after producing drawings, ceramics and sculptural wall pieces—many of which involved a "tough, ambiguous depiction of traditionally female imagery" (Douglas Crimp, 1972) for 11 years, Hannah started to insert her own image into her art. I don't know what experiences or conditions in her life precipitated this. Was she pushed towards it by critics such as Phyllis Derfner, who wrote responding to her show of cunts fashioned out of washing machine lint at Feldman in 1972:

"There is some wit in this but it is swamped by aggressive ideology… The ideology is that of women's liberation. Female bodies have been shown, but only in an oppressive, 'sexist' manner. Wilke's forthright repetitious presentation of the most intimate image of female sexuality is intended to be a cure for all this. I don't see how it is supposed to work. It is boring and superficial."

Unlike Judy Chicago and her bloated vaginal renditions of Great Cunts In History—a show that every mother in the world could take her daughters to—Hannah never was afraid to be undignified, to trash herself, to call a cunt a cunt. "I want to throw back to the audience everything the world throws at me" (Penny Arcade, 1982). Hannah later told the *Soho Weekly News* how she'd collected 'material' for this work over several years by doing laundry for Claes Oldenburg, her companion at that time. Even then Hannah was a neo-Dadaist. Claes Oldenburg, Great Male Universal Artist, shanghai'd.

In 1974 Wilke made her first videotape, *Gestures*. Created one day after the death of her sister's husband, *Gestures* was, among other things, an expression of grief and dismay, a reaching for the body after death. The critic James Collins gave it two thumbs up in *Artforum*. "Every time I see her work I think of pussy," he declared. An early champion of Wilke's work, Collins described *Gestures* thusly:

"Erotically Wilke's video was more successful—'hornier'—than the sculpture. Why? Well she's actually in it for a start. The video is probably the best thing in the show because by being in the pieces, using just her head and hands, she gives the folding gestures, particularly, more meaning. Stroking, kneading, preening and slapping her face were interesting but the folding mouth gestures were the naughtiest. Because she's sensuously breaking a cultural rule and that's one definition of erotic. Pushing at her lips and then folding them back… Using her mouth as a surrogate vagina and her tongue as a surrogate clitoris, in the context of her face, with its whole psychological history, was strong stuff!…

"Wilke's position in the art world is a strange paradox between her own physical beauty and her very serious art. She longs to fulfill her sexuality; but her attempt to deal with this dilemma within the women's movement has a touching air of pathos about it."

But don't you see, the paradoxes in Hannah Wilke's work are not pathetic, they're polemic. (It's like that night, Dick, when you called me "passive-aggressive" on the phone? Wrong!) *Gestures* throws the weirdnesses of male response to female sexuality wide open.

Meanwhile, Hannah-in-the-work was exploring much more personal and human ground.

"Ree Morton told me that when she saw the video she almost cried," Wilke recalled several years later. "I exposed myself beyond posing and she saw past it. She saw the pathos beyond posing."

From this point on, Hannah willingly became a self-created work of art.

In *SOS Starification Object Series (1974-1979)* she turns to face the camera in 3/4 profile, bare tits and jeans unzipped with one hand on her crotch. Her eyes are bare and heavy. Her long hair's set in housewife rollers, obviously a home job. Eight bits of chewed-up gum, shaped to simulate vaginas are stuck across her face like scars or pimples. "Gum has a shape before you chew it. But when it comes out, it comes out as real garbage," she later said. "In this society we use people up the way we use up chewing gum." In her presence, Hannah always was extremely beautiful.

In 1977 she made another videotape called *Intercourse with…* in which the answering-machine messages left by her boyfriends,

friends and family play as she removes the names of the most troubling, spelled out in Pres-type, from her naked body. "Become your own myth," she started saying.

Like every other work of art, Hannah became a piece of roadkill for the artpress jackals. Torn literally apart. Her naked body straddling interpretations of the hippie-men who saw her as an avatar of sexual liberation and hostile feminists like Lucy Lippard who saw any female self-display as patriarchal putty.

Hannah started using the impossibility of her life, her artwork, and career as material. If art's a seismographic project, when that project's met with miscomprehension, failure must become its subject too. In 1976 she produced a poster modelled after the famous School for Visual Arts subway ads that read:

"Having a talent isn't worth much unless you know what to do with it." Hannah reproduced it with a photo of her fucked-up self. Portrait of the Artist as an Object: she's wearing a crocheted apron that doesn't hide her naked tits at all and clutching a Mickey Mouse doll. The now famous chewing gum vaginas are arranged like tiny scabs across her body. In a later poster called *Marxism And Art*, Hannah's wearing a man's shirt flung wide open to reveal bare breasts, chewed up cunts and a wide man's tie. "Beware of Fascist Feminism," the poster reads.

From the very start, art critics saw Hannah's willingness to use her body in her work as an act of "narcissism" ("A harmless air of narcissism pervades this show…" *New York Times*, 9/20/75). This strange descriptor still follows her beyond the grave, despite the passionate efforts of writers like Amanda Jones and Laura Cottingham to refute it. In his review of *Intra-Venus*, Hannah's posthumous show, Ralph Rugoff describes the artist's startling photos of her naked cancer-ridden body as "a deeply thrilling venture into narcissism." As if the only possible reason for a woman to publically reveal herself could be self-therapeutic. As if the point was not to reveal the circumstances of one's own objectification. As if Hannah Wilke was not brilliantly feeding back her audience's prejudice and fear, inviting them to join her for a naked lunch.

A few smart men like Peter Frank and Gerrit Lansing recognized the strategy and wit of Hannah's work, though not, perhaps, the boldness and the cost. The fact she was a genius. At any rate, the controversy around her work never agglomerated into major stardom. By 1980 Guy Trebay was sniffing in the *Village Voice* that Hannah's vagina "is now as familiar to us as an old shoe." Has anybody ever said this about Chris Burden's penis?

No one apart from Hannah's closest friends and family recognized the sweetness and idealism at the bottom of her work. Her warmth. The human-ness of her female person.

In an amazing text written in 1976, Hannah proved to be her own best critic:

"Rearranging the touch of sensuality with a residual magic made from laundry lint or latex loosely laid out like love vulnerably exposed…continually exposing myself to whatever situation occurs… Gambling as well as gamboling… To exist instead of being an existentialist, to make objects instead of being one. The way my smile just gleams, the way I sip my tea. To be a sugar giver instead of a salt cellar, to not sell out…"

Hannah Wilke Wittgenstein was pure female intellect, her entire gorgeous being stretched out in paradoxical proposition.

In 1979, Claes Oldenburg, Hannah's partner since the late 1960s, changed their door-locks while she was out one day and married someone else. She recreated the collection of 50 rayguns she'd collected for his work and posed naked with them in a series of 'performalist self portraits' called *So Help Me Hannah* in which she "demonstrates" and overturns her favorite classic citations of male philosophy and art.

Hannah Wilke on Ad Reinhardt: sitting naked in a corner, feeling hopeless, head in hands, high-heeled legs apart. She's surrounded by toy pistols and bazookas. "WHAT DOES THIS REPRESENT/WHAT DO YOU REPRESENT" the title reads.

Hannah Wilke on Karl Marx: Posed shakily on the pistons of a combustion engine in her strappy high-heeled sandals, naked body part of the machine, Hannah lunges forward in profile, toy guns in hand. EXCHANGE VALUES. (Exchange *values*? Whose?)

The insertion of Hannah Wilke's complex human presence throws all slogans into question. Her beauty is compelling, but as in *Gestures*, her presence circumvents the pose.

"I have long since resolved to be a Jew... I regard that as more important than my art," R.B. Kitaj and Arnold Schoenberg declared. Hannah Wilke said: "Feminism in a larger sense is intrinsically more important to me than art." No one ever called these men bad Jews.

The bitterest irony of Hannah Wilke's career is that her imitators who risked much less became art stars of the early '80s. "Wilke's projection of herself contrasts markedly with the more impersonal impersonations of...the recent work of Cindy Sherman, whose 'dress up' masquerades are *au fond* no less narcissistic, but somehow easier to accept or digest as art because they disguise the self and parody the suffering, pain and pleasure we sense as real in Wilke's art," Lowery Sims argued in a New Museum catalog in 1984. But by then art history had already labelled Wilke dumb, her imitators smart:

Judith Barry and Sandy Flitterman, 1980: [Because Hannah Wilke's art] "has no theory of the representations of women, it presents images of women as unproblematic. It does not take into account the social contradictions of 'femininity'." (*Screen*: 35–39)

Catherine Liu, 1989: "Wilke is well known for appearing nude in her work. She projects a hippylike comfort with her own nakedness. But her self exposure, which translates as some kind of rhetoric of sexual freedom for women, is too facile, too simple a formulation. The work of artists like Cindy Sherman and Aimee Rankin has shown female sexuality to be the site of as much pain as pleasure." (*Artforum* 12/89)

"Because we rejected a certain kind of theoretical language, people just assumed that we were dumb," the poet Alice Notley said to me in Paris last year. Hannah Wilke spent a great deal of energy throughout her life trying to prove that she was right. If art's a seismographic project, when that project meets with failure, failure must become a subject too. Dear Dick, That's what I realized when I fell in love with you.

"Of course, Hannah did become a monster," I said to Warren Niesluchowski. Warren's a friend, an artworld personality and critic, a smart and cultivated guy. We were sitting on Mike Kelley's patio at a barbecue, catching up on news. Warren knows everyone in the artworld. He'd known Hannah since they met in 1975 at the Soho restaurant Food.

Warren chuckled. "Yes, she did. But of the wrong kind. Not a monster on the order of Picasso, or—" (and here he named several other famous males). "The problem was, she started taking everything so personally. She refused to take a leap of faith. Her work was no longer art."

In 1985 Claes Oldenburg threatened an injunction against the University of Missouri Press. They were preparing a book of Hannah Wilke's work and writings to accompany her first major retrospective.

In order to protect his "privacy," Claes Oldenburg demanded that the following items be removed: 1) a photograph from *Advertisements For Living* that depicted Claes together with Hannah's eight year old niece. 2) Any mention of his name in Hannah's writings. 3) Reproduction of a collaborative poster, Artists Make Toys. 4) Quotations from a correspondence between him and Hannah that was a part of Hannah Wilke's text, *I Object*.

Claes' fame and the University's unwillingness to defend her made it possible for Oldenburg to erase a huge portion of Hannah Wilke's life. *Eraser, Erase-her*—the title of one of Wilke's later works.

I explained to Warren about the difference between male and female monsters. "Female monsters take things as personally as they really are. They study facts. Even if rejection makes them feel like the girl who's not invited to the party, they have to understand the reason why."

Monstrosity: the self as a machine. *The Blob*, mindlessly swallowing and engorging, rolling down the supermarket aisle absorbing pancake mix and jello and everyone in town. Unwise and unstoppable. The horror of *The Blob* is a horror of the fearless. To become *The Blob* requires a certain force of will.

Every question, once it's formulated, is a paradigm, contains its own internal truth. We have to stop diverting ourselves with false questions. And I told Warren: I aim to be a female monster too.

Love,
Chris

ADD IT UP

Dear Dick,

Last weekend I went up to Morro Bay and dropped acid for the first time in twenty years. The night before I'd dreamt about poverty. No matter what the rich may say, poverty is not just lack, it's a gestalt, a psychological condition.

I dreamt about Renee Mosher, an artist-carpenter-tattooist who lives in upstate New York, the Town of Thurman, the same town she was born in. Renee has two grown daughters who she's raised alone. She's 39 or so and in the dream just like in life, she looked old and frightening. In the dream we were best friends, we told each other everything. But waking up, the impossibility of it—returning to an adolescent state where you choose your friends for who they are, and not their circumstances—flooded through me like bad blood. When you're old, essentialism dies. You are your circumstances. Renee's house is getting repossessed next month because she hasn't paid her taxes for three years. Notices pile up, sometimes she opens them. And what's the point of even trying? Even if she finds a way to pay, the taxes'll just add up again. She can't afford to keep the house. She'll move into a trailer. She'll walk away. A blood vessel burst in Renee's eye while she was installing a kitchen window at my house. The doctor at the clinic said it was her gall bladder. That cost her 60 dollars. When Renee gets sick she misses work and loses pay. The poor do not write faxes, hire lawyers or cut backtax deals with Warren County. They get sick, they feel crazed, they walk away.

"Rich people are just poor people with money," my socialite boss said 15 years ago in New York. But it's not true. There is a culture of poverty and it's not bridgeable.

John & Trevor'd travelled with a Warirapa shearing gang in the North Island of New Zealand since September. The job was lucrative and hard: start at 5, knock off at 5, seven days a week unless it rained. All spring long John and Trevor talked about the trip they'd take at Christmas when the job ran out. They'd put John's '61 V-8 Holden on the road and take off on a drinking/driving/whoring tour around New Zealand. They talked about the trip so much we all felt like we were going, too. They left Pahiatua on Christmas Eve. But on Boxing Day the car got totalled in a drunken wreck. They spent all the shearing money that they'd saved just paying off the bondsman.

"The most important entitlement," I think you wrote, "remains the right to speak from a position."

The acid came from San Francisco and it was nice in a California kind of way. Mustard sunlight reflected like a digital display over splashing waves; tall seagrass dancing in the dunes. Is poverty the absence of association? LSD unlocks the freeze-frame mechanism behind our eyes, lets us see that matter's always moving. Or so they say. But I was conscious while the grass and clouds were pleasurably roiling that they'd only be roiling in this way for seven hours. Unlike all the famous California acidheads, I was disappointed, underwhelmed, because drug-induced hallucinations are so visual and temporal.

What're pictures compared to living's endless tunnels, poverty grief & sadness? To experience intensity is to not know how things will end. This morning a Vietnam vet living with a hoard of dirty kids in a shack next to the Eagle Rock dry cleaners offered me 2000 dollars on the spot for my 1000 dollar car. Why? Because it (a 1967 Rambler) reminded him of his dead mother, the car she used to drive. We grasp at symbols, talismans, triggers of association to what's forever gone.

(For years I tried to write but the compromises of my life made it impossible to inhabit a position. And "who" "am" "I"? Embracing you & failure's changed all that 'cause now I know I'm no one. And there's a lot to say...)

I want to write to you about schizophrenia—("The schizophrenic believes that he is no-one," R.D. Laing)—even though I haven't got a wooden leg to stand on in relation to this subject, having never studied it or experienced it firsthand. But I'm using you to create a certain schizophrenic atmosphere, OR, love is schizophrenia, OR, I felt a schizophrenic trigger in our confluence of interests—who's crazier than who? Schizophrenia's a state that I've been drawn to like a faghag since age 16. "Why are all the people I love crazy?" went a punk rock song by Ann Rower. For years I was the best friend, confidante, of schizophrenics. I lived through them, they talked to me. In New Zealand and New York, Ruffo, Brian, Erje and Michelle, Liza, Debbe, Dan were conduits for getting closer. But since these friendships always end with disappearances, guns and thefts and threats, by the time we met I'd given up.

When I asked you if you'd been to school you acted like I'd asked you if you still liked fucking pigs. "Of *course* I've been to school." After all, your current job depends on it. But I could tell from all the footnotes in your writing that you hadn't. You like books too much and think they are your friends. One book leads you to the next like serial monogamy. Dear Dick, I've never been to school but every time I go into a library I get a rush like sex or acid for the first few minutes when you're getting off. My brain gets creamy with associative thought. Here are some notes I made about schizophrenia:

1. Sylvano Arieti writes in *The Interpretation of Schizophrenia* that schizophrenics operate within the realm of "paleologic": a thought-system that insists against all rationality that "A" can be both "A" and "not-A" simultaneously. If LSD reveals movement, schizophrenia reveals content, i.e., patterns of association. Schizophrenics reach past language's "signifying chain," (Lacan) into the realm of pure coincidence. Time spreads out in all directions. To experience time this way is to be permanently stoned on a drug that combines the visual effects of LSD with heroin's omnipotence, lucidity. Like in a Borges world, where one moment can unfold into a universe. In 1974 Brion Gysin and William Burroughs recorded their experiments in time-travel via an awareness of coincidence in *The Third Mind*. It's a self-help book. By following their methods (e.g., "Divide a notebook into three columns. Record at any given moment what you're doing, what you're thinking, what you're reading…") anyone can do this, i.e., can leave them "selves" and enter fractured time.

2. Ruffo was a 42-year-old man waiting to receive a full-frontal lobotomy in Wellington, New Zealand. He was an unmistakable sight in Wellington's limited cast of "characters"—big and bear-like, tufts of straight black hair, bad teeth, broad smile, an energy and openness behind brown eyes that wasn't English, wasn't "European." No matter what the season Ruffo wore a brown tweed overcoat wrapped around him like a cassock over sharkskin pants. Diagnosed

incurable by New Zealand's Mental Health, Ruffo was the most civil kind of "schizophrenic." He never raved; in fact, he never spoke without considering the impact of his words with exquisite care. While privately he may have been delusional, Ruffo wasn't bent on delivering any particular message. He'd discovered no conspiracies, and if voices spoke to him from radios, TVs or trees, he never translated them. His friends were his constituents, but unlike other politicians Ruffo was supremely patient. If plans were being made for him, perhaps they were for his own good. The Social Welfare agency that sent him checks hoped that once relieved of half a brain, Ruffo would become employable and self-supporting. He had no bitterness about this.

Southerly winds and rain pelted Wellington for six months of the year. Winters were gargantuan and mythic. Some years guide-ropes were installed downtown so that the city's lighter residents would not be swept away: thin people in oilskin parkas floating over cars on Taranaki Street, drifting like balloons from the city to the harbor, clear across the Cook Strait to the South Island above the Picton Perry. Every year or so an article by a distinguished cultural celebrity (a writer or a broadcaster who'd travelled "overseas") would appear in the *New Zealand Listener* likening Wellington to London or Manhattan. The entire city was delusional.

Sometimes after the floods a fine sparkling day would crack out of nowhere like the 8th Day of Creation, and these were days Ruffo would emerge in his overcoat from his bed-sit on Ohaka Terrace like an animal from its lair. I always felt better after running into him. Unlike most people in this self-consciously provincial burg, Ruffo was intelligent and curious. When he looked, he really saw you. His was a civilizing presence, transforming Wellington into Joyce's Dublin.

If Ruffo trusted you, he'd invite you to his room, a bedsit carved out downstairs of a woodframe house that the landlord must've abandoned years ago to Social Welfare. You reach it walking down a brambly rutted concrete path. In fact Ruffo was a gifted artist. Hardly anyone in New Zealand at that time painted without institutional sanction, three years of art school, then a gallery, but Ruffo did: he painted silkscreens, stagesets, cartoon-posters for his friends with theater groups and bands.

Back in Wellington years later, I learned that Ruffo had been blessed eight years ago with the lobotomy and he was still in town. In fact, he had a show up at the Willis Street Community Center Gallery. I used the money that I'd made from talking at the university about the semi-names I'd worked with in New York to buy my favorite. In it, an '80s-style Babbitt in a nice gray suit grins into a receiver at the red phonebox on the corner of Aro Street and Ohaka Terrace. The mouthpiece is a human ear. The street is a cacophony of traffic but there's still a faint mangle of bush peeping out through all the blobby colored cars. Yellow clouds stretch out across a blue-pink mackerel sky. In Ruffo's postmodern Wellington, One Dimensional Man still meets Katherine Mansfield.

The privilege of visiting Ruffo was always mixed, a little bit, with sadness. His basement room was dark and strewn with garbage. Digging through newspapers and dirty clothes to make a pot of tea, Ruffo never put an optimistic cast on things. He was a schizophrenic realist. He never had false hopes about an art career. If he was feeling really bad he'd disappear, not be at home, but he was never mean. Visits proceeded according to his rules, along a Continental model. He didn't talk about himself, he didn't pry into your life or problems. Visiting him was like travelling in another country. I didn't mind this 'cause I wanted him to teach me how to be. I loved him. I was 16 and a foreigner.

3. According to David Rosenhan, schizophrenia is a self-fulfilling diagnosis. In his experiment, eight sane people gained admission to psychiatric hospitals by claiming to hear voices. Though from that point on they acted "normally," the staff used everything they said and did as proof of the original "psychosis."

4. Since schizophrenics are at home in multiple realities, contradictions don't apply to them. Like cubist chemists, they break things down and rearrange the elements.

5. I like the phrase "paleologic" because it sounds Egyptian. At the end of *AC/DC*, a play by Heathcote Williams, the character Perowne performs an operation known as self-trepanning. Perowne, a vagrant mathematician, just gets bored by all the sex & mindfuck antics of his druggie friends. Because he doesn't pine for "human warmth" he doesn't dabble in psychology. Perowne's more interested in the flow of systems. Trepanning, as pioneered in London by Bart Hughes and Amanda Fielding, entails the drilling of a hole inside the skull. Bleeding from the wound expands the capillaries around the trepan-subject's pituitary gland. The Third Eye opens. I don't know how they figure out the spot or the exact depth of the incision, but Amanda Fielding made a movie where she does it to herself in a kitchen. And in the play, when finally Perowne trepans himself, his speech explodes. He rants, he sings in hieroglyphics.

6. Félix Guattari, co-author with Gilles Deleuze of *Anti-Oedipus —Capitalism and Schizophrenia*, objected to Arieti's use of the word "paleologic" in describing schizophrenia. "Paleologic," Félix said once, "implies returning to a vague primeval state. But on the contrary—schizophrenia is highly organized." Félix of course was expanding on his analogy between capitalism and schizophrenia.

Both are complex systems based on paradox in which disconnected parts operate according to hidden laws. Both rationalize fragmentation. Capitalism's ethics are completely schizophrenic; i.e., they're contradictory and duplicitous. Buy Cheap, Sell Dear. Psychiatry tries its hardest to conceal this, tracing all disturbances back to the Holy Triangle of Mommy-Daddy-Me. "The unconscious needs to be created," Félix wrote in *Mary Barnes' Trip*. A brilliant model.

Still, Perowne's gentleness reminded me of Ruffo's.

7. Schizophrenia consists of placing the word "therefore" between two non-sequiturs. Driving up to Bishop last week I had two beliefs: I wouldn't get a speeding ticket; I will die within the next five years. I didn't get a speeding ticket, therefore—

(When your head's exploding with ideas you have to find a reason. Therefore, scholarship and research are forms of schizophrenia. If reality's unbearable and you don't want to give up you have to understand the patterns. "Schizophrenia," Géza Róheim wrote, "is the magical psychosis." A search for proof. An orgy of coincidences.)

Two hours ago I took a break from writing this to take a walk before the sun went down. I had an urge to play Willie Nelson's "Crazy" on the *Red Hot Country* CD before going out, but didn't. When I turned the bend on 49th Terrace, my usual walk, *Crazy* sung by Patsy Cline was pouring, I mean POURING, out the windows of a house. I leaned back against a fence across the street and watched the house lift off. An operatic, cinematic moment, everything locked into a single frame that gets you high. Oh Dick, I want to be an intellectual like you.

8. Do you remember that night in February at your house while you were making dinner, I told you how I'd become a vegetarian? I was at a dinner at Félix's loft with Sylvère. The Berlin Wall had just come down. He, Félix and Tony Negri and François,

a younger follower of Félix's in French broadcasting, were planning a TV panel show about the "future of the left." Sylvère would moderate a live discussion between Félix and Tony and the German playwright Heiner Müller. They needed one more speaker. It seemed strange that people would be interested in any conversation between such a homogenous crew: four straight white European men in their 50s, all divorced and now with childless younger women in their early 30s. Sometimes coincidence is just depressingly inevitable. No matter what these four men say, it's like they've already said it. In Félix's book *Chaosophy* there's a great discussion on schizophrenia between him, Deleuze, and eight of France's leading intellectuals. All of them are men. If we want reality to change then why not change it? Oh Dick, deep down I feel that you're utopian too.

"What about Christa Woolf?" I asked. (At that moment she was founding a neo-socialist party in Germany.) And all Félix's guests—the culturally important jowelly men, their Parisianally-groomed, mute younger wives just sat and stared. Finally the communist philosopher Negri graciously replied, "Christa Wolf is not an intellectual." I suddenly became aware of dinner: a bleeding roast, prepared that afternoon by the bonne femme, floating at the center of the table.

9. There's a lot of madness in New Zealand. A famous poem by Alistair Campbell, *Like You I'm Trapped*, was written to his unnamed suicidal wife who'd been diagnosed as schizophrenic. *Like You I'm Trapped* claims the poet's right to project himself into another person's psychic situation. It's a beautiful poem but I don't know if I believe it. There's a lot of madness in New Zealand because it's a mean and isolated little country. Anyone who feels too much or radiates extremity gets very lonely.

Winter, sometime in the '70s, on Boulcott Terrace, downtown Wellington: I'm visiting my girlfriend Mary McCleod who's been in and out of mental hospital several times for no good reason. Mary's a part-time student, full-time resident of Paul Bryce's halfway house for "schizophrenics." Except for the respectful silence that falls on each of Paul's platitudinous remarks (Paul's a licensed therapist), Boulcott Terrace runs more or less along the lines of every other Kiwi hippie commune. Anyone who wants to can move in or out so long as they pay their rent and food money to the kitty. Perhaps Paul's read up on R.D. Laing and Kingsley Hall, though this really isn't likely. Boulcott Terrace is not so much an experiment as an out-let for misguided hippie altruism. It's an offshoot of Jerusalem, the poet James K. Baxter's rural Catholic commune. Outside it's howling wind and rain. Every southerly comes tearing through the broken lead-glass windows. A bunch of residents, mostly guys, sit around a three-bar electric heater in the living room drinking tea and beer. A typical Boulcott Terrace evening.

Mary's 22, a big pouty blonde dabbling in witchcraft. Long stringy hair falls all around the baggy thrift-store coat she wears to hide her babyfat. I'm drawn to Mary because she is so wantonly unhappy. Apart from this we don't have much in common but this is not a problem because in this world there're hardly ever any private conversations. Suddenly there's a rustling in the brush that masks the trashed French windows. It's Fuckwit Nigel, the most seriously crazy of the crew, smushing his face against the glass and licking it. A chorus of "Ouggghhhh, Gross! Fuck Off" goes up around the room. Paul fills me in on Nigel's sad case history. Later on that night Nigel puts his fist straight through the window.

Years later I see Paul in a hardware store on Second Avenue. In his late 30s, neat and trim, he's much diminished. Paul's visiting

New York to take a psychodrama class. He lives in Sydney. I throw my arms around him, feel as I'm embracing him like I'm reaching down a hall of mirrors back into the past. Encountering any piece of Wellington in New York City is magic, cinematic synchronicity. I want to tell Paul everything that's happened since leaving. I'm overwhelmed. But since Paul's never really left and Wellington, for him, isn't frozen in the mythic past, he isn't.

10. Last winter when I fell in love with you and left Sylvère and moved back alone up to the country, I found the second story that I'd ever written, 20 years ago in Wellington. It was written in the third person, the person most girls use when they want to talk about themselves but don't think anyone will listen. "Sunday afternoon, again, again," it led off. "The possibilities are not endless." Names and actual events were carefully omitted, but it describes the heartbreak and abandonment I'd felt after spending Christmas Eve with the actor Ian Martinson.

I met Ian at a late night party at the BLERTA house on Aro Street. BLERTA was a travelling rock & roll roadshow commune—a bunch of guys and friends and wives. They toured around the country in an old bus painted with cartoons by Ruffo. Ian Martinson had just directed a short TV film of Alistair Campbell's poem *Like You I'm Trapped*, and I'd reviewed it for the daily paper. I was the only girl who'd showed up at this party on her own, the only journalist, non-hippie, the only person under 21, all serious disadvantages, so I was incredibly flattered when Ian hung around the edges of the chair near me. Fane Flaws rolled around the carpet like a drunken centipede, Bruno Lawrence kept the party going with a string of dirty jokes. Ian Martinson and I talked about New Zealand poetry.

Around 3 a.m. we staggered up the road to my place for a fuck. "Aro" Street means "love" in Maori. Words left us the minute that we left the party. We were just two people walking up the street outside our bodies. Both of us were pretty drunk, and there was no way of making that transition, to sex from conversation, but anyway we tried. We took our clothes off. At first Ian couldn't get it up, this pissed him off, and when he finally did he fucked me like a robot. He weighed a lot, the bed was old and squishy. I wanted him to kiss me. He turned away, passed out, I may've cried. At 8 a.m. he got up without a word and put his clothes on. "This must be the most sordid Christmas that I've spent in my whole life," the Catholic Ian mumbled, leaving.

Six weeks later *Douglas Weir*, the first TV drama produced by New Zealand's brand new second channel, aired. The aviator Douglas Weir was played with subtlety, brilliance and conviction…by Ian Martinson. Sitting up that night at the typewriter in my bedroom, writing a review for the Wellington *Evening Post*, I felt like Faye Dunaway being slapped by Jack Nicholson in *Chinatown*. I was a journalist…a girl…a journalist …a girl. Hatred and humiliation gathered, soared out from my chest into my throat, as I wrote ten paragraphs in praise of Ian Martinson. That year he won Best Actor.

This incident congealed into a philosophy: Art supercedes what's personal. It's a philosophy that serves patriarchy well and I followed it more or less for 20 years.

That is: until I met you.

11. On April 19 I called you at 10 p.m. and 1 a.m. from my apartment in the East Village. You weren't home. The next night I tried again three times between 11 p.m. New York Time and midnight. Long distance bills fill the gaps left in my diaries. The next day, April 20, a Thursday, I left New York and drove upstate to Thurman. Freezing wind, stripped trees, gray thunderheads. It was

the beginning of Easter weekend. That night between 9:30 and 11:30 EST my time I tried your number four more times but hung up on your machine without leaving any message. Every call to you, according to my phone bill, was preceded by a desperate phone call to Sylvère in New York City. These calls lasted for durations of 6:0, 19:0, 1:0 and .5 minutes. At 1:45 a.m. (10:45 p.m. for you) I tried again. This time your phone was busy. I sat and chainsmoked at my desk for 20 minutes. And when I called your number once again at 2:05 a.m. this time it rang and you picked up, I finally reached you.

12. In a science fiction story whose name and author I forget, a group that's organized around utopian feelings sanctions, sanctifies group sex by describing elements of sex as Gifts from Aliens... "the touching gift," "the whispering gift." I am convinced that I've received "the writing gift" from you.

13. Schizophrenics have a gift for locking into other people's minds. Direct current flows without any spoken language. Like the *Star Wars* robot that can unlock any code just by reaching into a machine, schizophrenics can instantly situate a person: their thoughts and their desires, their weaknesses and expectations. And isn't "situation" such a schitzy word, both noun and verb?? "The schizophrenic... will suddenly burst out with the most incredible details of your private life, things that you would never imagine anyone could know and he will tell you in the most abrupt way truths that you believed to be absolutely secret," Félix said in an interview with Caroline Laure and Vittorio Marchetti (*Chaosophy*). Schizophrenics aren't sunk into themselves. Associatively, they're hyperactive. The world gets creamy like a library. And schizophrenics are the most generous of scholars because they're emotionally *right there*, they don't just formulate, observe. They're willing to become the situated person's expectations. "The schizophrenic has lightning

access to you," Félix continued. "He internalizes all the links between you, makes them part of his subjective system." This is empathy to the highest power: the schizophrenic turns into a seer, then enacts that vision through his or her becoming. But when does empathy turn into dissolution?

14. When my phone bill came in May I was surprised to see that that night—the night of April 21, the night of our last-ever conversation—we'd talked for 80 minutes. It hardly felt like 20.

15. No one, and schizophrenics least of all who do it best, can live in this heightened state of reflective receptivity forever. Because this empathy's involuntary, there's terror here. Loss of control, a seepage. Becoming someone else or worse: becoming nothing but the vibratory field between two people.

"And who are you?" Brion Gysin's question, asked to ridicule the authenticity of authorship ("Since when do words belong to anybody? 'Your very own words' indeed. And who are you?") gets scarier the more you think about it. In Minneapolis when I collapsed with Crohn's Disease after realizing Sylvère didn't love me I lay on a stranger's couch feverish and doubled up with pain, hallucinating through swirling particles to a face behind my face. Before they stuck the tubes down through my nose I knew "I" "wasn't" "anywhere."

16. Calling you that night was torture that I'd pledged myself to do. "I have to let you know," I said, "how I felt last weekend in LA after I saw you." (It'd been ten days and my body was still locked up with sickness). "If I can't tell you this I'll have no choice except to hate you in my heart, perhaps in public."

You said: "I'm sick of your emotional blackmail."

But I went on, and told you how when I got back to New York that Wednesday, April 12, I had three different kinds of rashes: a rash that made my eyes swell closed, a rash across my face and a different rash around my body.

You said: "I'm not responsible."

Somehow on the plane that Tuesday night I'd been able to exorcize the stomach pain that'd started in LA the night before, the night I called to say goodbye, the way you'd asked me to. Pacing in the tiny space behind the cabin, shouting down the Airphone to Sylvère as the plane flew over Denver, I'd barricaded myself against another Crohn's Disease flareup but the somatic body won't be denied, it's like a freeway. Open up an extra lane of traffic and it'll fill up too. On Wednesday morning I crashed with rashes, tears, a yeast infection and cystitis. A malady diffuse enough for Dr. Blum to write five separate prescriptions. I got the drugs and drove upstate. And now it was overcast Good Friday.

17. Because identifying so completely with someone else can only happen by abandoning yourself, the schizophrenic panics and retreats abruptly from these connections. Connect and cut. Connecticut. Schizophrenics reach beyond the parameters of language into the realm of pure coincidence. Freed from signifying logic, time spreads out in all directions. "Think of language as a signifying chain." (Lacan) Without the map of language you're not anywhere.

"Even if everything between us was 80 percent in my own mind," I said, "20 had to come from you." You disagreed; insisted everything that passed between us was my own fabrication. I wondered if that's possible. Granted, fan-dom is an engineered psychosis. But what went on with us was singular and private. And by the end of 80 minutes the conversation looped around. You listened; you were kind. You started talking in percentages.

Schizophrenia is metaphysics-brut. The schizophrenic leaves the body, transcends himself, herself, outside any system of belief.

Freedom equals panic because without belief there is no language. When you've lost yourself to empathy, a total shutdown is the only way back in.

And when does empathy turn into dissolution?

18. On Wednesday, April 5 I left New York to "teach for a week" at Art Center in Los Angeles, hoping I might see you. All winter, spring, I was shuttling between the rural poverty of upstate New York to Avenue D, New York, to Pasadena. That Wednesday afternoon I took a cab to JFK, upgraded my ticket in the Admiral's Club Lounge, caught the 5, got in at 8 to Los Angeles. I picked up a rental car and drove out to a motel in Pasadena. My entire existential-economic situation was schizophrenic, if you accept Félix's terms: schizophrenia as a paradigm for the internalized contradictions of late capitalism. I wasn't travelling as Chris Kraus. I was travelling as the wife of Sylvère Lotringer. "You may be brave," you said to me that weekend, "but you're not wise." But Dick, if wisdom's silence then it's time to play the fool—

That night I got lost on the 405, found myself driving towards your house in Piru. I turned around, cut back across the 101 to Pasadena. I didn't have to be at school 'til Friday but I came in Wednesday night 'cause I thought it would increase the chance of seeing you. Besides, on Wednesday night I'd been invited to a party for my friend Ray Johannson's 40th birthday.

At 10p.m. I checked into the Vagabond Motel on Colorado. I ran a bath, unpacked my clothes, then called you. Your phone rang eight times, there was no answer. I washed and styled my hair, then called again. This time your answerphone kicked on. I didn't leave a message. I smoked a cigarette, then thought about an outfit for Ray's party. Wisely, I decided against the Kanae & Onyx gold lame rubber jacket. But after getting dressed (black chiffon shirt, English military pants, black leather jacket) I reached another impasse. If I left a message on your answerphone I couldn't call again. No, I had to talk to you directly. But could I skip Ray's party just to sit beside the phone? Finally I decided to wait until 10:30. If you weren't home I'd leave and call you in the morning. At 10:35 p.m. I called again. You answered.

"Lived experience," said Gilles Dleuze in *Chaosophy* "does not mean sensible qualities. It means intensification. 'I feel that' means that something is happening inside me. It happens all the time with schizophrenics. When a schizophrenic says 'I feel that I'm becoming God' it's as if he were passing beyond a threshold of intensity with his very body... The body of the schizophrenic is a kind of egg. It is a catatonic body."

You didn't sound surprised when I told you I was calling from LA. Or maybe you just sounded non-committal. At first your voice was cold, detached, but then it softened. You said you couldn't really talk... But then you did, you did. I don't remember which conference in which European country you'd just got back from. You said you were exhausted and depressed. Two nights ago you'd narrowly escaped a DUI driving on Route 126 and you'd decided to stop drinking.

"I feel clearer now than I've ever felt before," you said, after 36 hours of sobriety. Waves of remorse pounded from my heart out to my fingers. I clasped the phone, regretting this entire schizophrenic project that'd started when I met you. "I've never been stalked before," you said in February. But was it stalking? Loving you was like a kind of truth-drug because you knew everything. You made me think it might be possible to reconstruct a life 'cause after all, you'd walked away from yours. If I could love you consciously, take an experience that was so completely female and subject it to an abstract analytic system, then perhaps I had a chance of under-standing something and could go on living.

"I never asked for this!" you said. And on the phone I was ashamed. My will had ridden over all your wishes, your fragility. By loving you this way I'd violated all your boundaries, hurt you.

Then you asked me how I was. Your way of asking ordinary social questions makes me think of Ruffo: it's way past simple listening. It's like you really want to know. Your attentive unshockability makes it possible to say anything. "I'm really fine," I said. But I wanted you to know how much good you've done me. "It's like—I've finally moved outside my head—I don't think I'll go back," I said. Three days before I'd written in my notebook: "Since knowing D. my eyes have moved into my ribcage. My body's turned to liquid glass and all the pieces fit..." And quoting Alice Notley quoting Donne: "No woman is an island-ess."

And then again, remorse. I wanted you to understand I'd never use this writing to 'expose' you. "Look," I said. "I'll change the names, the dates, the place. It'll be a past-tense narrative about cowboy love. I'll call you 'Derek Rafferty' instead of Dick."

You sounded less than thrilled. Was there any chance of redeeming things, this situation?

(A month before I'd sent you the first draft of a story called *The Exegesis*. On page 1 there was a line: "'You were so wet,' Dick ____'d said, glancing at his watch..." ...You freaked. "But that's my NAME!" you howled into the phone. And then you'd told me how, when you were writing your first book, you worked so hard to protect the peo-ple who you wrote about by concealing their identities. "And those were people who I *loved*," you'd said. "You don't even know me.")

My feelings for you were so strong I had to find a way to make love selfless. So even though I'd travelled all this way just hoping I might see you, if seeing me was bad for you, I wouldn't. It was April, the season of blood oranges, emotion running like the stream behind my house upstate, turbulent and thawing. I thought about how fragile people get when they withdraw from anything, how they become bloody yolks protected only by the thinnest shell.

"So—" you said.—"Did you want to see me?"

And this time (if morality's repressing what you want over what you think is right) I responded morally: "I think the question's more, do you feel like seeing me? 'Cause if this is a bad time for you, I think we should forget it."

But then you said: "Ah, I just have to check my schedule for the next few days."

You said: "Why don't you call me back around this time tomorrow?"

It was 10:52. My hand was wet from holding the telephone so tightly.

19. *Love has led me to a point*
    where I now live badly
    'cause I'm dying of desire'
    I therefore can't feel sorry for myself
    AND—

20. My hand was wet from holding the telephone so tightly. I was sitting on the edge of the double bed in the motel room. The bedside lamp glared back into the room against the windows.

By the time I got out to Silverlake, 11:45 p.m., Ray's party was already breaking up. Ray introduced me to Michelle Di Blasi, a writer-filmmaker who'd been all over New York in the early '80s. Where are they now? (a favorite conversational routine among survivors, sightings of the once-famous waiting tables, picking garbage…) But Michelle looked great, and on the plane that afternoon I'd been reading one of her new stories. It was the kind of story everybody likes, about a tough girl who becomes a truer version of herself by uncovering her vulnerability. It was the kind of story people like because its universe is played out in the story of one person. It was the kind of story (dare I say it?) that women're supposed to write because all its truths are grounded in a single lie: denying chaos. Michelle was nice: smart and open, radiant and charming.

The crowd was thinning out. Ray Johannson sat down and drank a beer with me and started to critique my writing. He said the "flaw" in all these stories is that I'm addressing them to you. I should learn to be more "independent." Everyone was disappointed that Amanda Plummer hadn't showed but I met another famous person's sister.

21. Last January when Sylvère and I had dinner at your house and I handed you a xerox of my first 120 letters you said, "I'm gobstruck." The other guests had all gone home and we sat around your table drinking vodka. The glass shattered when you poured Sylvère a shot. The three of us agreed to meet for breakfast the next day in Antelope Valley at Five Corners Diner.

Sylvère and I found you already sitting there at 9 a.m. and it was a gloomy fucking morning. The worn-out raincoat you were wearing reminded me of the record that you'd played the night before, *The Greatest Hits of Leonard Cohen*. It's geometrically impossible to arrange a group of three in anything but a straight line or a triangle. Sylvère sat next to you, I sat across. The conversation circled nervously. Sylvère was elusive, you were cryptic. I could hardly eat my oatmeal. Finally you focussed sharp and looked at me and asked "Are you still anorexic?" An allusion to my second letter. "Not really," I demurred, hoping you'd say more. But then you didn't, so I blurted out: "Did you read them? Did you really read my letters?"

"Oh, I glanced through them," you said. "Alone this morning in my bedroom. With all this rain, I found it very film noir…"

I wondered what you meant (I didn't ask) but now I'm right there too: shuttling urban & alone the night of April 5 between the airport and the rental car, the car and the motel…fixed points on a floating grid. The motel phone, the ashtray. The stupid Heidi-in-Bavaria waitress costumes at the restaurant party, a Tyrolean horror-show, the dregs of food, the conversations. Taking foolish stabs at girlfriendhood to Michelle Di Blasi by burbling on about the problems of my film. CUT-CUT-CUT. Robbe-Grillet meets Marguerite Duras and suddenly you're nowhere. Dennis Potter's Singing Detective stumbles up out of a basement bar sometime in the '70s and rounds a corner into wartime London. Paint it Black, Noir. Time's an unsealed envelope and crime's a metaphor for anguish, private symphonies of intensity exploding in the dark.

22. Of course it's no surprise when Félix Guattari talks about love in the same breath as schizophrenia. Here's a passage that I found three weeks ago when I started writing this and now it's August and I can't find the citation, and anyhow it's my translation, i.e., a cross between what he wrote and what I wanted him to say:

"It's like this: someone falls in love and in a universe that once was closed, suddenly everything seems possible. Love and sex are mediums for semiotizing mutation."

I disagree, at least I think I do, about the "semiotizing" part (Dear Dick, Dear Marshall, Dear Sylvère, What is semiotics?). Love and sex both cause mutation, just like I think desire isn't lack, it's surplus energy—a claustrophobia inside your skin—

Félix goes on: "Previously unimagined systems unfurl themselves in a once empty world. New possibilities of freedom are revealed. Of course none of this is ever guaranteed."

And now IT'S GETTING VERY LATE. It's August and since July 6 when I started writing this I've been in an altered state, have lost 10 lbs, etc.

This morning when I took a walk I thought about a talk I'll give next fall (I've been invited to your school) about poetics. I want to play video I edited two years ago for Jim Brodey's funeral. Jim was a quote-minor New York poet who died of AIDS after living in the street. In the tape he talks about Lew Welch, a quote-minor San Francisco poet who would've drunk himself to death if he hadn't suicided first in the '70s. I want to hand out copies of Alice Notley's brilliant essay *Dr William's Heiresses* where she talks about how female poets like herself who externalize and twist internal daily life have hardly any female ancestors. The critic Kathleen Fraser thought that for not inventing some, Alice was a bad feminist. Alice Notley proved the possibility of writing poems no matter what; Kathleen Fraser is an academic. "No woman is an island-ess," oh… The message is, IT'S GETTING VERY LATE. Be glad you're in a California art school but don't forget you live by compromise and contradiction 'cause those who don't just die like dogs.

I have to find a way of ending this, of getting to the point.

23. I wasn't really that surprised to get your answerphone on Thursday night when I called back, (April 6, 10:45 p.m.) the way you'd asked me to, just short of 24 hours later.

Desire, claustrophobia. If I left a message I'd have to wait in the motel room, wondering if you'd call back. So I hung up and smoked some pot and went outside. The pot was very strong and I started flashing back again to 20 years ago (I know, I know).

Remembering what it felt like to be 20, overwhelmed by feeling and sensation, lost for words. While having lots and lots of words to talk about *Douglas Weir* and Ian Martinson, Angola, China, rock & roll—the host culture, male. My schizophrenia. Is this letter all about the past? No, it's about intensity. R.D. Laing never figured out that "the divided self" is female subjectivity. Writing about an ambitious educated 26-year-old "schizophrenic girl" in the suburban 1950s: "…the patient repeatedly contrasts her real self with her false compliant self." Oh really.

That night I sat on a curb in sleeping Pasadena, stoned and spinning, writing notes about the bungalows.

Later on, I left this message on your answerphone: "Hi it's Chris. Just calling back to see if you still want to get together. If the timing isn't good for you, just let me know. I'll be in 'til 9 tomorrow morning." The normalcy of this message sounded totally surreal.

The philosopher Luce Irigaray thinks there is no female "I" in existing (patriarchal) language. She proved it once by bursting into tears while lecturing in a conference on Saussure at Columbia University.

24. According to Charles Olsen, the best poetry is a kind of schizophrenia. The poem does not "express" the poet's thoughts or feelings. It is "a transfer of energy between the poet and the reader."

25. The next morning—Friday, April 7—you returned my call.

26. It was 8:30 a.m. The Violent Femmes song *Add It Up* was cranked up on a cheap cassette and I was getting ready to go to school. "Hello Chris," you said, "it's Dick." Your accent sounded strained and bitter. It was the first time I'd ever heard you speak my name, or yours. "Look," you said. "It turns out I've got a previous engagement this evening. So how about the weekend? Why don't you give me a call tomorrow morning around this time?"

A tsunami wave inside my body rolled. The telephone became a schizophrenic instrument, the "therefore" placed between us, two non-sequiturs. I had to take control.

"No!," I said, then curbed the violence of it. "I'm only here 'til Tuesday and there're other things I need to do. If we're going to get together it'd be better if we could make a plan right now."

You suggested that we meet for lunch the following afternoon.

27. David Rattray was a 26-year-old American junkie when he started translating Antonin Artaud. He'd read Artaud in French at Dartmouth College, but in 1957, living on his own in Paris, he decided to become him. At the old Bibliothèque Nationale in Paris, the cataloging system held a list of every book checked out by every reader. Artaud was fairly freshly dead. And isn't scholarship just a stalking of the dead by people who're too stoned or scared to chase live bait? That year David Rattray read every single book checked out by Antonin Artaud.

This afternoon (August 12) I went over to the Occidental College Library. It was about 102 degrees. I wanted to look at Katherine Mansfield's famous story *At The Bay*, set in Wellington, New Zealand. I was hoping that its qualities—time frozen soft in green and blue—would help me write about the lunch we had in April, that Saturday afternoon. The third floor of the library was cool and empty and all of Katherine's books were there. Among them was a gorgeous Knopf edition of Mansfield's *Bliss and Other Stories*, the sixth printing, published in the year she died, 1923. Its dark green cover, thick lead type sunk deep on creamy pages, cheerful green and orange endpapers, threw me back into a time when books were friends. I sat down between the stacks and started thumbing through the pages. They were as intimate, delicious and inviting as Venusian skin.

I checked out *Bliss* and another book of Katherine's *Collected Stories* around 3 p.m. I had to try and eat, so I drove to 50th and Figueroa, a green and orange stucco restaurant, Chico's Mexican Taquitos. Waiting for the soup I opened *Bliss* at random to page 71, the opening of a story called "Je Ne Parle Pas Français." Chico's only other customers were two guys named Vito and Jose, as thin as me and both fresh out of "rehab" (four days of tranquilized withdrawal) at a nearby public hospital. A woman sitting, reading all alone will always be a receptacle for passersby to rant on. Vito sat down next to me. "Heroin's sooo good," he said. "But, you see, it's very bad." Now that he was clean, he thought he'd try his luck in Laughlin. He'd heard there were plenty of good jobs in the casinos. He'd save some money, try and join his wife and baby girl. "I don't know why I have such a fancy for this little cafe. It's dirty, sad." Page 71 of *Bliss* found Katherine sitting by herself one afternoon at the close of World War I in a French cafe.

"Don't talk so much," Jose told Vito. I was sitting like a schoolteacher with all my library books, offering advice on kicking. When Vito left he said "God bless." And at that moment I was overwhelmed with love for Katherine, whose letters from this time (Paris, Spring, 1918) had been suppressed after her death by her husband because they were "too painful."

"I don't believe in the human soul, I believe that people are like portmanteaux," she writes at the opening of this story, as if anybody cared. "*Bliss* was so brilliant...," Katherine's friend Virginia Woolf wrote to Janet Case, "...and so hard, and so shallow, and so sentimental that I had to rush to the bookcase for something to drink."

Katherine, Queen of the Biscuit Box School of Writing, the brave colonial girl, determined to live in London, even though the checks sent by her bank-director father from Wellington, New

Zealand didn't take her very far. Wellington, the capital of New Zealand, was a city of unpaved roads and horses. Men wrote heroic verse about the land. But there she was in Paris: 28 years old, alone, tubercular and hemoraging for the first time; willing to take a crack at it, at being "right" and making the most absolute of statements.

Katherine, who capitalized words like Life and wrote themes on love and rhubarb, indulged by D.H. Lawrence and lots of other men because she was sincere and pretty. Katherine the utopian space cadet, whose entire literary project was to capture heightened states of adolescent feeling ("bliss"). Katherine, who tried so hard in London to be best-friends with Virginia Woolf, who hated her, because Katherine was the kind of naif-imbecile that the literary men adored and championed at her expense.

"My God, I love to think of you, Virginia," Katherine wrote in 1917, "as my friend…we have got the same job and it is really very curious & thrilling that we should both be after so nearly the same thing…" even though she later wrote John Murray that she found Virginia's writing "intellectually snobbish, long and tiresome." In 1911, her first year in London, Katherine posed uncomfortably for a portrait. Thick eyebrows, pointed nose, neck craned forward…in this photo she was not a pretty girl. Her life there was one big flourish of bravado, her impetuosity, "pores and vapours" which (according to Virginia Woolf) "sicken or bewilder most of our friends."

Yet seven years after Katherine's death, Virginia admitted she still dreamed of Katherine, who had a quality she "adored and needed," so in a sense she loved her too. This afternoon the thought of Katherine trying to be "right" in London made me get all clutchy, and Dick, that isn't all:

No matter where you go, someone else has been before.

Because like me, Katherine Mansfield fell in love with Dick.

On page 85 of "Je Ne Parle Pas Français," she writes:

"It was impossible not to notice Dick. What a catch! He was the *only Englishman present* (italics mine), reserved and serious, making a special study of literature and instead of circulating gracefully round the room he stayed in one place leaning against the wall, that dreamy half smile on his lips and replying in his low soft voice to anybody who spoke to him."

But unlike you, this Dick had no "previous engagements." Straight off, he invited Katherine out to dinner. And they spent the night at his hotel,

"Talking—but not only of literature. I discovered to my relief that it wasn't necessary to keep to the tendency of the modern novel... Now and again, as if by accident, I threw in a card that seemed to have nothing to do with the game, just to see how he'd take it. But each time he gathered it into his hands *with his dreamy look* (my emphasis) and smile unchanged. Perhaps he murmured: 'That's curious.' But not as if it were curious at all."

Dick was Katherine's perfect schizophrenic listener. As Géza Róheim wrote, Dick was dreamily empathic because "a lack of ego boundaries makes it impossible for him to set limits to the process of identification." And Katherine flipped:

"Dick's calm acceptance went to my head at last. It fascinated me. It led me on and on 'til I threw every card I possessed at him and sat back and watched him arrange them in his hand."

By that time both of them were very drunk. Dick didn't judge. He just said, "Very interesting." And she was overwhelmed,

"...quite breathless at the thought of what I'd done. I had shown somebody both sides of my life. Told him everything as sincerely and truthfully as I could. Taken immense pains to explain things about my submerged life that really were disgusting and never could possibly see the light of day."

Have we talked enough about the schizophrenic phenomena of coincidence?

Last week at school Pam Strugar wondered why the brilliant girls all die. Both Katherine Mansfield and the philosopher Simone Weil lived lives of passionate intensity. Both died alone of tubercular starvation in rooms attached to flakey "institutes," dreaming in their notebooks about childhood happiness and comfort at the age of 34.

It moved me so that tears came into my eyes.

For weeks they had been talking about Butterfly Creek. "Let's go to But-ter-fly Creek!" Eric Johnson intoned, mimicking the plummy baritone of his father, the Reverend Cyril Johnson.

All January long there'd been record heat in Wellington. Miraculously still and cloudless days, sunlight glinting off the cars on Taranaki Street. That January all the offices shut down at 3 p.m. Clerks and typists mobbed the sandy crescent beach at Oriental Bay.

High up on The Terrace overlooking Willis Street, even the fieldstone stucco'd walls and lead-glass windows of the Vicarage gave no protection from the heat. But the Vicar and his wife, Vita-Fleur, who'd emigrated here from England after Cyril'd finished university and seminary school, were prepared for this colonial eventuality. All summer long Vita-Fleur made ginger-beer for her children. The recipe'd been handed down by her mother, an Anglican missionary's wife who'd spent 16 hellish years in Barbados. Five great stone jugs of ginger-beer sat outside the kitchen-garden on The Terrace:

enough to last at least that many New Zealand summers. Mother to Laura, Eric, Josephine and Isabel, Vita-Fleur was a large, conservatively-dressed, pigeon-breasted woman who'd married well. No more trundling round the globe to dark-skinned colonies. Cyril was acerbic, brilliant and everybody knew that he'd eventually be made a bishop. And Vita-Fleur's mission was to set a good example of wifely domesticity at St. Stephen's, the largest Anglican church in Wellington. Wellington is the capital of New Zealand. New Zealand is the cultural center of the whole Pacific Rim. Therefore, Vita-Fleur was a a role model to at least one third of the world.

> *God of Nations*
> *At our feet*
> *In these bonds of love we meet*
> *Hear our voices we entreat*
> *God Defend New Zealand*

(All rise, hats off, for the singing of the National Anthem at the 8 p.m. show on Saturday night at the Paramount on Courtney Place. Jaffas rolling down the aisles... Because the Paramount shows "popular" films, the audience is often mixed with Maoris...)

It was 2 p.m. that January Sunday afternoon at the Vicarage and the dinner plates had just been cleared away. Eric Johnson and Constance Green sat on the floor beside the window seat in the living room playing records. Both were in their teens. They had an ongoing debate about the merits of English folk-rock versus American rock & roll. Eric played Lydia Pence and Fairport Convention; Constance countered with Janis Joplin and Frank Zappa. Every 15 minutes the grownups (Cyril, Vita-Fleur and Constance's parents, Louise and Jaspar Green) hollered from the bloated depth of armchairs to "TURN THE RECORD DOWN!" Eric's sisters were reading *Elle* and English *Vogue* in their rooms upstairs, and Carla, Constance's little sister, was outside playing in the garden. Dull-dull-dull. But for Eric and Constance, the promise of this summer afternoon was still not killed.

The Greens had only just arrived in New Zealand in December, emigrating from a Connecticut suburb about 20 miles northeast of Westport/Greenwich, Episcopal nirvana. The Johnson's knowledge of geography did not extend to all the differences contained within the twenty miles between Bridgeport and Old Greenwich. Jaspar and Louise, both Anglophiles, were both still thrilled with their move to Wellington, which compared to Bridgeport was an epicenter of English-speaking culture. Meanwhile Eric and Constance circled round each other like two strange animals. Neither had met anyone like the other before.

That summer, Eric was permanently "home" from Wanganui Boy's Collegiate. He'd been expelled. After putting up with six years of torture—beatings from school prefects, classmates, even younger boys; being picked last for every team; weeping in the toilets, the School decided Eric "lacked character." That is, he wasn't using queerness as a means of negotiating power in Wanganui Boy's Collegiate hierarchy. He was a full-time queer. The very sight of him—blonde tousled hair, gray shirt tails, pale and thin as a pre-Raphaelite Ophelia—became disruptive to the school. "Sent down" (from Wanganui back to Wellington, New Zealand) at 17, Eric wanted to go straight to university. His parents refused. He was socially "not ready." They insisted he attend the new, optional seventh-form, created for future math and science majors. Eric rebelled. In desperation, Cyril agreed to let Eric choose from any school in Wellington.

At 14, Constance was a jumble of orange polyester miniskirts, plastic earrings, dirty words. Louise and Jaspar, hoping to raise her shabby self-esteem, also decided to let Constance choose a school. She'd be going into Sixth Form. Constance and Eric's first revelation to each other was that they'd both enrolled at Wellington Trades and Tech. It was a decision they'd each made separately and perversely and to the horror of their parents so of course they bonded instantly.

Located at the edges of the city's only slum, Wellington Trades and Tech had an impressive Latin motto carved above the door: *Qui Servum Magnum*. But no one there could read it since the school had not taught Latin for at least 20 years. "He Who Serves Is Greatest." Well, the future was no secret: lifetimes spent in auto body shops and typing pools. So everybody made the most of those last three years of school, getting stoned and fingerfucking each other in Biology and Study Hall.

Unlike his parents, who were impressed by the Green's Connecticut credentials, Eric knew straight off that Constance's cultural pretensions were strictly trailer-park. Tough-talking Constance became Eric's creature, his Pygmalion. Their first job was to get rid of her hideous American accent, replace it with the educated Yorkshire intonations he'd picked up from his Dad. Eric told Constance what to read and what to listen to. Sometimes they reviewed scenes from her past life for Eric's judicious editing. Eric approved of Constance's political transgressions—suspended from elementary school for reading Lenny Bruce and leafletting for the Black Panthers. But all the rest would have to go—the shoplifting, the biker gangs and blowjobs, the arrests for drug possession, breaking and entry—were just too tacky.

All summer long Eric and Constance had the most fabulous adventures, unfolding like the pages of an Enid Blyton storybook.

Nights, they hung out at the Chez Paree. Afternoons they caught the trolleybus and rode out around the bays, scaling volcanic rocks to watch the sunset. One day they packed a picnic lunch and went hiking in the hills above Karaka Beach, scene of Katherine Mansfield's famous story "At The Bay." Eric did a wicked impersonation of Mansfield's alter-ego, Kezia, and they laughed so hard they didn't notice when a Tasman fog came rolling in. Cyril himself drove out to find them. He looked so Midlands-serious with his torch and oilskin parka, like the man in the Gorton's Fishcake ads, that Eric and Constance punched each other in the ribs to keep from laughing on the long ride home. "What a Dag!" (New Zealand slang for laugh or sheepshit), Constance learned to say. Eric had a color photo of a hippie-gypsy couple hitch-hiking beside a wheatfield, torn out of one of Laura's *Vogues*. Could this be him and Constance?

Cyril's voice droned on in favor of the Diocese's liberal stand against apartheid to general clucks and nods. "Let's go to Butterfly Creek!" Eric said again. "You drive out through Petone, turn right on Moonshine Road, drive past the Eastbourne Cattery. Did you know it's owned by Alexander Trocchi's former wife? She moved out here from London. You park up in the hills, and for the first two hours walking it's native bush, all dark and jungly. And then you come out to a clearing, a meadow really, and there's a brook and waterfall. And everywhere you look there's butterflies."

They walked deeper into the bush, along a narrow track shaded by macrocarpa trees and kowhai. They'd left the meadow and its brilliant sun behind. The ground was cold and damp. Hardly any light penetrated the broad umbrella canopy of punga ferns. The boy stopped to catch his breath. He looked up in the sky through a tiny crack in the deep green foliage. And he was overcome with wondrous signs.

28. Your "previous engagement" Friday night, April 7, turned out also to be mine. And here things start to get a little strange. Our "previous engagement" was an opening of the Charles Gaines/Jeffrey Vallance/Eleanor Antin show at the Santa Monica Museum. The Antin piece, an installation called *Ghost Story— Minetta Lane*, had just been moved out here from the Ronald Feldman Gallery in Soho. *Ghost Story* was the piece I wrote to you about last January in *Every Letter Is A Love Letter*. The piece I'd Fed-Ex'd out to you in February before arriving on your doorstep in Antelope Valley. The piece that, if you'd read before I got there, might've made you be less cruel.

My stomach flipped when I saw your yellow Thunderbird in the Main Street parking lot. I moved closer to my friend and escort Daniel Marlos as we crossed the street and entered the Museum courtyard. "He's here!" I said. "He's here." And sure enough, I saw you talking to a group of people as I crossed the room to buy a drink. You saw me too—threw up your hands as if to shield yourself from danger. Then you pointedly ignored me as you circled round the room.

The Gallery rocked back and forth like a drunken boat. I felt like Frederic Moreau arriving late and uninvited at Monsieur Dambreuse's elite salon in Flaubert's *Sentimental Education*—a paranoiac treasure hunt, incriminatory, clues planted everywhere around the seasick room. Everywhere I looked I found you, eyes turned away, yet seeing. I couldn't move.

Finally I resolved to talk to you. After all, we weren't enemies. We had a date for Saturday afternoon. I waited 'til you were alone with just one another person, a young man, a student. "Dick!" I said. "Hello!" You half-smiled and nodded, waiting. You didn't introduce me to your friend, your creature. Waited for me to start some conversation, so I burbled on about the show. When this dead-ended I stopped short. "Well," I said. "I'll see you later." "Yes," you said. "I'll see you very soon."

That night your Thunderbird got broadsided and my rental car got towed. Coincidence Number Two. And isn't schizophrenia just an orgy of it? You got drunk after the opening, spent the night at a motel.

29. Eric Johnson caught a Railways bus from Wellington to Ngaruwahia. It's sometime in the early '80s. Félix called these "the Winter Years." Eric is now 34 years old. He doesn't have a bank account and he's carrying about 50 dollars. In desperation, after counselling, Vita-Fleur and Cyril finally cut off his allowance. "I'm looking for a job of work," Eric says to anyone he sees. Voice rattling through his hollow chest and craggy body, he looks like Hamlet's father's ghost wandering the moors in King Lear's storm.

Katherine Mansfield craved a slice of life so badly she invented it as genre. Small countries lend themselves to stories: backwaters where the people stuck there don't have much to do besides watch each other's lives unfold. Eric's carrying an army surplus ruck-sack, an oilskin parka and a wool jersey knit by Vita-Fleur. The rest of his possessions are a sleeping bag, one extra pair of longs, a knife and a canteen. After 13 years of vagrancy, more or less, Eric knows a thing or two about survival. The bus lets out on the Main Street of Ngaruwahia's downtown.

"Jerusalem! A Golden Land!" was how he'd described this place years ago to Constance. Ngaruwahia, with it's wide river, rolling hills, was the scene of Maori legends about ancestors as mythic as Greek gods. There'd been a rock festival here 15 years ago, then a commune. But now at 4 p.m. with thunderheads rolling in across this late spring sky, Eric curses the very size of it. Walking, walking, past used appliance shops and greasy burger bars. Eric was back from travelling "overseas." He'd got as far as Sydney, failed. Somehow he never caught the drift of what it was he was supposed to do. Social work? Ceramics class? He'd never met the right people. For every affirmation there were a hundred qualifying negations. Sort-of-raping Constance in the backroom of Bert Andrew's country shack when they were two years out of school had been his only foray into heterosexuality. And yet he wasn't queer. He'd figured that one out in Family Therapy. Voices spoke; they never told him what to do. Eric walks ten blocks down Main Street to the edge of town, sticks out his thumb to hitch a ride to Vincent's, keeps walking. At least it isn't raining.

A week before in Wellington Eric'd had the most confusing visit from Constance Green, who he hadn't seen now in eight years. She'd tracked him down on one of her whirlwind trips from the East Village in New York by phoning Cyril Johnson, now Archbishop of the Auckland Diocese. Shallow, flighty Constance, still a welter of opinions and hip clothes, asked Eric if she could shoot a video of him. "About what?" he asked cautiously. "Oh, you know, *you*," she'd said. He turned her down, mobilizing his large voice behind his chiseled features: "Why should I let you make fun of me?" This stopped her cold. Perhaps the distances between them were not so interesting.

⋅✦⋅⋅✦⋅⋅✦⋅

30. On Saturday, April 8 we spent a perfect afternoon together. You arrived at the motel around noon and I was kind of shaky. Instead of going to the gym that morning I'd stayed home writing about Jennifer Harbury. She was in the news that month after almost singlehandedly bringing down the military government of Guatemala. Jennifer, an American leftist lawyer, had spent the last three years demanding that the Guatemalan army exhume the body of her husband, a disappeared Indian rebel leader. Jennifer's story was so inspiring...and I was glad to've discovered it, even though my only motivation to write about her story was to take the heat off you. I'd cut back and forth between Jennifer and Efraim, me and "Derek Rafferty." You'd been so horrified to see your name in the last two stories and I thought if I could write about how love can change the world then I wouldn't have to write about you personally.

Fuck her once, she'll write a book about it, you or anybody else might say.

I was becoming you. When I pushed you from my thoughts you came back into my dreams. But now I had to prove my love for you was real by holding back and considering what you wanted. I had to act responsively, responsibly...I was spewing words and syntaxes I remembered reading in your book, *The Ministry of Fear*.

31.   *Why can't I get just one screw*
        Why can't I get just one screw

Believe me I'd know what to do
But you won't let me make love to you

Why can't I get just one fuck
Why can't I get just one fuck
Bet it's got something to do with luck
But I've waited my whole life for just one
DAY...

32. We talked awhile and drank some fruit juice. You liked the way I'd rearranged things in the motel room. (It was crammed with talismans and artworks that my LA friends had given me, thinking rightly that I needed some protection.) We looked at Sabina Ott's scratched-up yellow drawing, Daniel Marlos' photo of people with banana-dildos in the desert. You were intrigued by this, by images of sex that weren't heterosexual, a bit disturbed that dicks could be the butt of jokes. The photos of Keith Richards and Jennifer Harbury—motifs for this bogus story about my fictional cowboy love for "Derek Rafferty"—scotch-taped to the wall didn't go unnoticed. We talked some more and you explained how you'd ignored me at the opening last night because everything was getting too referential. I understood. Then both of us were hungry. We ate lunch at a soul-food restaurant up on Washington and I told you all about the failure of my movie. Then you confessed how, over the past two years, you'd stopped reading. This broke my heart. Outside the storefront restaurant the East Pasadena Saturday afternoon was clanging. You paid the bill, then we drove my rental car up to the wilderness preserve above Lake Avenue.

"Let's go to But-ter-fly Creek!"

Walking up the dirt track along the still-green mountain, everything between us flattened out. You seemed so open. You told me all about yourself at 12 years old, a young boy sitting at the edge of a playing field somewhere in the English Midlands, reading stories of great emperors and wars in Latin. You'd read your way into the world just like my husband. You told me other things about your life and what you'd left behind. You were so unhappy. Emotional seduction. The sun was very warm. When you took your shirt off you seemed to be inviting me to touch you but I refrained. To yearn responsibly. You had the softest palest skin, an alien's. "The Pacific starts here," I said. The landscape on the hill reminded me of New Zealand.

Run down catch'em at the top of the stairs
Can I mix in with your affairs
Share a smoke, make a joke
You gotta grasp and reach for a leg of hope

Words to memorize, words hypnotize
Words make my mouth an exercise
Words all fail the magic prize
Nothing I can say when I'm in your thighs

There weren't any butterflies on the hill in Pasadena. But come out to a clearing, and there's a waterfall, and then I told you how I admired you, and you said or you implied that what I'd done had helped you burn through some things in your life. And everything seemed as pliant as a macrocarpa branch, fragile as an egg.

33. In the blinding sunlight of the Vagabond Motel parking lot you asked me if I'd call again before I left LA. Perhaps we could have dinner. We embraced, and I was first to break away.

34. Sunday, April 9: Writing in my notebook after visiting Ray Johannson in Elysian Park: Bliss.

35. And so I called you up on Monday night. I was booked to leave at 10 p.m. on Tuesday. "The schizophrenic reacts violently when any attempt is made to influence him. This is so because a lack of ego boundaries make it impossible for him to set limits of identification." (Róheim) The schizophrenic is a sexy Cyborg. When I reached you you were cold, ironic, wondering why I'd called. I hung up sweating. But I couldn't leave like this, I had to try and make it better.

I called you back, apologized, "I—I just felt like I had to ask you why you sounded so distant and defensive."

"Oh," you said. "I don't know. Was I defensive? I was just looking for something in my room."

Visions of you vision of me
Things to do things to see
This's my way to cut it up
You better wait a minute honey
Better add it up

I threw up twice before getting on the plane.

36. Dear Dick,

No woman is an island-ess. We fall in love in hope of anchoring ourselves to someone else, to keep from falling,

Love,
Chris

DICK WRITES BACK

Chris finished writing *Add It Up* before the end of August. The next morning she accidentally cut her right hand on a broken glass. The cut left a bumpy scar. She knew that *Add It Up* would be the last letter.

Chris posted it to Dick after getting back from the hospital. She wanted a response, and fast, because things were finally happening with her film and she'd be travelling, starting in September. Perhaps the only reason Dick had never written back was she'd failed to express her feelings for him forcefully? Surely *Add It Up* would convince him. She waited for his letter, but by Labor Day, Dick still hadn't phoned or written.

Once again her husband, Sylvère Lotringer intervened, phoning Dick and soliciting his compassion. "If nothing else, you must agree that Chris' letters are some new kind of literary form. They're very powerful." Dick hesitated.

On September 4, Chris went to Toronto to put *Gravity & Grace* through the lab. Stumbling into bed after watching the final answerprint at 5 a.m. a few days later, Chris wrote to Dick: "This is the happiest day of my life." She never mailed the letter.

She went back briefly to LA before leaving to premiere her film at the Independent Feature Market in New York. Still no word from

Dick. Sylvère phoned again and this time Dick promised he'd write Chris a letter.

The Independent Feature Market was a nonstop trial of screenings, meetings, cocktail parties. *Gravity & Grace* wouldn't screen until Day Four. On the first day of the Market, Dick left Chris a message asking her address. He'd like to send his letter via FedEx. The next day Dick left Chris another message, saying that his houseguest had accidentally erased her message. "This time I've instructed him not to touch the answering machine, so if you call back, I promise you, I'll get your message."

Dick's Fedex arrived before 10 a.m. on the day of Chris' screening. She stuck it in her bag and promised not to read it. But as the taxi rounded Second Avenue, she scrutinized the airbill, changed her mind and ripped it open.

There were two white envelopes inside the package. One was addressed to her; the other to her husband, Sylvère Lotringer. She opened Sylvère's first.

September 19

Dear Sylvère,

Here's the book on altered states and trance that I told you about. Georges Lapassade writes in Italian and French and I suspect this book also available in French. However it hasn't been translated into English. See what you think. The other, more mysterious tract on tarantulism seems to have vanished for now. If and when it turns up I'll send it on.

I apologize for being so resolutely incommunicado and for not following up sooner on this and other matters. I really didn't want to cause either you or Chris unnecessary pain. A large part of the silence and awkwardness between us is undoubtedly attributable to what I still believe to be the unwarranted and uninvited aftermath of your overnight stay at my home at the end of last year when weather reports had indicated you might not be able to make it back to San Bernardino. In retrospect I feel I should have been absolutely unambiguous in my response to the letters you and Kris sent over the following months instead of opting for bemused silence. I can only say that being taken as the object of such obsessive attention on the basis of two genial but not particularly intimate or remarkable meetings spread out over a period of years was, indeed still is, utterly incomprehensible to me. I found the situation initially perplexing, then disturbing and my major regret now is that I didn't find the courage at the time to communicate to you and Kris how uncomfortable I felt being the unwitting object of what you described to me over the phone before Christmas as some kind of bizarre game.

I don't know how our connection stands now that you've both received this package. Friendship, as far as I'm concerned, is a delicate and rare thing that's built up over time and is predicated on mutual trust, mutual respect, reciprocal interests and shared commitments. It's a relation that ultimately is lived out, at least, as if it were chosen not taken for granted or assumed in advance. It's something that has to be renegotiated at every step, not demanded unconditionally. In the circumstances it may be that, for now at least, too much damage has been done on all sides for the kind of negotiated rapprochement that would be needed if we were to restore the trust in which real friendship thrives. That said, I still have immense respect for your work; I still enjoy your company and conversation when we meet and believe, as you do, that Kris has talent as a writer. I can only reiterate what I have said before whenever the topic has been raised in conversation with you or Chris: that I do not share your conviction that my right to privacy has to be sacrificed for the sake of that talent.

Regards,
Dick

A strange coincidence. Sylvère already was familiar with Georges Lapassade (the name means "fling" in French argot). In fact, Sylvère knew Lapassade very well. In Paris, 1957 trance-master Lapassade was at the Sorbonne, practicing an early form of psychodrama. Among the puzzled volunteers was a first-year student by the name of Sylvère Lotringer, who was waiting to leave school the following year with the French *mouvement* to lead a Zionist kibbutz in Israel. Georges Lapassade was fascinated by this ambitious youth who had no personal ambition.

The rhetoric of therapy revolves around belief in personal choice. Until then Sylvère never thought he had any. Georges Lapassade suggested the unthinkable to Sylvère: that he refuse to go to Israel and leave the Zionist *mouvement*. Under the guidance of Lapassade, Sylvère wrote a formal resignation letter to the comrades who'd been his extended family since age 12. And so he never went to Israel and stayed in school.

The taxi was approaching Houston Street. Eagerly, Chris opened the envelope addressed to her and started reading. It was a xerox copy of Dick's letter to Sylvère.

She gasped and breathed under the weight of it and got out of the cab and showed her film.

Afterword by Joan Hawkins

THEORETICAL FICTIONS

Critics OFTEN don't seem to like Chris Kraus' "NOVELS" much. I say "novels" (in quotes) because I'm not entirely sure Kraus' works belong in the generic category of "novel." Rather, as Sylvère Lotringer has noted, Kraus' prose works constitute "some new kind of literary form," a new genre, "something in between cultural criticism and fiction" (*I Love Dick* 258, 43). Kraus herself has called an early manifestation of this genre-bending "Lonely Girl Phenomenology" (137). I prefer to call it theoretical fiction.

By "theoretical fiction" I don't mean books which are merely informed by theory or which seem to lend themselves to a certain kind of theoretical read—Sartre's *Nausea*, for example, or the **nouveaux romans** of Robbe-Grillet. Rather, I mean the kind of books in which theory becomes an intrinsic part of the "plot," a mover and shaker in the fictional universe created by the author. IN Kraus' "novels," debates over Baudrillard and Deleuze and meditations on the Kierkegaardian Third Remove form an intrinsic part of the narrative, where theory and criticism themselves are occasionally "fictionalized."

BUT although theory plays such a key role in Kraus' books, theoretical discussion is often erased from reviews of HER work. *I Love Dick*, her first book, is generally described as the story of Kraus' unrequited love for cultural critic Dick Hebdige.

"Who gets to speak and why…" Kraus writes, "is the only question" (191). I would modify that as follows: who gets to speak, who gets to speak about **what**, and **why** are the only questions. Certainly they're the questions which even favorable critiques of Kraus' work have led me to ask. Why are Kraus' "novels" mainly inscribed within a genre she has termed "the Dumb Cunt's Tale" (27)? Why do even art reviewers tend to edit, censor, filter out certain key aspects of her work? I can't answer these questions, BUT I can try to redress the balance a little BY TALKING about the aspects of Kraus' art which I believe have OFTEN been overlooked.

I Love Dick is divided into two parts. Part One: Scenes from a Marriage lays out the parameters of the love story—the unifying emotional and narrative device of the book. It reads, the late Giovanni Intra writes, "like *Madame Bovary* as if Emma had written it." Certainly, *Madame Bovary* is the literary analogue that Chris and her husband Sylvère use. In one memorable segment, Sylvère writes to "Dick" about his wife, "Emma," and signs himself "Charles." "Dear Dick, This is Charles Bovary" (110–112). Chris joins in the conceit when she tells the reader, in an expositional aside, that "sex with Charles did not replace Dick for Emma" (113).

But *Madame Bovary* isn't the only literary reference. "I'm thrown into this weird position," Chris tells Dick in her first letter to him. "Reactive—like Charlotte Stant to Sylvère's Maggie Verver, if we were living in the Henry James novel—*The Golden Bowl*" (26–27). And when he's not thinking of Flaubert, Sylvère refers to Chris' infatuation with Dick as the '90s equivalent of a Marivaux comedy. But since much of the plot is driven by letters, written by a couple who are attempting to seduce a third party into some kind of love-art projet, the book also bears a slight resemblance to *Liaisons Dangereuses*. Like *LD*, *I Love Dick* is self-reflexive as hell, as Sylvère and Chris continually critique and comment upon each other's prose, arguments, and plot-lines. Like *LD*, *I Love Dick* establishes a fictional territory where adolescent obsession and middle-aged perversity overlap and intersect, a territory where the relationship between "always for the first time" and a sort of jaded "here we go again" can be explored (in one letter Chris even refers to herself and Sylvère as "libertines," a term that invokes both Laclos and Sade). And, as in *LD* where the relationship between Valmont and the Marquise de Merteuil is the one that really counts, the most compelling and enduring relationship in *I Love Dick* is between the two people who initially seem to have grown a little too used to one another. As one perceptive critic observes, the reader-voyeur ultimately cares less about whether Chris sleeps with Dick than whether she stays with Sylvère (Anne-Christine D'Adesky, *The Nation,* 1998).

For anyone who likes to read literature, *I Love Dick* is a good read. But the literary references should also cue us to the textual savvy of the people who populate the piece. These are people who dig each other's references (32), who analyze and critique each other's prose, who are very aware that the literary form itself "dictate[s] that Chris end up in Dick's arms" (67). So it's strange that critics have tended to treat *I Love Dick* as more of a memoir than fiction, as an old-fashioned text which we could read as though the past twenty years of literary theory about the signifying practices of language had never happened.

"There's no way of communicating with you in writing," Sylvère writes to Dick at one point, "because texts, as we all know, feed upon themselves, become a game" (73). And it's this self-cannibalizing, self-reproducing, viral and ludic quality of language and text that critics seem to have largely ignored in writing about the book.

I Love Dick opens with the account of an evening Chris Kraus, "a 39-year-old experimental filmmaker," and her husband Sylvère Lotringer, "a 56-year-old college professor from New York," spend with "Dick...an English cultural critic who's relocated from Melbourne to Los Angeles" (19). Dick, "a friendly acquaintance of Sylvère's," is interested in inviting Sylvère to give a lecture and a couple of seminars at his school (19). Over dinner, Kraus writes, "the two men discuss recent trends in postmodern critical theory and Chris, who is no intellectual, notices Dick making continual eye contact with her" (19). The radio predicts snow on the San Bernadino Highway and Dick generously invites the couple to spend the night at his house. "Back at Dick's, the night unfolds like the boozy Christmas Eve in Eric Rohmer's film *My Night at Maud's*," Kraus notes (20). Dick inadvertently plays an embarrassing phone machine message left for him by a young woman, with whom "things didn't work out" (22). Sylvère and Chris "come out" as a monogamous hetero-married couple. Dick shows them a videotape of himself dressed as Johnny Cash, and Chris notices Dick is flirting with her. Chris and Sylvère spend the night on Dick's sofabed. When they wake up the next morning, Dick is gone.

Over breakfast at the Antelope IHOP, Chris informs Sylvère that the flirtatious behavior she shared with Dick the previous night amounts to a "Conceptual Fuck" (21). Because Sylvère and Chris are no longer having sex, Kraus tells us, "the two maintain their intimacy via deconstruction: i.e. they tell each other everything" (21). Chris tells Sylvère that Dick's disappearance invests the flirtation "with a subcultural subtext she and Dick both share: she's reminded of all the fuzzy one-time fucks she's had with men who're out the door before her eyes are open" (21). Sylvère, "a European intellectual, who teaches Proust, is skilled in the analysis of love's minutiae" (25). He buys Chris' interpretation of the evening, and for the next four days the two do little else but talk about Dick.

The couple starts collaborating on **billets-doux** to Dick. At first they just share the letters with each other, but as the pile grows to 50 then 80 then 180 pages, they begin discussing some kind of Sophie Calle-like art piece, in which they would present the manuscript to Dick. Perhaps hang the letters on the cactus and shrubs in front of his house and videotape his reaction. Perhaps Sylvère should read from the letters during his Critical Studies Seminar when he visits Dick's school in March? "It seems to be a step towards the kind of confrontational performing art that you're encouraging," he writes in one of his darker notes to Dick (43). When Chris finally does give the letters to Dick, "things get pretty weird" (162). But by that time, the letters have become an art form in and of themselves, a means to something that has almost nothing to do with Dick.

"Think of language as a signifying chain," Chris writes, referencing Lacan (233). And here you can literally see the signifying chain at work, as Chris' letters to Dick open up to include essays on Kitaj, schizophrenia, Hannah Wilke, the Adirondacks, Eleanor Antin, and Guatemalan politics. "Dear Dick," she writes at one point, "I guess in a sense I've killed you. You've become Dear Diary…" (90).

If Chris has metaphorically "killed" Dick by turning him into "Dear Diary," Dick—when he finally writes back—erases Chris. Despite the fact that he appears to have had sex with her at least twice and has shared several lengthy conversations ("long distance bills fill the gaps left in my diaries," she writes at one point, 230), he continually maintains that he doesn't know her and that her obsession with him is based solely on "two genial but not particularly intimate or remarkable meetings spread out over a period of years" (260). At the close of the book, as almost every reviewer notes, Dick finally responds by writing directly to Sylvère but not Chris. "In the letter," Anne-Christine d'Adesky writes,

> he misspells her name as Kris, and seems mostly concerned with salvaging his damaged relationship with Sylvère. He expresses regret, discomfort, and anger at being the **objet d'amour** in their private game and clearly hopes they won't publish the correspondence as is. 'I do not share your conviction that my right to privacy has to be sacrificed for the sake of that talent,' he tells Lotringer. To Chris, he is more curt, sending only a xeroxed copy of the letter he wrote to her husband. It's a breathtaking act of humiliation, an unambiguous Fuck You.

But it's also the appropriate literary conclusion to an adventure that was to some degree initiated by Sylvère. The first love letter in the book was written not by Chris but by her husband. And one of the things the "novel" unveils is the degree to which women in the classic Girardian triangle function as a conduit for a homosocial relationship between men as noted by Sedgwick. "Every letter is a love letter," Lotringer writes at one point, and certainly his first letter to Dick reveals a desire for intimacy that exceeds the usual hetero-friendly-professional correspondence. "It must be the desert wind that went to our heads that night," he writes, "or maybe the desire to fictionalize life… We've met a few times and I've felt a lot of sympathy towards you and a desire to be closer…" (26). The homosocial tone of the letter, as well as Sylvère's fear that he sounds like a love-struck girl sets up "the game" as one of competition and intimacy between men. No wonder Chris—whose crush on Dick supposedly initiates the adventure—feels "reactive...the Dumb Cunt, a factory of emotions evoked by all the men" (27). When Dick finally writes, he reinforces Chris' peripheral position. Ignoring everything that has passed between Dick and Chris, he responds to Sylvère's initial letter to him, in language which illustrates—as d'Adesky notes—that he's "mostly concerned with salvaging his damaged relationship with Sylvère."

On the simplest level, then, *I Love Dick* is a more complicated piece of work than the reviews would indicate. Through the use of letters, taped phone conversations, and written exchanges between Chris and her husband, it deconstructs the classic heterosexual love triangle and lays bare the degree to which—even in the most enlightened circles—women continue to function as an object of exchange. By saying this, however, I don't mean that it's simply another illustration of Eve Sedgwick's arguments in *Between Men*. Sylvère and Chris are too theoretically savvy to unproblematically present text/language as a transparency through which the real might be read. It's never clear if the style of Sylvère's letter is dictated by his feelings for Dick or by his awareness that the "form dictates" certain expressions of sentiment (67). What is clear is that "the real" is not exactly what interests Chris. "The game is real," she tells Dick in her first letter, "or even better than, reality, and better than is what it's all about" (28). Sylvère thinks Chris' evocation of the hyper-real here is "too literary, too Baudrillardian." But Chris insists. "Better than," she writes, "means stepping out into complete intensity" (28). And it's that intensity which Chris craves.

"Lived experience," Félix Guattari writes in *Chaosophy*, "does not mean sensible qualities. It means intensification" (235). And while Kraus doesn't quote Guattari until late in the text, his presence is already felt in the first letter. In fact, what's interesting is Chris' idea that you can somehow use Baudrillard's notion of the hyper-real, the simulacrum, to get to Deleuze and Guattari's notion of intensification. And that perhaps is the theoretical drive behind the entire project, as the letters and the simulacrum of a passion which receives little encouragement emerge as the truest and best way outside the virtual gridlock and into Deleuzian rematerialization of experience.

Given that Sylvère and Chris' stated goals ARE the desire to fictionalize life and to surpass the real, it's curious that the aspect of *I Love Dick* that is most frequently discussed in reviews is its connection to the banal, its status as a **roman à clef**. *New York* magazine revealed that the "Dick" of the book is Dick Hebdige, and rumor had it that Hebdige tried to block publication of *I Love Dick* by threatening to sue Kraus for invasion of privacy. As a result of this publicity entirely too much attention has been focused on Dick, who—as d'Adesky notes—remains "a mystery man" in the text itself. The fact that he doesn't return messages, Chris points out, turns his answerphone, and to some extent the man himself, "into a blank screen onto which we can project our fantasies" (29). In an interview with Giovanni Intra, she has called Dick "every Dick…Uber Dick…a transitional object."

Certainly he is Virtual Dick. It's difficult to know whether certain things that Kraus describes in the book ever really happened. And Dick's works, which at times are named and quoted in the book, are fictionalized. Real works are given fictitious titles and some quotes attributed to "Dick" appear to have been written by other people. This may have been done to further blur the real Dick's identity and so avoid a lawsuit. The net effect, though, is curious, since the camouflage of Dick's work continually refers back to Kraus and Lotringer themselves. In a postscript to one of Sylvère's letters, Chris asks Dick to send a copy of his 1988 book, *The Ministry of Fear* (42; the "real" book is Hebdige's *Hiding in the Light*). AND THEN THERE IS the reference Kraus makes to "Dick's" *Aliens & Anorexia*, A NOVEL SHE WOULD PUBLISH THREE YEARS LATER. "And then in *Aliens & Anorexia* you wrote about your own physical experience, being slightly anorexic," she writes. Then she quotes from "Dick's" work:

> If I'm not touched it becomes impossible to eat. Intersubjectivity occurs at the moment of orgasm: when things break down. If I'm not touched my skin feels like the flip side of a magnet. It's only after sex sometimes that I can eat a little. (136)

Later she quotes again from "Dick's book."

> Anorexia is an active stance. The creation of an involuted body. How to abstract oneself from food fluxes and the mechanical sign of the meal? Synchronicity shudders faster than the speed of light around the world. Distant memories of food: strawberry short-cake, mashed potatoes… (136) "This's one of the most incredible things I've read in years," she says. (137)

Dick Hebdige hasn't written a book called *Aliens & Anorexia*, but Chris Kraus has. And I don't know if Hebdige is slightly anorexic, but Kraus has written that she is. In *Aliens*, she WRITES

> anorexia is not evasion of a social-gender role; it's not regression. It is an **active stance**: the rejection of the cynicism that this culture hands us through its food, **the creation of an involuted body…Synchronicity shudders faster than the speed of light around the world. Strawberry shortcake, mashed potatoes.** (163)

The observations about food fluxes and the "mechanical sign of the meal" are a paraphrase of Deleuze—whom she quotes in *Aliens* (163). BUT the stuff about intersubjectivity appears to have been written specifically for Dick.

"Intersubjectivity occurs at the moment of orgasm," Kraus writes IN *Aliens*, "when things break down." But intersubjectivity in the text occurs through intertextuality, when distinctions between original and citation become blurred. The lines in *Aliens & Anorexia* aren't attributed to "Dick." Given the context, it's hard to say who is quoting from whom, BUT MY guess is that Kraus attributes her own language to "Dick" in *I Love Dick*—and in that way acknowledges what she explicitly states elsewhere in the text. It is through her love for Dick that she begins to write, through her passion for him that she finds her own voice. And in that sense he can be seen as an "author" of her work. But this doubling up of language and self-referentiality is also an elaborate part of the "game"—a reminder that even (or perhaps "especially") critical texts are unstable, are signifying chains which feed off themselves. Even critical texts can be/should be seen as "fiction."

ONE OF THE QUESTIONS KRAUS STRUGGLES WITH IS HOW TO RECONCILE WRITING WITH THE IDEA OF A FRAGMENTED SUBJECT. IT'S ONLY IN THE SECOND HALF OF THE BOOK THAT SHE SETTLES INTO THE FIRST PERSON PRONOUN. "For years I tried to write," she tells Dick in the middle of a long piece on schizophrenia, "but the compromises of my life made it impossible to inhabit a position. And 'who' 'am' 'I'? Embracing you & failure's changed all that 'cause now I know I'm no one. And there's a lot to say…" (221). RECALLING THE FAILURES OF HER EARLY NOTEBOOKS, SHE CONFESSES TO DICK:

Whenever I tried writing in the 1st Person it sounded like some other person, or else the tritest most neurotic parts of myself ... But now I think okay, that's right, there's no fixed point of self but it exists & by writing you can somehow chart that movement. That maybe 1st Person writing's just as fragmentary as more a-personal collage, it's just more serious: bringing change & fragmentation closer, bringing it down to where you really are. (139)

It seems as though reading the "real" Dick Hebdige's work enables Kraus to find a way of talking about art, a way that makes sense to her. "You write about art so well," she tells him in *I Love Dick* (133). But she does, too. The essay-letters in the second half of the book "Every Letter is a Love Letter" are linked to Kraus' obsession with Dick (her drive to his house the first time she plans to have sex with him is intercut with her memories of/meditations on Jennifer Harbury's hunger strike on behalf of her Guatemalan husband, for example). But the essays also take on a life of their own, independent of Dick. And they are essays, not just "riffs," as d'Adesky calls them. The piece titled "Kike Art"(186–204) is easily the best thing on Kitaj I've ever read, and her meditations on Hannah Wilke and Eleanor Antin are wonderful pieces of art criticism/history. I particularly like the way that she invites us, throughout these essays, to consider who gets "accepted" into the art world pantheon, who doesn't and why. Again and again SHE ASKS US to go back to those moments we consider "avant-garde," and read them through a slightly different lens. She invokes theory, SEEMS TO FEEL COMFORTABLE IN A THEORETICAL SKIN, without using theoretical language.

When Roland Barthes in 1970 sat down to write an enthusiastic review of one of Kristeva's early works, he chose to call it "*L'étrangère*," which translates approximately as 'the strange, or foreign, woman.' Though an obvious allusion to Kristeva's Bulgarian nationality (she first arrived in Paris in 1966), this title captures what Barthes saw as the unsettling impact of Kristeva's work. 'Julia Kristeva changes the place of things,' Barthes wrote, 'she always destroys the latest preconception...she subverts authority' (qtd. in Kristeva 150). I think a similar argument can be made about the "alien" nature of Chris Kraus and the unsettling impact of her work. "She always destroys the latest preconception...she subverts authority."

Kraus tends to perform theory and, through the performance, she demonstrates how much it matters. "Every question, once it's formulated," she writes, "contains its own internal truth. We have to stop diverting ourselves with false questions" (218). It seems to me that that quote might be used to summarize the critical project of theory in the past decade. It certainly could be used to summarize the critical projects of the other writers (INCLUDING DICK HEBDIGE) who haunt this book.

As this edition of *I Love Dick* goes to press, *Torpor*, a new Chris Kraus title, is being released by Semiotext(e). Ending where *I Love Dick* begins, *Torpor* serves as a kind of prequel to the earlier book. But since it plays more directly with time and tense than *I Love Dick*, the book also serves as a kind of sequel—a nod to some distant maybe—future.

"There is a tense of longing and regret, in which every step you take becomes delayed, revised, held back a little bit. The past and future are hypothesized, an ideal world existing in the shadow of an if. *It would have been*" (*Torpor* 157). If there is a temporal space in which *Torpor* unfolds, this is it—an always already perhaps.

"It is 1989 or 1990" when the book begins. "George Herbert Walker Bush is President of the United States and the Gulf War has just begun in Saudi Arabia" (16). Jerome Shafir and Sylvie Green (the Sylvère and Chris of *I Love Dick*) are traveling through the former Soviet Bloc, "with the specious goal"—the book jacket tells us—"of adopting a Romanian orphan." But throughout and around this frame tale, other stories and histories unfold. Jerome's past as a "hidden child" of World War II—one of the Jewish children protected by Gentiles during the deportation (itself the hidden shadow story to France's "official" World War II *resistancialist* history) haunts the story and the couple. "You'll write a book," Sylvie would have told Jerome, "about the War. You'll call it *The Anthropology of Unhappiness*" (33). Interconnected with that tragic personal and sociopolitical history is the unfolding present of the Romanian Revolution, which Jerome and Sylvie watch on television, and then experience firsthand as they drive through the impoverished East. And there is the story of the couple itself—Sylvie's abortions, Jerome's "other" family (his ex-wife and daughter), the *realpolitik* of academe and the art world, the punk past, and post *I Love Dick* future.

Animated by what Gary Indiana calls a "complex and terrifyingly nimble, restless intelligence," *Torpor*—like *I Love Dick*—deftly interweaves the personal with the political, in such a way that none of us is let off the hook. Which is not to say that the book is lugubrious or grim. Jerome and Sylvie, the book tells us, "have become a parody of themselves, a pair of clowns. They are Bouvard and Pecuchet, Burns and Allen, Mercier and Camier" (47). And just as Beckett's most stunning humor "derives from his description of torturous relationships" (Rosen 208), Kraus' humor frequently attaches to the travails of this middle-aged childless couple. There's a lot of comedy—particularly at the beginning—and (as in *I Love Dick*) part of the book's power is the way that that comedy gets refracted into some future hypothesized space where a great deal is at stake.

Torpor is a great companion piece to *I Love Dick*—a way of looping back to a moment before the end of the novel you hold in your hands and an elucidation of the allusions you find here. The story of Félix and Josephine, "French Theory's Sid and Nancy," is elaborated and played off against the story of Jerome and Sylvie. The connections between Continental Theory and the '80s art world are teased out, and the way the Holocaust haunts both French Theory and *belles lettres* is given more explicit shape and dimension. "And don't you think the most important question is *How does evil happen?*" Kraus writes in *Dick*. In the first novel, that question emerges late in the text, as Chris describes the Coca Cola strike in Latin America and writes to Dick about her trip to Guatemala. Here, it emerges ruthlessly early, as the narrator juxtaposes factual information about Romania against the sometimes comic sensibilities of a "torturous relationship."

Like *I Love Dick*, *Torpor* is beautifully written. Kraus has a way of ending paragraphs, shifting down into a statement so succinct it causes me to pause every time.

"In the months before she left Jerome," Kraus writes, "she'd started writing love letters to a man who didn't love her. In L.A. she continues writing to this man, and then she just continues writing" (280–281). *Torpor* confirms the promise of *I Love Dick* in a way that few prequels/sequels manage to do. If, like me, you find you love Chris—keep reading.

Works Cited

—D'Adesky, Anne-Christine. "*I Love Dick* (Book Reviews)." *The Nation*. June 1, 1998.

—Guattari, Félix. *Chaosophy*. New York: Semiotext(e), 1995.

—Hebdige, Dick. *Hiding in the Light*. London, Routledge, 1989.

—Intra, Giovanni. "A Fusion of Gossip and Theory." *artnet. com Magazine*. November 13, 1997. Accessed April 30, 2006: http://www.artnet.com/magazine_ pre2000/index/intra /intra11–13-97.asp

—Kraus, Chris. *Aliens & Anorexia*. New York: Semiotext(e), 2000.

—Kraus, Chris. *I Love Dick*. New York: Semiotext(e), 1997.

—Kraus, Chris. *Torpor*. Los Angeles: Semiotext(e), 2006.

—Kristeva, Julia. *The Kristeva Reader*. Ed. Toril Moi. New York: Columbia UP, 1986.

—de Laclos, Pierre. *Les Liasons Dangereuse*. New York: Doublday, 1998.

—Rosen, Steven J. Samuel *Beckett and the Pessimistic Tradition* (New Jersey: Rutgers UP, 1976

—Sartre, Jean Paul. *Nausea*. Trans. Lloyd Alexander. New York: New Direction, 1964.

—Sedgwick, Eve Kosofsky. *Between Men*. New York: Columbia UP, 1985.